BEAUTIFULLY RESTORED

—•—

TRISHA MADLEY

CONTENTS

DEDICATION

This Book is Dedicated to the special women in my life;
who are the first to jump at the chance to read my stories.
Nina Faieta
Mary Balmer
Kathy Blinkiewicz
Amy Dobbs
Maria Longo
Amanda Zickafoose

And as always, to my daughters...
Madison and Hayley

1

—·—

"M rs. Dawson, Mr. Dawson's been in an accident." Rose, our housekeeper, barges into my bedroom, causing me to sit straight up in bed. It has to be the middle of the night.

Rose is standing in front of me as my eyes open, focusing on her. "What's happened? Is he all right?" The memory of that horrible night starts to replay, but Rosa prevents the movie reel from continuing.

"He's fine, but he's destroyed the blue car and he's taking it out on the kitchen. Mr. Andrew has gone home for the night. You have to go down to him before he hurts himself!"

I place my hand on her shoulder. Her dark espresso-colored eyes are wide and unsure. It's my job to make her feel safe. After all, she didn't marry this man, I did. In fact, she has been the most decent person in the Dawson household.

"It's okay, Rose, I'll get him to calm down. Do you know what he did?"

"He came in and was carrying a piece of the car, a bumper, maybe? He's been going on and on about the gate being in the wrong place."

There is only one reason why the gate that's been surrounding our ridiculously large mansion would be in the wrong place—Mr. David Dawson is officially drunk, and at some point in his venture, decided that the one-of-a-kind, million-dollar Bugatti needed to be driven, and he brought some vodka along for the ride.

I pat Rose on the shoulder. She nods. She's used to dealing with his emotional outbursts and knows this isn't the first—or the last—time we'll have to deal with this. Only she's the lucky one, she can quit anytime, but me...well, I'm married to the man with no chance of parole.

I drag my body from the warmth of my bed and slip on my floral robe. It's fluffy and comforting, although the pleasure will soon dwindle and I'll be entering my own personal hell.

What in the world is wrong with this man? I can't even count the number of times he's wrecked his precious babies, his stupid cars. The Bugatti, though, is a one-off car, irreplaceable. He's rambled on about if I ever scratched it, how impossible it would be to fix. How I'm never allowed to drive it because it's too much car for me, blah, blah.

Rose leaves while I stand and look at my disheveled, yet rosy, complexion. I'm so tired; I worked twelve long hours today and didn't want to be disturbed. It's honestly one of the *many* reasons why my husband and I have separate bedrooms.

No matter, nothing matters but the man wreaking havoc on my beloved kitchen. I can hear banging coming from downstairs. God only knows what he's taking his stupidity out on now. The sound of something crashing sweeps up the stairs and startles me, bringing me back to my reality. Wasting no more time, I leave my bedroom and rush down the two flights of stairs.

My foot almost slips out of my slipper, causing me to stumble just as a loud thud causes me to pick up the pace.

When I reach the kitchen, my heart lurches and drops to the floor. He's cleared the counters and cabinets, leaving the remnants on the floor. The pot rack above the island sink remains empty, while the pots and pans that once hung there were tossed aimlessly to the marble floor.

And in the middle of the chaos is the man I married. Blond hair, blue-eyes, full of charm and charisma—and the cruelest person I've ever met. David Dawson. My husband.

"This is all your fault, if you hadn't taken my life from me, my freedom. I could be better. I could be a good man," he slurs but I understand every word. He blames me for the way his life turned out. Today I'm lucky, it's just words being slung at me, usually he grabs the closest item within his reach and hurls it in my direction, always careful not to hit me so I remain the perfect wife—on the outside— but he doesn't give a damn what he's done to me on the inside.

He talks this way every time he's drunk...and most of the time when he isn't. I'm blamed for things I haven't done and things I have done. He believes his life is miserable because of me and reminds me how I've had a part to play in how his life has gone wrong.

I've done all I can to make it up to him, to make him feel better, but nothing I do or say can stop his pain...or mine.

Gathering my strength and bracing myself for whatever reaction I'm going to have to deal with, I start picking up the broken remnants of my kitchen.

"David, what happened?"

His ice-filled eyes wreak havoc on my nerves because before he even speaks, his eyes answer for him...me. Emerson Marie Dawson, his wife, is what happened to make his life the way it is, and I agree with him for only one reason. I've ruined a part of him, but he's done far more damage to me than I could ever do to him.

"What do you think? I tried pushing in the brake pedal and my leg didn't work because I only have one that works right. My new robot leg is a piece of shit."

His head falls into his hands while he moves his head back and forth as if trying to erase a memory.

"Let's get you into bed. I'll take care of everything," I say while cautiously walking toward him. He's like a feral animal; one quick move and it'll send him away...or worse.

"You're a selfish bitch. This," he motions to his prosthetic leg, "Is all your fucking fault. You did this to me."

He's right, I did. I made him lose his freedom, his independence, and his entire world as he knew it, but that's why I've stayed. It's also the only reason why I'll continue to remain in this dark marriage.

"Come on, let's go to bed."

"No! I'm staying at my fucking kitchen table. You're going to have to watch me suffer. You're selfish, you're the reason I'm like this. You did this to me, to us," he says with no emotion other than disgust on his worn face.

He lowers his head and rests his cheek on the table as he exhales a sigh of relief.

This is my cue to leave him alone. He's ready to pass out. I'll clean up the rest of the mess while he's in la-la land. Unfortunately, I can't clean up the mess of his life. I leave the kitchen and walk down the hall and straight into his study. I quickly and quietly close the door. When I hear the silence, my stomach hurts and churns that familiar feeling of panic, pain, but most of all, guilt.

I take a few deep breaths to calm myself. I've learned from years of therapy that breathing is my only friend. Andrew has the night off, otherwise David probably wouldn't have gotten this far in his night of destruction.

Parker, the new hire, must have either quit or been fired. I'm sure Andrew told him about how David gets, but it probably was too much for him to handle if he witnessed it firsthand. It would be for anyone.

Sitting at the large cherry desk, I rummage through the stacks of paper to see if anything might have set him off. I don't have to scour long when the answer stares back at me. On the desk is a picture of our wedding night, and another of him with his father.

I take the picture of us and slip it into my robe pocket. No matter how many times I try to hide it or destroy it, he finds it. Damn technology! It makes it easy for the worst night of someone's life to never disappear.

The phone is to my left. Picking up the receiver, I dial the only person who can help me. I don't even hear it ring a single time before Andrew's voice says, "Yes, sir."

"Andrew, it's Emerson. He's destroyed his Bugatti."

"Damn it, that idiot. One night I want off and he goes pissing it all away. Where is he?"

"Passed out in the kitchen. I don't know all that's happened yet. I'm not the person he needs to see right now. I'm sorry to bother you at home, but do you think you could come over?"

"Of course, doll, I'm already leaving my place. Luckily, my lady's used to this. We actually had a bet of how long he'd last. Eight hours is more than we thought." He laughs and I can hear Shelly in the background, "Damn it, only two more hours and I would have won."

Andrew is the only person in the world I trust. He knows me and David and what really happened to us so many years ago. Luckily, Shelly has been willing to share her husband with me over the years. She knows what a horrible man David has turned into, and is my biggest supporter and confidant.

This is probably the first time I've smiled today. Thank God for friends.

Thankfully, Andrew and Shelly live only five minutes away. I decide to stay in the study because I'm safe in here. Because this is not my first time dealing with my childish husband, I pull up the surveillance footage on the computer. As I watch, I'm stunned. He only made it out of the garage before wrecking the yard completely. By wrecking, I mean, watching the Bugatti in the video drive over bushes, through the two water fountains while water sprays at the camera, and taking out the family sculpture of his great grandfather.

Clicking out of the video in frustration, I lean back and close my eyes to calm my nerves. It only lasts a few seconds when the banging begins. It seems sleeping beauty hasn't found sleep after all.

"Emerson!" he yells, "Emerson! Where are you?"

I steel my nerves and walk up to the door, speaking sternly. "Andrew will be here soon. Wait for him and he'll fix whatever you broke."

"He can never fix what *you* broke. I used to feel so lucky to be your husband but now...I can't say that. I can't say anything good about you." I can hear the slur in his voice along with the venom.

My heart sinks for the millionth time. I've only ever tried to make him happy and make up for the one night I can never take back. I still am unsure of the details of that night. I can't remember, but I know I was the one driving.

The banging on the door startles me again. It's not his hand, but his foot kicking the door.

I back up as far as I can. But before I can find a secure location, David kicks the door in and stumbles through, almost falling over, but his hand reaches out, making contact with my robe. Yanking it, he causes my head to bang into his forehead. "Ow!" His face is disturbingly close to mine, and his boozed, vomit-laced breath is suffocating me.

"I've got you, you can't hide from me. Look me in the eyes. You coward! Look at my leg, it isn't fucking real, it's nothing but metal. Metal. You cunt! You did..."

"Enough!" Andrew demands, and David is violently ripped away from me.

I close my eyes, and count to one hundred. Focusing on the numbers...nothing else, breathing one, breathing two, breathing three..."

By the time I've counted to four hundred, Andrew is standing before me.

He's staring at me quietly, not saying a word, but the look on his face tells me all I need to know. The very upbeat man I've grown to admire is now wearing a scowl.

He wants me to leave David, but I can't, and he knows it's a lost cause.

"He's in his room and it's locked. Don't go near it. Go to your room and lock the door—both the deadbolt and chain. I'll stay the night and we'll figure out what to do in the morning." He smirks, "I know his dad is going to be pissed about Great-Grandpa Dawson."

I give him a bleak smile.

He pats my shoulder. "You okay?"

"No, but what can I do about it?"

"I can't believe you're still blaming yourself and believe it's his right to treat you the way he does. I only work here for you, you know that, right? But one day I might not be here to save you. You need to leave him. You don't need his money or his companies."

"I can't leave him. I took a vow...richer or poorer..."

"Sickness and health, I know, but those vows don't include abuse. He may not punch you in the face, but the way he mentally abuses you is far worse. He lies and cheats on you, and yet you still believe you should stay...why?"

I shrug and the tears fall. "It's my fault he lost his leg."

He puts his hands in the air, "One day you will see it wasn't your fault and you will be pissed at all the time you wasted here...wasted on him."

He's probably right, but that day isn't coming anytime soon.

2

— · —

He's still asleep from last night. Andrew has worked his magic and calmed David down. The landscapers are already busy repairing the fence and restoring the yard into their pristine condition. The statue and fountains are a different story. They will need special care in their restoration that we don't currently have on staff.

The Dawson family has more money than any family should, and along with that comes immense power.

Power and influence that haunts me in every aspect of my life.

David's father, Edward, has already been contacted and is covering up his son's mistake. David's done much worse, and this is a tiny mishap compared to all the other times.

Edward will be here in a few hours, and I'm not looking forward to seeing him. He's almost as horrible to me as David is, only he doesn't call me names, just issues veiled insults—but David's mother, Beatrice, is the worst in the Dawson clan. She hates me and has told me those exact words on more than one occasion. She holds me responsible for her son's leg being trapped, crushed, and eventually amputated, but here I am trying to control my temper and act in an appropriate manner as she stands in front of me.

Her short hair is perfectly styled by her very own hair stylist. The same stylist who lives in their mansion, which explains why she can look this put together at eight-thirty in the morning? She's wearing a long, black caftan, from her own designer caftan company.

"This is ridiculous, do you not know how to make him happy so that he will not look for happiness elsewhere? These little episodes he has could all be stopped if you paid more attention to him and gave him more affection." Mrs. Dawson rolls her eyes and makes a deep-throated sound of disgust.

I don't dare say a word. It doesn't matter what I say or do... she doesn't care. Nothing I ever say will change her opinion of me or her son.

"David's car needs to be fixed. It is one of those special cars of his; we can't just have any greasy mechanic fix it. David informed me that there is a person in South Carolina who can fix it, and only he can do the job, but David doesn't want it to be out of sight, nor do I. You don't know who's going to try to steal it when it's so far away."

"I'm sure it'll be fine," I make the mistake of saying.

"You would say that seeing as you can't even take care of my son properly. So that's why I'm sending you with the car for the duration of the repair. You're not to leave its side."

I huff. "You're kidding me, right?"

Mrs. Dawson looks both amused and shocked at the same time. "Of course, I'm not kidding. David doesn't want some dirty hoodlum trying to steal his car, his million-dollar car. Surely you feel the same way."

"Actually, I don't. We have insurance, if they want to take it, let them have it. After all, he doesn't care enough about his precious car to not wreck it so this shouldn't be my problem."

She steps closer and wedges her finger close to my face. "Darling, if you babysitting a car makes your husband happy, you will do it!"

I let out a chuckle; I can't believe what she's asking me to do. "I will not."

Her finger now pokes at my shoulder. "Safe to say that you like your job, your reputation? I've been very generous considering what you did to my son. I'll make it all go away. Everything you have worked so hard for will...vanish."

I can feel the blood drain from my face. This isn't the first time she's threatened me, but my career is the only thing that brings any kind of joy to my life. I'm starting my own cosmetics line, and I can't risk her ruining it for me.

"I'll talk it over with David...once he wakes up," I concede.

She backs away from me, retracting her claws, and smiles. "Good. I knew we could compromise. I'll be sure to give Andrew all the details."

I don't say another word, nor does she. Mrs. Dawson, in her perfectly styled clothing and slim figure, turns and walks away from me. This is my cue to do the same and retreat to the only part of the property no one ever visits.

I walk from the sitting room of the mansion to the chapel at the very end of the yard. It takes me at least ten minutes to get to my sanctuary, but when I do, I feel relieved, free, and most of all, at peace. Scanning the small building that's as big as a garden shed, but is made of large, multicolored stones in brown, beige, and even some pieces of brick, I can finally breathe. The random pieces of rubble are beautiful to me. I couldn't believe my luck when I found it. The Dawson's only built the chapel for Great Grandmother Dawson when she could no longer attend church. Regardless the reason, it's here and I love it.

The door is a beautiful deep red, but it is naturally antiqued. To unlock the door, I have to use the original skeleton key. As I insert the key, I pull out the iron rod circle door handle. The bouquet of the comforting smells of candles, incense, and essential oils like peppermint, jasmine, and lavender—all my favorites—waft out.

I'm the one who consistently cleans and handles the upkeep of the chapel, as well as took it upon myself to fill it with artwork and statues.

I was raised Catholic, and have had the chapel adorned with saints, crosses, the Virgin Mary, and many angels. I feel protected and loved in this environment, my safe haven, hidden away from the penance and the burden that's become my life.

I settle into the first pew of the five that were installed. They actually came from the Vatican. I'm not sure how the Dawson's managed to get them, but I don't care. This is one of the few gifts I've gotten from this marriage, and the pews were here long before I was ever born.

I spend a few hours praying, meditating, and reading. Although it's not the Bible, I still love a great story. Anything to take me out of my world that allows me to get lost in another.

Interrupting my reading, Andrew walks in the chapel.

"I thought I'd find you here. What are you reading?"

"A romance novel." I grin, peeking up from my glasses.

He smiles but I see the sarcasm behind his twinkling hazel eyes.

"So, the Bugatti has extensive damage. He never even made it out onto on the road but managed to total it by simply driving around the yard." Andrew shakes his head in astonishment. "So, we need to take it to be repaired, but there's a problem," He pauses, but I already know what he's going to say. "David has to oversee the rebuild since it's more of a project than I initially thought, but Mrs. Dawson told me that you were going." A part of me is pleased, this news means, he'll be gone with his love until it's fully restored. This project could last weeks, maybe even months, so Mrs. Dawson is wrong, and her son will have to go in my place to ensure his precious Bugatti is restored to its glory.

"I see that smile on your face, but I'm about to wipe it off. Mr. Dawson doesn't want David leaving after his little adventure last night, and I don't blame him." I can feel my cheeks fall. "So Mrs. Dawson's idea for you to stay with the car still stands."

Although I should be annoyed at his comment, I'm not. "I know, I was hopeful that he'd have to go but since I was duly informed by the queen, I don't have a choice. What am I supposed to do...babysit it? I hate those cars!" I can feel my face starting to heat, though. Rage is creeping through my veins at Beatrice dictating what I have to do.

"Calm down, killer, we're in church." His large physique makes the room look much smaller. He might even be able to split a pew in two if he isn't careful.

I take in a deep breath. "So, what's the plan? Please tell me you have a plan to get me out of this?"

"No, you don't want to get out of this, it's the best thing to happen to you. It's a vacation, Emmy. You don't have to work, or see that prick every day, only stare at a car occasionally. Van, at the shop in South Carolina, is cool as shit. He won't care what you do, or if you're even there."

"I'm sure he loves the idea of someone watching over his shoulder as much as I like Mrs. Dawson looking over mine." I cringe just thinking of it.

"Yeah, he'll fucking hate it, maybe even tell you all about it, but he's a good guy. Rough around the edges, but he'd do anything for anyone. I'll drive you there, it's about eight hours away."

"What?" I whine.

"We'll be there before you know it. Daddy Dawson said he'll send David in a week or so after he gets some rest to check on the car and relieve you. Then you can come back to this fucking prison." He waves his hand around the chapel.

"I don't want to go. I can't leave work. I'm getting samples of my line in a few weeks, and I need to oversee it." I huff. "I hate him...and her!"

"Vacation, doll. Relax. Have fun. I promise you'll have a great time, and you'll get to be a normal twenty-something woman. Not treated like a child or employee...or prison inmate."

Four hours later, Andrew and I are on our way to Bradley Restoration in a huge truck, and behind us we're towing the Bugatti. Of course, the Bugatti is in an enclosed trailer because, of course, it is. The only thing missing from the preparation to make sure it was secure was bubble wrap. If we would've had more time, I think David would've found enough to encase his precious baby completely.

I'm by no means a car person. I haven't had my driver's license renewed in years, and I don't really need to drive because Andrew is usually around to take me where I need to go—which usually consists of only work and home.

Andrew's listening to country music and I'm enjoying the peacefulness of being away from Dawson Manor. Watching people going about their day; driving to work, stopping for coffee, buying groceries, and having lunch with friends is something that makes me smile...but also reminds me that my life is not as it should be.

"So, I know this guy, Donavan. Most people call him Van. Anyway, you'll probably be staying at his place." His head is trained on the road ahead, but the eye I can see is focused on my reaction. He looks to be holding his breath, and he should be because I'm going to explode.

"Why on earth would I stay with a stranger? I'm sure there are hotels or a lovely bed and breakfast nearby? Doesn't the Dawson family own some property there or something?"

His voice is apologetic, "It's a small town and Mr. Dawson set up the accommodations already; plus, there will be no one to drive you around."

"You're not staying?"

Of course, he's not. He has a wife to go home to. I'm so stupid.

"No, I'm going to take the truck back. They don't want the truck left here." He shoots me a knowing look.

By here he means with me, in case I decide to drive away and leave his precious Bugatti alone, even though I don't have a valid license.

He's cautiously watching the road, and this time is avoiding looking over at me.

"Fine. Am I supposed to sleep in the Bugatti, or on the floor of the garage?" I can't hide my sarcasm.

"No. Van's a great guy and you'll be staying with him. He's got a small house behind the garage with a few spare rooms. He'll be too busy working on the car to bother you. Besides, he's not like that, he's a great guy."

I look over at him, "You keep saying that 'great guy' comment, but somehow, I'm not buying it."

"I told you he's rough around the edges, he might not be super happy that some rich chick is coming to oversee his work, but he'll get over it."

"Rich chick?" My lips purse like I just tasted something bitter. "How do you know him anyway?"

"As you know, the only thing David and I have in common is cars. This dude is the best when it comes to building and restoring cars. I've visited his place a few times for David and well... we just hit it off. I even hang out with him and his crew when I'm doing something for David or the OG, Mr. Dawson."

I chuckle at his OG remark. "Then why aren't you babysitting the car?" He lets out a breath, like he's preparing for something, or maybe a confession. "What?" I ask.

"I sort of...well...I declined and suggested you go."

"You what? Why?"

"As a favor to you. Because you need to get away from that life, Emmy." He places a hand on my knee. "You need to see how real people live and have fun for the first time in your life. I know that you'll have a great time. Even if you don't talk to a soul, at least you'll be out of that toxic environment."

I can't stop the huff that is my reaction to this mess. Only the Dawson's would have me babysit a stupid car...and why did we need to drive so far away?

I sigh. "Well, I guess I'll just barricade myself in the guest room."

"Sounds like your best bet, but who knows, he might introduce you to something new."

"Yeah?"

"Yeah." He nods. "You could use a dose of normalcy in your chaotic world."

I roll my eyes and lean my head against the window. He's going to start his speech, I can hear the tone in his voice, the brother-to-sister talk. Only I have no idea what it's like to belong to a loving family.

I was given up for adoption as an infant and adopted by Doris and Chester Kane. They were both in their mid-forties when I came to live with them at six months old.

Mother Doris, as she loved to be called, didn't pay much attention to me. I was only adopted because she didn't want to be the only woman in her circle of friends to never have a child. After my shine had worn off after a couple of weeks, a nanny was hired. Nanny Marie, whom I consider my mother figure, still talk every day.

My adoptive father also had no time for me, or my mother, for that matter, not while keeping up with his thriving law firm and the many mistresses he had around town. My adoptive parents had two sides: either they never talked or screamed at each other.

We were a very dysfunctional family and still are. I only speak with them at holidays and at charity events they attend that the Dawsons host. I've grown accustomed to people treating me poorly. Maybe one day I'll find the courage to leave this mess. I just don't think there is anything out there better for a person like me. A person who thought she found her happily ever after, a new family that loved her; only to have found out that the furthest thing they feel for me is love.

When I met David at our local country club, I thought my life would change. He was so handsome, charismatic, popular, and self-confidant. So, when he picked me, I couldn't believe it. I thought no one would love a girl like me.

He fell for the Dawson name, the power and the business deals between him and my father. Now there is nothing to be gained by being married to me. Somedays I dream of a different life, but I'm so afraid to be alone.

I was so lonely as a child...wasn't allowed to have friends. My father did not want me introduced to potential bad influences. So, I concentrated on schoolwork, learned everything about the family business, and now have used that to start my own business up.

Andrew's words hit me hard. Something new? Fun? One day, I hope the guilt I feel will fade and I'll get to leave this life behind.

But now that he has no use for me, he's turned into a monster. He's a selfish, conceited man who thinks the world should adore him as much as his mother does.

Andrew stops the vehicle at a gas station and gets out. I take this moment to get out and stretch as well.

As I round the vehicle, Andrew is shaking his head. "Why you wore a suit is beyond me. You are free from that prison you put yourself in, you don't have to wear its uniform while you are on *parole*."

I roll my eyes and walk past him into the convenience store. An older gentleman opens the door and nods his head. I reply properly and head toward the ladies' room.

As soon as I enter, my body relaxes at the feeling that nobody can see me and that I'm blissfully alone. I love moments like this where it's just me with only my thoughts for company.

I don't have to be someone I'm not. I don't have to be composed, put together, cold, and above all, strong.

My eyes flash to the woman in the mirror. Her chocolate locks are perfectly twisted into a tidy bun that sits as it does every day atop her head. Her makeup is minimal, but she wishes it would be different. She loves the photos she sees of models in the magazines and online. The ease with which their beauty is accentuated by their dramatic use of color. Her clothes are as bland as her personality. Dry and blandly, matter of fact. A navy-blue blazer, white button-up shirt, while the only hint of life is a vintage flower brooch with a purple stone in the center.

Her appearance is that of a fifty-year-old. She wears this armor of fabric as a shield, protecting her from the possibility of someone noticing her. A single tear leaks from her left eye and she knows nothing in this reflection is real, but it will always be like this.

I'm brought back to reality by the knock on the door. "Hurry up, I have to piss."

My composure returns and I deactivate the emotions that were stirred, and move to open the door, letting the offending party know exactly how rude she is.

Only when the door opens, it's a tall woman with bright pink hair and a face painted in the image I was just wishing were colored on my face.

She pushes past me, heads for the stall, and I exit.

My mind is processing the image. She is beautiful and carefree, allowed to do what she wishes, say how she feels, and do what she wants without any guilt or regrets.

I envy her in this moment, she is everything I wish I could be.

When I reach the massive truck, Andrew is screwing the gas cap lid on. I hear the twist and the tear of the receipt.

It's my cue that we're done here, and we're off to the new fate that awaits me.

3

— · —

"Wake up, sleepyhead, it's time for your adventures in babysitting to begin," Andrew says annoyingly while pulling my scarf from my face. I want to punch him in the face for letting the light shine in and waking me up.

"Asshole." The best reply he will ever receive for such an act.

"Ah, come on. We are three miles or so away. I thought you might want to freshen up before we get there and ah, maybe change into something less...professional and more age appropriate."

I look down at my navy suit jacket and realize that I'm going to be spending my time with a bunch of greasy mechanics and at some point, my clothes will be destroyed by the simple task of sitting in a chair. However, I didn't bring anything other than suit skirts or suit pants. I did toss yoga pants into my suitcase, but I'm sure I'll be fine.

"I'm sure I can take it to the cleaners, Andrew."

He chuckles. "I'm talking about relaxing and blending in with a new environment. You don't have to act perfect here. Let your hair down, drink a few beers, have a one-night stand, or tell someone to fuck off, anything. You're free, free from the Dawson's clutches temporarily."

His words sink in. I can do whatever I want and not have to be on task all the time. I'm free. The emotion that the word freedom evokes in me strangles my breath. I can feel tears fighting to get out, but I hold back.

"Thank you for the suggestion." I say sarcastically. "I can't believe you just said that to me."

"You can be happy, Emmy. David wasn't the only one who was hurt in that accident, and it wasn't your fault, no matter what they tell you." He grabs my hand and clutches it tight.

I look up at him and he smiles. His smile is so sincere, so compassionate, it makes me realize how lucky I am to have friends like him and Shelly in my life.

We sit in silence for the next few miles to the repair shop.

My mind wanders to the contents of my suitcase. He's right, I can wear what I want; I won't have to always be proper. I used to wear jeans all the time. I only wear t-shirts to bed; how nice it would be to wear them anywhere I wanted to.

I ponder how to wear my long brown hair. Before I married David, it was almost blonde from the amount of time I spent on the beach, in the sun.

Bringing me back to reality is the sound of the monster truck quieting.

The image of a small shop in a rundown neighborhood and dilapidated cars scattered about the premises is not the image that's before me. No...the image before me is a large metal structure with large windows that touch from floor to ceiling with an enormous sign that reads, "Bradley Restoration."

I guess when it comes to their babies, the Dawson men don't just let anyone handle them.

This car shop looks straight out of the hot rod magazines like the ones David leaves around the house. Glass windows encase the prettiest cars I've ever laid eyes on. The vibrant colors of reds, blues, blacks, silvers, all gleaming under the sun's reflection. Sunglasses will be useful in this type of atmosphere.

Andrew opens the door for me. "It's a great shop, isn't it? Wait till you meet Van, you're going to love him."

"Oh yes, you keep saying that. You know me, grease monkeys are my thing," I say snottily.

He points, getting in my face, "You say shit like that, and somebody's going to get your ass. I love you, Emmy. But shut up. These are good, hard-working people, not the Dawson's."

I'm stunned at his response, I thought it might make him laugh, but I touched a nerve it seems, a very delicate one.

As I jump from the truck, my heels awkwardly wobble, but somehow, I manage to stay vertical.

Andrew grabs my hand rather briskly, he must still be aggravated by my comment. Got it: *Grease monkey stricken from the record.*

We approach the large, spotless glass doors with metal, car-shaped handles. I inwardly chuckle thinking that I'm entering a little boy's fantasyland.

There are numerous cars and trucks in many colors and styles. I know nothing about cars. From what little knowledge I have, some are very old, and some are new, but most of them I've never even seen before.

The rows of cars are off to both sides of the red carpet that leads to the front counter where a woman sits with long, dark purple hair. She's dressed in a Bradley's Restoration t-shirt and jean shorts, wearing dark makeup, and her blue eyes sparkle and narrow on me.

"Hey, Drew, we've been expecting you." She smiles, but it doesn't quite touch her eyes. No, her eyes are focused on me.

Her bright lips pout, her arms crossed, and eyes still narrowed. This girl is defending her territory. I'm not sure what territory she thinks

I'm going to impose on, but from the looks of her, she's not about to let me find out.

"Vi, I thought you would eventually change your hair color now that purple is the new thing. You never follow a crowd."

"Did you ever think that maybe they were following me?" Her cocky attitude is making me like her less and less. She still only stares at me as she talks. *What the hell?*

"Right, Vi. Violet this is Mrs. Emerson Dawson, David Dawson's wife. I told Van about the whole situation. We got the Bugatti loaded on the trailer," he informs her.

"Well, look at you, brought the wifey from her throne to take care of her husband's baby."

My eyes bulge directly out of their sockets. "Excuse me?" I ask rather politely despite the attitude, which she has just addressed me with. "Wifey...or maybe stick up your ass is better? You think you can drop off your car, spy over our shoulder and look down on us just because we don't come to work in a suit." She exaggerates the last word and then turns to look at her compact mirror and scrubs her finger across her two front teeth.

I'm momentarily paralyzed. No employee or associate has ever disrespected me in such a manner as Violet. I knew babysitting this car would make them uncomfortable, but I didn't imagine they would be furious.

Andrew steps in. "Knock it off, Vi. I don't care who you are, this is still a client, a special client."

"Violet! In the back!" I hear a stern voice from behind me.

I watch as she shrinks under his authority and scuttles away through the door that must lead to an office. When I turn around, I see who has caused her to act this way, who she's protecting by releasing her fury on me, because I've never seen a more beautiful man in all my life.

Dark eyes greet me first, long eyelashes frame them, and a few stray black curls fall over his perfectly arched eyebrows. The black hair cut into layers that haphazardly falls in a mass of soft curls, begging to be touched. His facial features could have been chiseled from granite. His jawline's spattered with facial hair, and the smile that plays on his plump rosy lips is full of fun.

"Sorry, about that, I had a fight with her earlier about some mistakes. I guess she hasn't gotten over it and has taken it out on you." He innocently shrugs his shoulders.

He and Andrew do the weird handshake-hug guy thing, I haven't quite figured out. I'm standing there like some sort of crazed fan. Mouth open, eyes wide, and star struck. Who is this man, a model?

"Van, this is Emerson Dawson, David's wife, and she's here to oversee the restoration," Andrew says proudly.

This is Van? I feel mortified. I'm here to babysit him and this car for my husband. What could he possibly think of me?

Van stretches out his hand for me to shake and says, "Nice to meet you Mrs. Dawson. I have a place set up for you to stay. You won't be here for long. The Bugatti is our top priority." His professional attitude and demeanor take me by surprise, but I can't tear my eyes off this beautiful man. I don't think I ever thought of a man as beautiful before, but I don't think there's another word to describe him. I'm momentarily paralyzed and feeling ridiculous. Dropping my head and shaking his hand is the only way to recover what little composure I have.

His hands are rough, dry, and fit perfectly in mine. They're stained black around the nails, in desperate need of washing, but for some reason, I don't mind.

He holds onto my hand until I look up at him, our eyes lock, and his smile fades as he lets go.

"Van, I got everything ready for you. Wait til you see this beauty. You won't believe it exists, and then you'll want to slap the shit out of Dawson for ruining such an incredible machine," Andrew explains, slapping Van on the back shoulder and directing him toward the doors.

Their backs face me as they pass through the doors and he fades into the sunlight, causing me a sudden pang of sadness.

"He's not into girls like you. Mousy, quiet book nerds aren't his thing. I bet you don't know how to party, or how to please your man. Van's definitely not for you," Vi says from behind me.

I turn around to look Maleficent in the face. A fitting name for her, a witch can't even compete with this bitch.

"Excuse me?" I ask in a threatening tone.

She's standing behind the counter in her t-shirt that's been cut into a V around the neckline, dipping down into what little cleavage she has, and short, ripped shorts. Even though she sports an amazing body and can kick my butt, all I want to do is destroy that disgusting grin on her face.

"Donavan Bradley isn't for you. Don't look...and definitely don't touch."

"I'm sorry, I'm a married woman. I have no such interest in him."

Violet grabs a strand of her purple hair and concentrates on the split ends. "I've heard that bullshit before. You'll be begging him to fuck you in one of those cars, and he'll do it because he's Van. But he's mine. You got me?" She points directly at my face.

I'm astonished at her honesty and hostility. I am married, not happily, mind you, but I will stay true to my marriage.

"I have no interest in Mr. Bradley, I am here to ensure that my husband's car is properly repaired. I will also be speaking with Mr. Bradley about your unprofessional behavior." I turn and whip my bun at her, then take a few steps forward to calm my nerves.

I can feel my heart beating fast, all the adrenaline is making me wish I could hit something. I've never punched a person before, but the thought of my fist meeting her jawline sounds intriguing.

Catching the glass doors out of the corner of my eye, my freedom is calling, so I take that as my cue to get the hell away from Maleficent. When I reach the metal car handles and fling open the doors, the fresh air I've been so desperately seeking isn't so fresh. Humid and suffocating is more like it. It reminds me that I am in the south. But I don't care at this point, anywhere is better than in there with her.

A group of men are standing by the trailer that we brought with us. I can hear excitement coming from them. Andrew's talking and pointing at objects on the car. Van has his finger up to his chin, listening and nodding. He is laser focused on what Andrew is telling him. I notice a man to the right of him; short but muscular wearing jeans with grease stains, t-shirt, and ball cap, writing on a notepad.

What a sight before me? These men are not like the men I'm used to. They are laughing, down-to-earth men, enjoying what they are doing but taking it very seriously. They each nod and add their two cents but touch the car as if it'll break. Van's hand glides over the mangled metal, bends down to eye level, and examines the area closer.

David and his friends gather around these machines to discuss the power behind them and what they will be buying next, but never lay a finger on them other than to get behind the wheel.

Andrew spots me and waves me over. "I'm going to be headed out in a bit and just wanted to talk with you for a second." He leads me by the shoulder to the front of the truck. "Please do me a favor, relax.

Van will be quick and he's good at his job, so sit back and let him do the work. Think of this as a vacation."

I can't help but roll my eyes. "I'm serious, if you find something new or someone who makes you happy, it's okay to let go of the guilt and grief. You did nothing wrong that night, and you've dealt yourself a life sentence that you don't deserve."

With those words he kisses me on the top of my head and walks back to the group of guys while I stand dumbfounded by what he just said. I know every word is true, it wasn't all my fault, but it's because of me that David is the way he is.

I'm so involved in my own thoughts it takes a horn to bring me back to present. "Hey, sweetie! You're going to get run over," a guy yells.

Turning to face the door, I realize that is the last place I want to be. Andrew is handing Van some cash, and they seem to be having a private conversation among the Bugatti being unloaded off the truck. I can't help but notice the tight expression on Van's face and how he seems to be soaking in every word Andrew is saying. When they finish, both turn to face me.

Crap.

Andrew walks away from Van and toward me. "Van's going to show you to your place. I don't want to freak you out, but it's more," pausing for longer than necessary, "modern than you're used to."

Right away I know what that means. "Am I staying in a tent?"

Van's voice filters through the warm air before I even notice he's standing beside Andrew. "No tent, but 'tiny, itty bitty living space', yes," he says as he brings his thumb and finger to emphasize his point, acting out the Genie impersonation from the Disney movie *Aladdin.*

I can feel my face flame. I'm not sure if it's the idea of living in a small space, or the cuteness of Van's Genie impression, or that I'm a married woman finding my full attention on a stranger.

I muster through my thoughts. "How small?"

"Follow me," Van answers my question, gesturing for us to follow him.

He takes a few steps ahead, and Andrew starts walking. I tug on his shirt to halt him. "What did you get me into?"

"Relax, it's as peaceful as your chapel, I promise." I think I hear him mutter under his breath, "Maybe smaller."

Rolling my eyes, I huff at his promise. There's nowhere as peaceful as my little chapel.

We walk what feels like miles around the metal building, but I take in the beauty of it. Large windows, workmanship of the simple things such as door signs or vintage Coke machines. It seems to have personal touches everywhere on the exterior. Among the beauty is the noise of restoration. Machines grinding, metal clanging, engines firing, and people laughing.

When we reach the very end of the building, I see what Andrew is talking about and I can't believe what's in front of me.

Three tiny houses in a row, with siding, window shutters, porches, and fences encapsulating a tiny yard. They aren't much bigger than a child's playhouse, but so much smaller than a house. There's also a rundown brown trailer beside them, but it doesn't take away from their beauty.

Van swings his head around and brushes the curls from his eyes. "These are part of my new business venture. Bradley Tiny House Design, and you, my dear, are the first resident. Well, aside from myself and my granddad." I can't help but look at him in awe. "They're beautiful."

"Really?" he asks in a high-pitched voice.

"Van, she lives in a mansion but spends most of her time in a shed," Andrew adds.

Scrunching his face, he says, "Huh?"

I hit Andrew on the shoulder, not wanting him to expose my secrets. "Can I see inside?" I ask, not filtering my thoughts at the imposition.

Oh my, what a beautiful sight. These tiny houses are a dream come true, and if they are half as beautiful on the inside as they are on the outside, I'm in love.

Van steps up on the porch to the gray tiny house with black shutters and white window frames. I gape at the small porch swing and window flowerpots.

When the door opens, I'm amazed at what I see.

"It's a little more than two-hundred-twenty square feet. But I kept it as modern and eco-friendly as I could," Van explains.

I walk into the tiny space and feel like I've walked into another world. The entire house is no bigger than my bedroom at home, but is as quaint as any house I've ever been in. Van's eyes shine with pride as he gives us a tour.

"This is your kitchen area with a small stove and fridge. There's a small table that folds down for extra space." He demonstrates by flipping it up and down.

As I look around, the functionality of the small space is incredible. Turning my body in a three-hundred-sixty-degree rotation, I'm able to cook, eat, do laundry, relax on a sofa, and use the bathroom.

"This is something, Van, but I don't understand," Andrew says.

"You know I like new business ventures. A friend came to me and expressed a need for affordable housing. I like it because people who are disabled can live independently. It also works well for people who can't afford a mortgage, a lot of land, or just want a small space."

He has good reasons for building these tiny homes; I get the feeling that there's something he's leaving out. His business is obviously extravagant; there's no need to live in a small house.

His light eyes find me. "You'll like it here. You can look after the progress of the car, have your own house and if you want, you can hang around the shop. I have some really great friends who pop in and out from time to time." Andrew raises an eyebrow at Van. "Okay, all the time." I didn't miss the edge in his voice as he said look after the car. This is the first time he's let on that he isn't as friendly as he seems.

"That's more of the truth," Andrew says, turning his attention on me. "I'm going to head out now. Give me a hug."

Andrew wraps his arms around me and squeezes me tight. I return the gesture, and a very specific feeling of sadness washes over me, not for Andrew leaving, but for me being on my own.

Whispering in my ear, he says, "I wouldn't leave you here if I didn't trust him. No matter what the Dawson's say, you're my priority."

He kisses me on the forehead and releases me. He gives one last wave before he walks out the door.

"I'll be out in a second," Van calls.

Interrupting is a skinny young kid, struggling to carry my luggage. He even has my toiletry bag hanging from his mouth. It's a Chanel bag, for God's sake.

"Matt, bring those over here," Van yells.

I can't bear to watch Matt juggle my bags, so I turn my attention back to the tiny house. I glance around and notice its minimal decorations and the functionality. The one thing I don't see is a bed. I wonder where it is hidden.

As if he's reading my mind, Van answers my unspoken question. "Look above."

My eyes are drawn up to see a loft directly above the kitchen area. I am fascinated by this small space. I'm not sure why, and it's starting to bother me. I live in a mansion, but here I am, lusting over this tiny space.

"I know it's not what you're used to, but I think you'll enjoy it." He sighs, and his voice deepens, "I'm not going to give you a hard time as long as you keep your opinions to yourself about how I restore the Bugatti. Andrew told me you had a tough couple of days, so just relax and hang out. I'll set up an office in the main shop so when Mr. Dawson visits, he'll think you've been keeping an eye on me, but I don't expect to be working on it in the main shop. I work mostly in the old shop."

I'm confused... I didn't notice another building. I guess I'm getting to see how protective over his work he is, but I don't blame him, I'm the same way about mine.

"Thank you for the accommodation, I'll be fine. I don't intend to get in your way as long as you do the work quickly and correctly," I say and mentally want to slap myself, embarrassed by the crude tone and snotty attitude. I remind myself I'm not talking to an employee. I've entered this world of people who are carefree, and here I am, Miss Stuffy Pants—or I guess, Stuffy Dress. They probably think I'm boring. Violet has obviously made that perfectly clear.

"Good, I'm glad. If you need anything else, we'll be in the shop." Van smiles, but it doesn't reach his eyes, giving a quick nod, acting as if my snotty nature hadn't affected him in the least, but his curt smile says otherwise. I watch as he casually strolls up to the shop with Andrew and Matt, slapping Andrew on the back and playfully chatting. Before I opened my stupid mouth, his smile was so good-natured, simple, and pure. He seems to be a happy guy. No malice behind his eyes, no intimidation or darkness, but I get the feeling that maybe me being here is going to cause that to change.

4

It's dark, I'm in my pajamas, ready to kiss this day goodbye and fall asleep. As I apply the last of my moisturizer to my face, a loud thumping comes from outside, making me jump, inhaling cream up my nose. Ugh!

I haven't paid much attention to the outside world since I walked into my new space. Organizing my things has been my priority. Mr. Bradley has done an efficient job at making the space functional, as well as comfortable.

The noise increases, causing my nerves to ignite. How's anyone supposed to get some sleep around here? I check my graduation gift from my parents, a Rolex with diamonds around the circumference of the watch. Twelve twenty-one, I peek out the tiny peephole. The number of cars in the parking lot has doubled. On my tiptoes, I push my face closer to the door, straining to see what's going on. I didn't notice earlier, but there's a smaller, wooden garage behind the main garage. The light beams from the garage door, revealing a large crowd of people gathered between the two shops. Lawn chairs, stools, motorcycles, and cars litter the area. There are people standing around with cans in their hands, others look like they are working on some car part on the ground, and some are walking back and forth between garages.

The sound of pounding on metal clanging makes me jump away from the peephole.

Damn it! Why on earth are they working so late? Don't they realize what time it is? I creep back over to look out again to see who thinks it's a great idea to bang on a car in the middle of the night.

Of course, in the middle of the circle of people is Van, with what looks like a hammer in his hand. His arm effortlessly swinging, striking the metal with ease. I can't help but notice his rhythm as he pounds. His mouth is moving but I can't hear what he's saying.

I'm hypnotized by the beat of his pounds, unable to look away, I can't help but notice his exposed arm, I can see that it's muscular from all the way over here. My smushed nose is making it difficult for me to get my eye closer to the hole so that I can see him clearer.

What am I doing?

Pushing away from the door, I catch myself acting as the official peeping Tom of Bradley Restoration. My breath is heavy, my heart's racing, my hormones running rapidly through my body, and there's a tingle between my thighs. *What's happening to me?*

I stare at the white door as if it has the answers. A few moments later, I screech as a knock answers my question.

My body freezes, but my head turns looking for someone to tell me what the hell is going on. There's another knock, this time a little louder.

I peek through the now familiar peephole. The object of my stalking is standing with his arms crossed against his chest, and his muscular arms are close enough to reach through the door and touch. Glancing at his face, I expect to see the friendly face I did earlier, but instead he's wearing a scowl.

I straighten my black satin pajama shirt, pulling it down farther so that my thighs aren't exposed. I take a deep breath and open the door.

"Hello," I say as business-like as I can manage.

He nods and walks past me, into the house. "I saw your light on," he says casually, but I'm still processing the smell of oil and grease mixed with a fresh soap scent as he passes by me. He asks another question, but I have no idea what he's said.

"What?" I ask, holding my breath.

"I asked, did we wake you? We must have, you look a little out of it."

"Umm...yeah, I mean, no. I was getting ready to go to bed."

"Well...I wanted to let you know, since you're overseeing my work, I'll need an extra week at least, maybe more. He really did a fucking number on the frame. It's going to take me longer than I thought." His face hasn't changed; he's still scowling at me. What happened to that smile he greeted me with earlier?

"Okay." I swallow and cross my arms, feeling uncomfortable with the look on his face.

"Okay, then. I figured you'd like to know as soon as possible so you could do whatever you needed to do to stay longer. I was talking with the guys, and they're not as cool with you being here. How about you just let me do what I do and go home." The side of his mouth quirks up a smidge, confidence practically radiating from his pores.

He finally gives me a hint of a smile, and it's at the notion of me leaving. A fire ignites inside me. "I'll be staying for the duration. No matter how long it takes you," I retort.

"Look...I'm not trying to be a dick here, but you're going to hate this place. We're not your crowd. I doubt you want to leave the comfort of this house and hang out in the garage and drink beer with us."

He was so right, yet so wrong, too. There's a part of me that wants to go over so badly and see what's going on. The idea of "hanging out" with him awakens something inside me, but was quickly doused when he insinuated that, "we're not your crowd." I never had the chance to have fun and be part of a crowd, or even have many friends. I jumped straight into a marriage that's been over for a long time.

"You're right." These are not my kind of people. I won't fit in their world. I'm here to make sure they do their job and to get home to my husband. "I also would like to get some sleep. Do you think you can tell your friends to turn down the music? Or maybe stop the pounding?"

He smirks, shaking his head. "Nope, I've got work to do, Mrs. Dawson. And I work to music." His body moves close to mine and my heartrate picks up a few beats, his hand reaches up to my face and my heart stops altogether. He swipes a rough finger across the tip of my nose. "You got something on your face." Heat creeps up my face as I realize what I must look like. I forgot to wipe off all the cream.

He laughs, wipes his finger on my silk-covered shoulder, and turns to open the door. "When you pull the stick out of your ass, you can hang out with us." He winks and closes the door behind him.

Fuming, I pound to the door and lock it behind him. A few moments pass and Van screams, "Let's party!"

****

As I lie on the soft mattress, I gaze up at the ceiling of the tiny house that's made of glass. Various windows, different sizes and shapes, but all provide the glorious view of blue sky and fluffy white clouds.

I drag my still tired butt out of bed and gather myself to get ready and face my day. I was so embarrassed after he left last night. Of course, I couldn't sleep because of that, and the noise didn't stop until almost four in the morning. I inhale, shrugging off the rough night.

Climbing down the wooden ladder, which is the only way to get down from the raised bed, I step into the kitchen. The smell of freshly brewed coffee greets my senses. Thank God I set the timer last night...I pour the coffee into a mug that says, 'Fuck off until I have a cup of joe'. Laughing to myself, this would never be appropriate in the Dawson mansion.

I turn around and open the wooden screen door, opposite the front door that leads to a row of trees, tall grass, and beautiful wildflowers. The colors are amazing: a rainbow of purple, blue, and pink sprinkles the green grass.

What a glorious morning as the sun gleams down on the beautiful view in front of me. I inhale the aromas that can only be described as heaven on earth. Fresh air, not mixed toxins. It's too bad I have nothing but drunks surrounding me. They were so loud and obnoxious. I swear Van told them to be as loud as possible.

I stop the thoughts and inhale again. I'm going to do what I came here to do and leave as soon as possible.

"It's something, isn't it?" Van says quietly. I jump at his words. "Sorry, I didn't mean to scare you, but I was having my morning cup of joe too." He raises his coffee cup that mirrors mine.

I never even noticed that the back porch was attached to the tiny house beside mine. Van sits in all his morning glory, shirtless and in black boxer briefs. His chest is glorious. Not a big, bulky, chest like a weightlifter, but defined and lean. My gaze can't help but follow down to his muscular abs. He must spend his extra time in the gym. The sight of him is as beautiful as the view I was admiring a moment ago.

His dark hair waves in the breeze, eyes squinting in the sun, but a peaceful smile plays on his lips. *There it is, that smile, his smile.*

I'm taken aback and mute.

"Everything okay?" he asks, but sits forward in his lounge chair, waiting for a response. His golden skin is like a precious gem that's begging to be touched.

"Sorry, yes. Everything is fine. You just startled me," I manage.

"Didn't mean to, I just thought I'd better say something before I seemed like some sort of creeper. How'd you sleep?" He chuckles while bringing the cup to his lips.

I manage, "Fine." I'm distracted by the way he makes sipping hot coffee look so sexy.

"Do you want to sit?" He taps the chair beside him.

It's then that I realize what I'm wearing; an oversized Superman t-shirt and underwear. I changed after he left, ruining my silk night-gown with my face cream. I'm sure he sees the look of embarrassment strapped on my face.

I tug down my shirt, "No, thank you. I'll see you in a bit."

Turning around, I pad into the tiny house as fast as I can, slamming the door shut behind me. He saw me in my underwear, oh God! They weren't even cute or sexy, almost granny panties. He's such a jerk. How many times can I embarrass myself in front of him.

It shouldn't matter, I have no right to be worried about what he thinks of me, but the reality is, David hasn't looked my way in months. He hasn't touched me since the accident. He hasn't even called to see if I arrived or if I'm in need of anything. No, he doesn't care about me, and I ask myself why I care so much, and the only answer that I ever get is: guilt.

I rummage through the suitcase in the corner and remove a bra and a fresh pair of underwear. I grab my suit that's hanging in the tiny closet space and place it on the hook on the bathroom door.

Bathroom? No, it's a small shower with a toilet inside the shower. I have to make sure to leave the lid closed so I don't overflow the toilet with my shower water.

I roll my eyes at the thought. What have I gotten myself into? Yes, this is a cute space, but it wouldn't work for my day-to-day life.

By the time I'm getting dressed, my elbows are sore from whacking them against the walls of the shower. I throw on my robe and begin putting on my makeup. Part of the Dawson Legacy is Dawson Cosmetics. They run several other ventures, including a multi-million-dollar jewelry empire, but I must say this is my favorite of all their companies, and I'm on track to be the head of the company. If I have a successful launch of my small line, it may become mine to run.

I enjoy being able to test out new products, have my makeup done by the finest makeup artists in the world. It makes me feel so beautiful for the short period of time I allow myself to be glamorous.

Being glamorous at the office doesn't get you taken seriously by employees or the Dawson family. I've been an accountant for years for Dawson Enterprises. My usual attire is a skirt suit, plain blouse, and heels. My love of shoes is the only way I let some of my personality shine. I do love my Jimmy Choo's.

When I'm finished, I glance in the mirror provided on the living room wall. I giggle to myself; living room, kitchen, bathroom, and dining room all within three-hundred-sixty degrees of the spot I'm standing in. I look professional in my cranberry suit and white silk blouse, and of course, my matching cranberry heels.

As I exit, I see that the shop has come to life again. Several cars have arrived, and the sounds of machinery have taken over the quiet morning.

Walking across the gravel parking lot in heels is no easy task. My ankles are wobbling with each step. I slow down to avoid hurting myself. Approaching closer, I can see into the large showroom window. Bright violet hair stands out among the vast array of colors.

The door chimes when I walk into the showroom.

Violet's smile is replaced with a venomous smirk as her eyes meet mine. *Great, this is all I need to start my day.*

I glance quickly at the cars lining my path to her. I'm not even sure what I'm supposed to be looking for. I have no idea about cars, and already know that my presence here is not welcome by Violet or Van.

"Hi, sweetie, you here to make sure Van knows how to do his job, or that he doesn't fuck up your precious car?" Her eyebrow raises. "You have no fucking clue what kind of car you have, do you?" she snips.

She's right, I don't give a shit about this car. It's David's and I want nothing to do with it, but because Mrs. Dawson feels this is part of my punishment and has threatened my future in the cosmetics firm, I'm glad to be away from the Dawson's. Although, I wish it was under different circumstances.

"Where can I find Mr. Bradley?" His name alone makes me inwardly cringe and want to hide at the thought of him seeing me half naked this morning.

"Sleeping Beauty hasn't come in yet. So, you're stuck with me." The wicked gleam in her eyes makes me believe I'm in for a rough time.

I take a moment to glance at the rest of her, besides her vibrant purple hair, she's wearing ripped jeans, a tank top with the shop's logo, and black high heel lace-up work boots. She has leather bracelets lining both wrists, and a small diamond garnishing her nose.

There couldn't be two more different people in one room.

I have dealt with meaner people than her. My mother-in-law makes her look as sweet as Snow White. I take a second to square my shoulders and gain the strength I need to stand up for myself.

"I was told that a workspace would be provided for me."

"Not anywhere near me, thank God. You're in the garage so you can hover over Van and the boys." Violet turns and pushes open the door behind her.

She takes both hands and cups them around her mouth and yells as she shakes her head, "Boys, your new boss is here."

Violet turns to me. "This is the shop. That desk over there is yours. Don't ask me to clean it off, I refuse to clean up for you, princess."

With eyes rolling, I don't reply and walk toward the desk covered with rags, boxes, random tools, and automotive parts of some kind, I guess, and who knows what.

I can hear hushed voices talking, but can't hear exactly what they're saying. I decide to block them out. Setting my bag on the ground, I start removing the contents of the desk. Before I even get the first box moved, Matt is beside me.

"Here, I'll get this cleaned off for you. Van told me to do that yesterday before I left but I forgot." Matt smiles apologetically.

He's probably right out of high school. He's slim with short blond hair and a cute smile. I bet he gets lots of attention from girls his age. He reminds me of a young bad boy.

We both start clearing off the desk, but I soon stand back because I have no idea where to put all of it.

He places some items on shelves around the shop, but mostly throws them in the trash. Matt finishes wiping down the table with a rag, and suddenly, a beautiful dark mahogany desk appears.

"Thank you, Matt."

"No problem, I just wish I would have remembered yesterday. Van's going to be pissed at me."

"I'll make sure that he won't be," I say, giving him a reassuring smile.

Matt walks away, and I settle my bag on the desk. Luckily, the black leather chair isn't covered in dust or boxes. The thought of grease suddenly stops me, so I swipe my hand along the seat of the chair making sure my suit won't be ruined.

Lucky for me, my hand is clean.

I sit down and take out my laptop. I have a ton of work to do for the makeup line, even though I'm not in charge yet.

One day, if I can believe Mr. and Mrs. Dawson, I'll be able to make decisions, or perhaps having some of my ideas heard, for the cosmetics division of Dawson Enterprises.

My laptop has kept me company for the last few years and it's certainly doing that now. The makeup division is in balance, and our jewelry division is balancing billions in profits. Peace fills me immediately. I'm good at my job; it's the rest of the world I have trouble with.

As I'm about to turn my attention to the makeup division and see what's new in the departments, I hear someone say, "What a fucking idiot," near David's car.

When I look up, Van's standing there staring at it. His back is to me. He's wearing a tight black t-shirt accentuating his back muscles. His arms look as if they're crossed in front, making his back muscles more defined. My eyes automatically follow down and I notice his jeans are worn, stained, and fit perfectly over his butt. As soon as the word butt pops in my head, my brain takes over and scolds. I immediately look away from him.

I sit back down and hide behind my laptop. I begin typing, not even sure what I'm typing, anything to pretend I didn't just check out Van's ass.

Within minutes, I hear more voices come into the room. A gravelly voice starts complaining about how early it is to be working. A man with long blond hair pulled back into a ponytail, beard, and carved jaw line is the one speaking. He is not my type at all, rugged, tattooed and so manly, but very attractive. *Do you have to be gorgeous to work here?*

I force myself to look away, continuing to concentrate on nothing on the laptop.

"Van, did you see what he did to the wheels. What a fucking idiot," another voice mocks.

"I just said the same thing. Let's get a list going of what he fucked up, and then see if we can get parts for the easy stuff, but I'm sure I'll need to fabricate most of them," Van answers.

I look up in time to see Van's face staring back at mine.

"I don't want to be a dick, but are you seriously going to sit here and watch us all day and night? Drew was vague, but I assume this is the last place you want to be in your overpriced suit." Van comes across as cocky, and I'm not liking it at all, nothing like the polite, shirtless neighbor earlier.

My instincts kick in. I've dealt with plenty of cocky, entitled assholes. Swallowing, I say, "I'm here to make sure you finish the car and finish correctly," assuming my serious businesswoman role.

Another man comes into the garage. He's tall, and his arms are large, but I don't think there is a spot on his arm not sporting a tattoo. His hair's cut short, and he's very handsome. Striking blue eyes narrow on me.

"Like you even know where to begin, empress." The man's sarcastic tone only fuels my response.

"I know that this car should be finished by the time my husband arrives, and if it's not you will all be sued." I feel my back straighten as I square my shoulders back. I can bark back too.

"Jake, back your Cadillac out!" Van says, then turns to face me. His eyebrows raise and dark eyes narrow as his head tilts, assessing me.

Instantly I regret my attitude. I've pissed him off...all of them, actually.

"You don't have to worry, it will be finished by the time he gets here. I already told you last night because of your husband's lack of driving skills, he's really fucked up this car and it's going to take more time. We restore classic cars here, not fix them so they look pretty. Whether you believe it or not, there is a big difference between restoring a car to its natural beauty and fixing a crashed car. I'm doing *this* car because I'm fucking good at what I do, and because you and your hubby are paying me a pile of cash, so I couldn't refuse. But I need you to understand something, this is my garage." He walks closer and slams his hand down on the desk, then bends to look directly into my eyes. "I don't take orders from you, and you have no say in what I do. Why your husband would send you to babysit his car is beyond me? But whatever, it's your life, just stay out of the way." Van's dark eyes trap me with his harsh stare.

I involuntarily shrink in my seat in response to being scolded. I'm surprised he hasn't passed out from his long-winded speech.

When his gaze releases me, I let out the breath I was holding. What on earth do I say to that? I knew he wasn't happy with me being here, but it's taken a turn for the worse.

"Van, you have to see what the moron did to the exhaust," Jake yells from across the garage.

Van is staring at the desk, not looking at me. He doesn't say a word, pauses, then turns to face Jake.

By the time I regain my composure, Van's already deep in conversation with Jake.

I'm not sure what to do next, so I close my laptop, gather my purse, and stride out the garage door.

My heels are making it difficult to walk at the pace my brain wants me to... which is light speed out of this garage, and this town. I'm not sure why his attitude is bothering me so much. I've taken much worse from David, sometimes within seconds of being in his presence. I don't even know Van.

"Mrs. Dawson, please stop." I hear another unfamiliar voice.

I don't answer and continue toward my destination to the other tiny oasis besides my chapel.

The voice calls for me again, but this time he's caught up with me. He's tall and slim, short blond styled hair and black-rimmed glasses. "Please don't worry about Van, it's not you...he's got some personal issues going on."

"I appreciate that, but we all have personal troubles, don't we?"

He stops at my words, but I continue.

When I reach my house, or *his* house, I slam the door behind me and dial Andrew.

"Hey, how's it going?" Andrew asks.

"How's it going? Let me tell you how it's going, I'm being treated like I'm some sort of criminal for watching them work. You need to pick me up now!" I can't help the disdain in my voice.

"I can't, I'm escorting Dawson senior around today. I'm on his watch until God knows when."

"Fabulous. Then let me tell you about your wonderful buddy and how he's treating me like a cockroach that's hanging around that he can't get rid of. So much for *Van's a great guy.*" I mock in Andrew's voice.

"Did you call him a grease monkey?" There's no humor in his tone.

"No, of course not..." The memory of my snotty tone comes back, and I confess, "but I may have told him he needs to have the car done in time."

"You can't boss these guys around, Emmy. You think they listen to any kind of authority, or give a shit if he takes his business elsewhere? I'll call Van, smooth things over."

I huff. "I think he should apologize to me. I can't believe you're taking his side."

"You've been stuck in the Dawson family too long. Just try to be...friendlier, okay?"

"Fine. I can't wait to get out of here. Any idea when David is coming?"

"Not yet, I'll let you know when I do. I'll talk to you later. Don't take the job literally, have fun, and be nice. Like a vacation."

My hope fades, I'm on my own. I've faced far worse; an insensitive mechanic can't be the worst thing I've ever dealt with.

"Don't worry about it. I can handle myself," I concede, but he's already hung up. I remove my suit jacket, heels, and climb up the ladder. Lying across the bed, I stare up at the sky and close my eyes.

"Vacation?" I say to the air, like that's even possible.

5

I'm not sure how long I've been staring at the sky, but it doesn't seem long enough. My satin shirt became uncomfortable, so here I lay with only my bra and skirt on. Climbing down the ladder, I grab a tank top from my suitcase resting on the kitchen counter. If I had my cell phone in hand, I'd hashtag it: tiny house problems.

Exhaling a breath of relief at the quiet, I open the fridge. I sigh, empty. I don't even know where there's a grocery store in this town, even if I did, how would I get there? I don't have a car or a driver's license. Dear Lord, I'd have to ask Van, or worse, Violet.

Turning to my right, I pick up my bag and rummage through it for some type of snack. I bought a bunch of junk food at a gas station on our way here.

Reaching for my favorite chips, the doorbell rings, followed by a knock.

Ugh...I hope it's not that guy with the glasses. He's the only one who isn't trying to be a jerk, but I can't take any more today. I peek at myself in the small mirror on the wall. My cleavage is showing, so I yank up my tank top to cover myself.

I open the door to see Van leaning against the doorframe, looking up to the sky while his dark curls move in the wind. His layered hair falls perfectly in motion with the breeze.

I'm staring, but I can't make my lips move.

"You going to invite me in?" He cocks his head to the side. "Never mind, I own this place." He walks past me, while I stand, immobile. As he turns to face me, his eyes seem to land on my tank top and he swallows, causing me to wish I hadn't ever taken off my shirt. I clear my throat. He takes his eyes off me.

"Sorry." I clear my throat again, extremely uncomfortable in the moment. "I didn't expect to see you after your little speech out there."

"Believe me…the less I have to deal with you, the better."

Ouch, that stung.

I must not have covered my hurt quick enough because his eyes soften, fixing his casual stance. "There's a problem with you staying in this house…I sold it." He pushes his hair back off his face.

"Oh…yeah?" Not sure what else to say, I add, "Congratulations, you must be very…happy?"

His eyes brighten, "Yeah, the dude's paying way too much but…it's his life." He shrugs.

"I suppose." With a glimpse of hope, I ask, "Can you tell me where there might be a hotel and I'll be out of your hair." Saying the word causes me to look directly at his hair again. I'm momentarily distracted wondering how his barber gets the layers to fall perfectly into place, framing his gorgeous features. I shake myself out of it as he begins to speak.

"That's the thing, there isn't a room available. We have a big show, a car thing in a few days, so all the hotels in the area are booked." He shoves his hands in his pockets and leans back on his heels, looking like he's about to deliver some horrible news. "So, um…" He pauses.

"Um, what? I can't leave, he'll make my life hell." I can't believe I just said that out loud and hurry to cover my mouth, in shock that it slipped out so easily.

"What do you mean?" Van stops his nervous stance and straightens his shoulders, stepping closer. "Hell? What kind of hell are we talking about?"

"Oh...you know, typical married people...hell." I end up stammering the words, waving my hand dismissively. His eyes narrow, but I don't think he's buying it.

"No, I don't know. I'm not married." Van swipes his hand down his face, inhaling as if he's calming himself.

I'm surprised he's getting upset. Trying not to overthink the situation, I say quickly, "I didn't mean it the way it came out, just he wanted me here to make sure things were done to his specifications. He's sort of a control freak."

Oh shit! That sounded far worse.

"A control freak?" He opens his mouth to say something but closes it. His face turns a shade of red that I haven't seen before, but he calmly manages to state, "Anyway, it's none of my business," he says under his breath. "You can stay at my place, there's a loft above the garage, or there's a house trailer near the old garage so you can have your own personal space." Van moves to the door, opens it, and steps out onto the porch. "See?" He turns to his right, pointing at the dark brown trailer that's falling apart. It looks as if it's been sitting here since the seventies. "But if you're not comfortable with that, you can stay on my couch."

"Your couch? No, I can't do that to you. I'm not going to take over your house." Oh my, there's no way I can handle being in his space, with him...alone. I can barely function as it is now.

"I've stayed on my couch many times. No big deal. Sorry, I know I promised Andrew I'd take good care of you. I wouldn't be keeping my word to him if I left you to fend for yourself."

I don't miss the way he emphasizes his promise to Andrew. This is becoming a big ordeal, and it's the last thing I wanted. I've only been here one day, and nothing is going according to plan. Not like anything was set in stone, but it did include having a place to stay. The only thing for me to do is suck it up and stay in the old trailer. I'm sure it isn't that bad. This tiny house is basically a trailer.

Conceding to my new fate, I say, "I'll stay in the trailer."

"You sure, you haven't seen it yet? No one has stayed there in years." He cocks his head to the side, "Well...except for when people get shitfaced and I kick their ass out of the shop." He laughs to himself.

"I'll be fine." I turn away from him, walking back into the house. "I'll get my things packed up." My voice cracks.

He shrugs, "Okay, then. Ace will be over to help you with your bags." He smirks, "If you change your mind, my couch is open."

I nod, turning back to shoving my makeup back into my toiletry bag.

A few minutes later, I look through the blinds to see where Van went. His back is to me as he's talking to Ace in front of the brown trailer, pointing at a cracked window. It looks awful. Peeling chocolate paint, front screen door falling off its hinges, and to top it all off, the trailer is sitting up on cement blocks.

I don't want to be uptight or entitled, but I'm having trouble erasing the images of several mansions and some of the world's most exquisite places I've vacationed, so the thought of living in a trailer that's falling apart and where people are banished to when they've had too much to drink, is making my stomach churn.

"What am I getting myself into?" I say out loud, falling back onto the bench.

I lie there for what seems like an hour, but probably is more like ten minutes, as the doorbell chimes. Sitting up, I head toward the door.

Ace stands on the porch, wearing a beaming smile. He rubs his hands together, "I'm ready to be of assistance."

I smile in return, his cute smile rubs off on me, helping me forget the huge mistake I'm about to make.

"This is all my stuff." I gesture to the few bags sitting on the counter.

"Good." He steps over and takes all three bags in one hand. His brow furrows, "Are you sure you want to stay in that..." He thumbs in the direction of the trailer.

"I'll be fine. It's as big as this place, and I've been fine here."

"Yeah, but that isn't like this. It's a shithole. I don't think Van's doing what's best for you."

I'm taken aback by his admission. "What do you mean?"

He shrugs. "I think he can find a better place for you to stay. You can even stay at my place. It's not much, but at least it doesn't smell...and it's clean."

I sigh, none of my options are good. I barely know Ace or Van, there's no way I should stay with either.

"I'll be fine, but thanks for the offer."

We leave the tiny house and walk to the trailer. It's stationed across from the older garage that's now filled with the Bugatti and its parts.

I turn my attention to the trailer as we get closer. Oh God, it's worse than I thought.

Ace takes the key out of his pocket and steps closer to the trailer. I can't help thinking why does he even lock it? Someone could probably just kick in the door. There are two wooden crates seated side by side for makeshift steps. Ace drops my bags onto the gravel, and I inwardly cringe at the thought of my luggage getting ruined.

He struggles getting the key to cooperate, but he finally kicks the bottom of the door and it opens. Ace gives me a faint smile. "It has a little trick to it."

As he opens the door, the scent of mold, rotten eggs, and a smell I can't even place, assaults us. "Shit!" Ace says, covering his nose. "That's fucking awful. It's way worse than I remember."

I stand on the crates, not wanting to move any farther, but I do. My eyes dart to the inside of the trailer. There's no way I can stay in this dump. Besides the horrid smells spewing out, the place is trashed, literally...papers, cans, food containers, and other random nonsense are scattered throughout the small space. There's a sink, fridge, and table at first glance. As I continue farther, the sink is filled with dishes and cups, covered in some type of mold that is now furry.

Ace must see the terror on my face. "You can't stay here."

"I don't want to stay with anyone. I'll be fine." But even I don't believe the stubborn words that continue to fall from my lips. "I know how to clean. It's either clean this or sit in there," pointing toward the shop. "With Violet staring holes into my forehead."

He laughs, his perfect white teeth gleaming back at me. I rake over his features. Ace is very handsome. He doesn't look like the other guys, very clean-cut, dressed in jeans and a blue and white pin-striped, button-up shirt. His hair is styled with some type of gel, unlike Van's whose haphazard locks fall into place all on their own.

I shake my head to stop my silly brain from concentrating on his hair, again. Jeez, what is wrong with me? *Get it together.*

Heels hitting the wooden crates cause me to turn my attention toward the door. Violet stands with a hand covering her mouth, and the other holds a stack of blankets and sheets. "Dear God, what the hell crawled up here and died." Her face crinkles. "Ugh...he must really not like you."

"Not funny, Violet, she can't stay here," Ace raises his voice.

"What? He's not making her? She doesn't want to stay at his place, this is the next best thing." She's right; I refuse to stay with him. Not only does it go against my marriage, but also, I can't seem to think straight around Van, and I don't want to continue to make a fool of myself around him.

"It'll be fine. I can clean it up. No big deal, I've stayed in worse." Lies, all lies. I never clean anything. Mrs. Dawson would have a fit if I cleaned up anything myself. "We have maids, dear," falls very easily from her lips.

Violet shrugs. "Whatever, I have towels too." She steps out for a second and then reappears with a few towels and washcloths. "Lucky for you, I do know the shower and shitter works. Ben used them a few nights ago when he couldn't hold his tequila."

I sigh a breath of relief; at least I don't have to use the bathroom in the shop. Thank heaven for small miracles.

She places the towels on the table and leaves without another word.

"Don't worry, I'll help you clean up in here. Let's start with the bedroom." Ace pads toward the room at the back of the trailer. I can't believe my eyes. It's actually clean. The mattress is almost white, and the tan carpet looks new, or at least not worn. He shrugs, "Huh? Not so bad?"

"See...I'll be fine. Thank you for your concern but I can clean it up with no problem."

"You don't always have to be so proper, you know." Ace's lips lift a fraction. "Just relax, we're not really that different from you." He touches my shoulder in a reassuring gesture, it doesn't help me relax, only makes me feel more uncomfortable. I'm not used to people touching me. Unlike Van, it doesn't send butterflies into chaos in my belly.

I give a polite smile, but back away from his touch. "I was raised that way. I can't help it."

He nods his head back and forth, raising his hands in surrender. "All right. All right. But I'm not leaving you with this mess. I'll just bill Van for the hours, and you should too. What an asshole making you clean up this place when you're paying for his new race car."

"Race car? He races?" The fact that he's using the money for a car doesn't bother me...no, it doesn't bother me at all. I'm taken aback by the tingle in my spine at the thought of him behind the wheel, speeding and taking a checkered flag.

Ace shrugs. "Yeah, ever since we were kids. He's an adrenaline junkie. He street races. More dangerous than any kind of racing you can do on the track."

The tingle in my spine turns to a lump in my throat. "I'm sure the vehicles are safe, mandated by officials?"

Ace's eyes crinkle and his boyish grin turns into a smirk. "There's nobody mandating the races besides the street racers. It's more of a...club, I guess is the best way to explain it to you, in terms you can understand. '*Jerk*,' I think to myself. "It isn't like NASCAR or Indy. If you don't follow the rules on the street...let's just say life gets a little more challenging."

"What do you mean?"

He huffs. "I shouldn't have said anything." He inches closer and places both of his hands on my shoulders, framing me with his body. "It doesn't matter, okay?" With his body this close to mine, and with such an intense look on his face, he seems much bigger in size and in presence. I back away, feeling uncomfortable, again. His hands fall and I turn to the sink.

"You can start in the fridge and I'll take the sink," I order while concentrating on finding the dish soap. Thankfully, within five minutes, his cell phone rings.

"Yeah. I'm with Mrs. Dawson," he says with a hint of authority. He takes his head out from the fridge and closes the door. "Right now?" He sighs, "Fine. I'll be right there."

He leans on the counter, his elbow supporting him. "I have to go. Van needs me to do some computer stuff. Do you want to come hang out over there?"

"No, I have too much to do. I really just want to get settled and go to sleep."

"Okay. Do you have your cell?"

"Yes, it's on the table."

He picks it up and taps the screen. "What's your code?"

"One, two, three, four."

He chuckles, "Really? You are a millionaire, and you don't have a more secure code?"

I give him a slight smile. "Nobody wants in my phone."

"Yes, they do, believe me. I just want to exchange numbers in case you need me. Change it when I'm gone." Both of his hands land on my shoulders, again, caging me with his body. "Please," he says softly.

I swallow, not sure if I should punch him or step back. Thankfully, he steps away.

He smiles, turns, and leaves the trailer.

What the hell was that about?

6

It's taken me five long hours to scrub mold off the plates, grime off of the counters, and God knows what else that was growing in the fridge, but the trailer is clean. I've wiped the walls, mopped the floors, and swept every inch of the trailer. I didn't know I had it in me.

Ever since I can remember, I've had maids, but never taken advantage of them. If something needed picked up or a chore done, I did it and continue to do so. However, I've never spent a whole day doing it. A sense of accomplishment comes over me. Grinning from ear to ear, I remove the mask from my face, able to breathe clean air for the first time in hours. The kitchen window's handle is the only one that isn't broken. I crank the handle, letting the window crack open and allowing some fresh air to drift in.

Dusk has come and gone. Finally, it's dark enough for me to get some sleep. I tread to the bedroom to unpack my things, again. It's nice to take my shoes off and walk from the tile floor to the carpet without being afraid of what I'm stepping on or in.

Changing back into my Superman t-shirt brings back the memory of a shirtless Van, carelessly drinking his coffee and his eyes drifting down to my legs. My stomach clenches in response. I roll my eyes at myself. I need to stop all this fantasizing. I'm a married woman, not a liar, or a cheater, so nothing is going to happen between us.

Gathering the sheets and blankets off the bed, I sniff them to see if I'm going to die from dust mites or bed bugs, considering Violet was the one who brought them to me. To my surprise, I inhale the fresh scent of fabric softener.

"She must have grabbed the wrong ones." I laugh to myself, but take a win where I can. Finally, comfy and cozy with a freshly made bed and clean space to call my own, I crawl into bed. Exhausted, my eyes close, finding sleep.

****

In a foggy haze, something tickles my face. The tickle runs down my neck onto my chest. A high-pitched squeak causes my eyes to flash open. A brown mass of fur sits on my chest; big, bright beady eyes stare back at me.

Oh...my...God! I scream at almost the same pitch as the mouse.

Within seconds, I jump up, flinging the covers off of my body and stand on the bed. The only light shines from the old garage, and it doesn't offer much visibility. I stand still, trying to focus on the bed, making sure the little rodent has run off. Instead, that same tickle that ran across my neck is now running across my toes.

I scream again, jumping off the bed.

The light in the trailer comes on. I blink to adjust to the light, as my eyes focus, Van stands in all his gorgeous glory. Shirtless, abs carved from stone and spattered with grease. His jeans hang low, a V hovering just above the seam mocks me as my gaze lingers.

"What the hell happened? What the fuck are you screaming about?"

I shake my head and take a breath. "A mouse," is all I can muster between being invaded by a mouse and a sexy, shirtless, abs-for-days mechanic.

"Are you fucking kidding me? All that for a little mouse."

"Yes! I woke up to that little mouse on my chest!" Fury rises in my voice. I glance at his face, careful not to notice his abs again. Out of my haze, I notice he's holding a metal bar, hand clenched tightly around the handle, making the veins on his arm pop out, exposing the detail of his muscles. He's like a walking Adonis.

He points at me with the bar. "You are such a..." He stops and drops the bar to his side.

"A what?" I retort, angry now.

"A princess, a spoiled rich brat. This is probably the first time you've ever lifted a finger to clean." He slings back at me, dropping the bar to the ground with a loud thud and crossing his arms.

Fury rises in my throat, causing me to step toe to toe with him. His crossed arms separate us, but I don't care. He's being an ass, and I'm going to let him know about it.

"I'm not a spoiled brat. You have no idea who I am or what my life is like. You're a grease monkey who got lucky that someone in your family was smart and actually made something out of nothing for you to inherit!" I yell, giving it back to him.

He sneers. "Grease monkey?"

As he says the words, Andrew's comments flash in my head.

"I'm...I'm sorry. I didn't mean it like that," I stumble, trying to find an apology.

"You know what, I was wrong. You are not a princess...you're a bitch!" I gasp. "That's right." He inches closer, his breath dancing against my face. His scent mixes in the air, causing me to glance at his mouth. The fire in my belly needs to be extinguished by his lips. I'm craving for him to douse the fire. "You know what else?" His voice lowers.

Looking up at his twinkling eyes, I breathe, "What?"

"With your hair falling from that bun," He reaches his hand to take a strip of my hair in his hand. "That's the sexiest little Superman t-shirt I've ever seen." Letting go of my hair, his hand floats down, brushing the collar, gliding his finger over to my shoulder and down to the bottom of my shirt. His voice becomes husky, "And with those black panties giving me a peep show, you almost make my dick hard...almost...but not really." He smiles, biting his lip as he backs away, wagging his brows.

"Argh! I can't believe you!"

"Me? You're the happily married *client* who is all hot and bothered. I can't help it you haven't been laid in forever."

"You're an ass!"

His back faces me, but he turns and adds, "I know, and let's keep it that way."

Oh no, he doesn't, this isn't over. He isn't getting away with treating me like that. I stride out the door after him. Forgetting about the severe drop-off from the doorway to the crates, I stumble. The gravel digs into the skin covering my knees while my fingernails scrape into the gravel.

"Jesus Christ!" echoes in the air.

I lift my head to Van hovering above me. "I'm fine," I spit. "Not like you care."

He bends down to my level, "Yeah...you look perfectly fine to me." He couldn't add any more sarcasm if he tried. *Ass!* "Here, let me help you up. You're not exactly what one would call graceful, are you?"

"I can get myself up." I shrug off his help by yanking my elbow from his grasp. I stand, wiping the gravel from my hands, bending down to swipe my knees. "You need to take care of this rodent problem."

He's laughing; the asshole is laughing in a vibrant, full-bodied way, touching his stomach as he bends over. "That was the fucking best."

"It wouldn't have been very funny if I would've gotten hurt and sued you, now would it?" A triumphant spirit wells inside of me.

He straightens, taking his hand off his belly, and shakes his head back and forth. "No, I'm not talking about your wipeout, I'm talking about how I got you to stay in the trailer and clean it. But I didn't expect a mouse to try to sleep with you. That was fucking classic."

"What are you talking about?"

"I'm talking about I've got an extra bedroom for you to stay in, and it is rodent free. Actually, it is pretty nice."

I don't believe this, not only is he laughing at me, but he did this on purpose.

"You set me up?"

Still laughing, he responds, "Damn right, I did. Somebody needed to knock you off your pedestal and help with that stick up your ass. Some old-fashioned elbow grease does wonders for a spoiled princess."

"So, you made me clean up your mess, and God knows who else's, and get attacked by a mouse, all so you could teach me a lesson." I step toward him and point my finger right at his chest. "Now look here...I'm paying you a very large sum of money to fix this stupid car, not for you to play jokes or games. Andrew went on and on about how you were a decent guy, but I'm beginning to think he's a bad judge of character."

As I glance away from his smug face, I notice we've gathered a crowd. Ace, Violet, Matt, Ben, and some others.

"I guess I can say the same about you. He didn't mention you were a bit of a brat."

I gasp.

Ace steps in between us. "Van, quit being a douche."

"This is none of your business, Ace." He has an edge to his voice.

"I'm making it mine. You're being an ass to a client. You'll be lucky if she doesn't call her husband right now and he sues you for harassment."

Van rolls his eyes, but his face softens.

Ace faces me. "I don't know what's gotten into him. He never acts this way...okay, he does, but not toward a client. Come on, I'll get the mouse out of the trailer."

"I'm not staying in there. I'm calling a car service and leaving ASAP." I go to grab my phone, but realize that it's not in my pockets, nor do I have pockets. I'm standing outside in just a t-shirt and panties.

"Don't worry. You can stay with me." Ace glances down at my thighs, but his eyes quickly jump up to my face.

Van turns to face us and inches closer, "No way. She's not staying with you. She'll stay with me. I've got plenty of room, besides...there's a hole in the roof of the trailer and we're supposed to get rain tomorrow." His lips quirk up in a smile... a genuine smile. "I'm sorry. I was just having a little fun. It's what I do, I truly didn't mean any harm." He bows as if he's bowing to royalty. "Not really...maybe a little."

"Really? Just joking? Do you realize how unprofessional this is? I could ruin your business in one minute if I wanted to."

He straightens and huffs out a breath. "I'm being unprofessional. How about you and your husband? Sending your wife to babysit your mechanic is about as insulting as you can get."

Stomping my bare foot into the gravel, stubbing my toe in the process, I shout, "I didn't want to come! He made me!"

Van's eyes widen, "Tell him to fuck off then and go home. You're a grown ass woman."

"It's not that easy."

"Yeah, it is." He steps closer, crossing his arms and lowering his voice so only he and Ace can hear. "What's really going on?"

I swallow. "Nothing."

He bites his bottom lip, and squints. "I don't believe you." He turns his head and says to Ace, "Get her shit, and bring it up to my place."

"Van..."

"Do it!" Van's voice raises.

Ace growls under his breath but walks back over to the trailer.

"Do you want me to escort you safely into the trailer?" Van asks sweetly, almost batting his eyelids. *Jerk.*

"No. I can manage."

"I'm sure you can. I mean, you didn't break anything, so that's a positive, right?"

I spin and poke at his chest, "Enough! Got it? Enough!"

Van puts his arms in the air in surrender. "Okay," he says softly.

"Imagine that—she bites back," Violet mutters under her breath.

I can hear others in the crowd mumbling among themselves, but I don't care about their opinions. I just want this night to end. I whirl back in the direction of the trailer and try to forget about the vast array of emotions that Mr. Donavan Bradley evokes.

I carefully step up on the crate and into the trailer. Ace is holding my yoga pants in his hand. "Here." He hands them to me.

"Thanks." I carefully slip them on, not wanting him to get more of a peek at my undies than he already has.

"You haven't unpacked too much. So, I just threw the few things of yours back in the bag." He pauses for a moment, "Do you want to stay at my place? I don't feel comfortable with you staying with him. He's being a real asshole. I've never seen him act like this."

"It's fine. I can handle it." As I say the words, I don't believe them. I have no idea how to handle him—or myself—when I'm around him.

7

— · —

Ace escorts me over to the older garage. As we inch closer, one of the garage doors is now closed. The crowd that had been milling around earlier seems to have disappeared. In all the chaos, I didn't notice anyone leaving.

"He has a really nice place. It's a loft, but it's nice. A hell of a lot nicer than that trailer." Relief washes over me as I let out a breath. "If you change your mind, you can give me a call. I'll be right over." He hands me a business card. Turning it over, it says Ace Monroe Racing. "You race cars too?"

"No, I turn them up."

"Umm...I don't know what that means?"

"It means he hooks the car up to a computer and pushes a button. Basically, tuning the car." Sneaking up behind us, Van answers for Ace, his tone less than enthused.

I roll my eyes, I can't help it. Can't he be nice for one second? I don't know why I apparently bring out the worst in him. For some reason, this fact hurts my heart.

Ace spins, standing toe to toe with Van. "I don't know what your problem is, but I've had enough of your bullshit!"

Van leans in, arms crossed, and his face reddens with each passing second. "You going to do something about it?"

Jesus, this is ridiculous. "Stop it!" Somehow, I manage to wedge myself in between them. They don't seem to notice. At least they're not throwing punches.

Ace doesn't say a word or even move. Van is equally poised to stay.

Van threatens in a low voice, "Go home."

Ace backs up and his eyes soften as he looks my way, pointing in my direction. "Call if you need me." He looks back at Van and nods. Van nods back, as if they're speaking in some sort of testosterone-fueled secret language.

Ace heads back toward the main shop. I spin to get answers from Van. "What is your problem?"

"Don't worry, princess, it has nothing to do with you." He nods to the garage. "Come on."

I huff but follow him into the garage. I don't really have another choice, it's not like I feel comfortable with Ace either. Something about him is...off.

The older garage is much smaller than the main garage. There are only two garage doors, and only one car inside, the Bugatti. To the left of David's car, I spot a few machines, but they look extremely old and worn. My curiosity piques at the one with a metal circle on the top and a smaller version on the bottom. "What is that?"

"An English Wheel."

It's all he says while I follow him to the side of the garage. We take the wooden stairs up to a small porch, stopping in front of a black, dented and peeling metal door, revealing its abuse. "I'll bring your stuff up after I show you around." He points down to the bottom of the stairs where my things are sitting. Ace must have set them down without me noticing.

"And?" He doesn't answer, of course, so I give it another try as we stand face to face. "What does an English Wheel do?"

"Shapes metal to fix your asshole husband's fucked-up car," he says, spinning to face the door to his apartment.

"Why are you being this way toward me?" He stops, causing me to bump into his back.

"What way?"

I can barely hear him because he has yet to turn and face me, his head pointed up to the night sky.

"A jerk! You have yet to be nice to me. I know you don't want me here, but I promise to stay out of your way. I plan on being invisible."

"Sounds good to me," he says, causing what little confidence I have to deflate, but I quickly bounce back, squaring my shoulders. "As long as you decide to act like an adult, we'll be fine from here on out," I say. Van looks over his shoulder and briefly nods. He takes a key out of his pocket, slides it into the lock, and the door opens.

He goes through, reaches up to his right, and the doorway brightens.

I follow a few steps behind him. As I walk through the doorway, I'm astonished at my view.

The apartment is huge. I can't believe it's above a garage. It's an open floorplan; the kitchen bleeds into the dining area that moves into a living room. The space is modern, with black and gray furniture, white kitchen cabinets, stainless steel appliances, and black laminate flooring.

"It's not much, but you'll be safe from Mickey Mouse here."

Ignoring his snide comment, I say, "This is really nice. I didn't expect much since you made me stay in mouse purgatory."

He crosses his arms and smirks. "You do have a personality, who'd a thunk it?" He laughs, shaking his head, then turns away from me, and heads into the kitchen.

I ignore his comment again, taking a look around. The white cabinets and black and white marble countertops are nothing short of beautiful. His kitchen is so clean, it actually sparkles. "I would have never thought you knew how to clean from the looks of that trailer."

"Yeah, well, at least I cleaned the trailer bedroom for you," he admits, twisting to place a plate on the counter in front of me. His black t-shirt stretches over his muscles, igniting the spark I thought had diminished. Van reaches over the center island and taps my jaw with his finger, "Close your mouth, it's not that astounding. I have OCD, and am not that big of a dick. Since you're staying here, we need to go over a few rules."

He turns his attention back to the counter, wiping the spotless plate with a towel. He cleaned the trailer bedroom for me? I'm not sure whether to be thankful or upset that he left the rest of the mess for me to clean.

Digging in the fridge, he sets out grapes, cheese, and strawberries. Then he moves to reach the top of the fridge, grabbing a box of crackers. The t-shirt rises with his arm, revealing enough skin to keep the flame burning. *Great, teenie bopper, get yourself under control!*

"Rule one, you sleep over there." Pointing to the black L-shaped couch. "My room is up there." He points again, but this time, he points up to the ceiling. As I glance up, a metal railing separates Van's bedroom from the rest of the apartment. A bed and dresser mock me.

"That's your room? There is no privacy. You can watch me sleep. You'll know every time I get up to use the bathroom." Oh no, I hope there is a private bathroom.

"Calm down, Ems." I jolt at my new name. I become even more aware of him at the sound of my name. "Bathroom has a door, and I can't see in it. I don't need to see you..." He puts a hand up to his mouth as if he's telling a big secret and whispers, "Take a piss."

"Ew...you're disgusting!"

He laughs, "Nah, it's easy to rile you up."

"I thought you said there was an extra room?" I ask.

"Yeah, the room with the couch. The living room."

I roll my eyes. Of course, he'd think this was a suitable room to sleep in.

"What's rule two?" I ask to put a stop to bathroom talk and his understanding of what an actual bedroom is.

He rubs his hands together, "Ahh...you're going to love these, I like a clean house, so you make a mess, you clean it. Rule three, I work a lot, so when I come home, I want the TV and couch. So, if you are sleeping when I get home, I'm turning it on and sitting on the other end of the couch, and I don't care if you wake up, got it?"

For a moment I think he's testing me, but he hasn't smirked or smiled. His eyes narrow, waiting for me to respond. "Okay."

"Last rule, I promise I'm done messing with you. I'd appreciate it if you'd give me some space. No more looking over my shoulder unless it's to hang out with everyone or to actually pick up a tool and help out."

We both smile, laughing at the ludicrous notion.

"Oh wait, one other thing."

"This is becoming a very long list."

"I know, but this is important. You're coming to the lake party tomorrow."

I scrunch my forehead. "I don't think so." I have no idea what this party entails. Plus, I don't go to parties. Especially with people I don't know well.

"Too bad, it's time for you to live a little. I know when I see someone who needs less working and more playing."

"We'll see," I say, not wanting to commit to anything permanent, but there's a glimmer in his eye that I just can't say no to.

"I'll go get the rest of your things, make yourself at home."

As he leaves, I purposely look down at my white leather flats to distract myself from watching the way his body moves. It takes everything I have not to check him out.

The door clicks closed, and I glance up, the anxiety lessening with his absence. The couch calls, I'm exhausted. A beige blanket and pillow are neatly stacked on the cushion. I would have never guessed he was so neat and accommodating by his earlier behavior.

The couch conforms perfectly to my body. I can't help but want to lie back and fall asleep. But I don't dare until Van is either gone or in his room. I'm still uncomfortable staying in his place. Maybe a little TV will settle me. Nothing like a little reality show to make me forget about my odd situation. Three remotes set on the table, and I have no clue which one will turn it on.

The door opens, pulling me from my thoughts. Bags slide through the door; Van follows, struggling to get the door closed. "Damn, Ems. Your bags are heavy. What the hell did you bring?"

"Not that much, really."

Putting his hands on his hips, he sighs. "I beg to differ. Anyway, I see you found your bed. Blanket and pillow are for you. Get comfy, I'm going to bed. It's been a long fucking day." He pauses, opens his mouth to say something, but doesn't.

Not sure what to say or do to stop the awkward silence, I say, "Goodnight."

He smiles, a pure, unfiltered smile, "'Night, Ems, hope you sleep well."

His smile hits my chest, causing my breath to falter. I swallow, gaining some composure and busying myself with making my bed for the night. Deciding to take the longer part of the couch, I lie my head on the flower pillowcase and smile at his girly fabric...until I wonder what girl gave it to him and how many girls have slept on it. The smile quickly vanishes from my face, replaced with a scowl. Ugh.

Van is making noise in the kitchen, but I close my eyes instead of concentrating on him. I try to fall asleep. No use, I can hear him shuffling near me. I thought he would've gone to his room. I open my eyes; within seconds he appears with a bowl of cereal, shoveling a spoonful into his mouth with milk dribbling down his chin while reaching for the remote.

The light from the TV stings my eyes. I close them to ward it away. Crunching and voices invade my efforts. "What are you doing? I thought you were going to bed."

"Remember rule three, TV."

Rolling over, I cover my face with the blanket. He continues to crunch, and someone blabbers on about a motor mount, whatever that is. The voice gets louder.

Ripping the covers off of my face, I say, "Are you trying to be rude, or are you just drowning out your obnoxious crunching?"

With a mouthful of cereal, he mumbles, "Unwinding before bed. You should try it. Maybe that stick will come out a little easier."

I sit straight up, thanking the good Lord I decided to keep my yoga pants on for this adventure. "You promised you'd be nicer to me. That isn't a nice thing to say."

He wipes the excess milk from his chin with the palm of his hand. "I promised I'd stop messing with you. I'm just telling you the truth."

"You wouldn't know the truth if it hit you in the head!"

Setting his bowl on the table, he turns and faces me. "I'm not a liar." His voice has a hint of aggravation.

"You're lying right now."

"How?"

I channel my best Van voice, "I built this great little house for you. Great accommodations...oh wait... I sold it. Now you can clean this shithole and sleep in a mouse-infested bed...oh wait, never mind sleep on my couch and I'll keep you up all night crunching my favorite childhood cereal." I finish, almost out of breath. "It's ridiculous the number of places I've stayed in such a short period of time."

"Cap'n Crunch, thank you."

"Ugh, next you're probably going to tell me you're having a girl come over and probably kick me out so you can have your fun time with her." My voice sounds much louder than I want it to.

Fun time? Oh my God, I want to kill myself. How stupid, fun time for him is sex and girls and more sex and cars and oh...I'm such a loser.

He chuckles. "I promise you won't interfere with my...what did you say? *Fun time?*"

My lips purse and I nod. It's all I can manage with my beet red face.

I need to change the subject, so I concentrate on the sold tiny house topic.

"When did you sell the house?"

He laughs. "Oh no, you're not getting out of this. What exactly do you think I do in my fun time?" His body moves closer to mine, practically wiggling his eyebrows at me.

I can feel my face flame. "Date?" My voice shakes, unsure of what can of worms I just opened.

Van leans in. "Are you thinking my fun time is..." His mouth is dangerously close to my ear, his breath heating my neck. He says in a low voice, "Sex."

"No." I push his shoulder to move him away from me and stand. I can't think when he's that close. Throwing the covers back on the couch, I tell him, "I'm exhausted, so either you sleep on the couch, or I do. What's your choice?"

He raises his hands in surrender. "Calm down. You can have your throne back, princess. I'm sorry, just a little fun time with you."

"Jerk."

"Aw...come on. I'm sorry. I swear. Look, I'll answer your question." His dark eyes look up at me, melting away all the anger that I have toward him. He pats the spot beside him. "Come on, sit, get comfy. I'll tell you a bedtime story."

I listen because all he has to do is ask and my body betrays me. That glimmer in his eyes and the sweet natural smile makes me want to make him happy. I settle back onto the couch and cover back up with the blanket, only this time I sit up, careful not to lie down. Van takes the end of the blanket and covers himself too. Anxiety blooms at the thought of him under the same cover as me.

"I didn't lie, I did have the house for you, but I sold it a few minutes before you got here. They paid over the asking price. I couldn't turn them down."

"That would be a bad business decision if you did. How did you even get into building these houses?"

"My grandfather, he had a stroke, and I couldn't stomach him living alone in a big house and getting into trouble, but I also couldn't put him in a nursing home, so he lives in the brick tiny house next door to the one you stayed in."

"Oh, I'm sorry, but what a clever solution. It probably gives him more freedom."

"Yeah, it's working out good. He can't get into trouble, but still can do what he wants, and he's contained. I can keep an eye on him. He's not completely immobile, but it makes his life easier."

My heart hurts for him. He looks so solemn when he speaks of his grandfather. I don't want to pry so I change the subject again.

"I bet he's proud of you. Both of your businesses are amazing. It's unlike anything I've ever seen before. I'm used to the world of cosmetics, but customizing cars is a very unique business."

Van seems to loosen at my words, leaning his head back on the cushion, getting more comfortable.

"You just don't know about cars. Everyone seems to be into customizing cars, but most people don't make a lot of money doing it unless they put their life into it. It's always been a way of life since I was little. My grandfather, my dad, and even my mom. My parents aren't involved any more, but my brother is, and it's been...hell." He knowingly looks me straight in the eyes.

I got what he was saying loud and clear, he's referring to my "hell" earlier.

"Is there anything I can help with? I mean, accounting wise or business advice?" I offer.

"No. It's complicated. He's jealous of the success I've been able to have with the shop, and now that my houses are flying out of here...he thinks he should get a piece of every pie."

He says it so casually, not affected, but underneath I'm sure there is more to this story, and I'm guessing it's not been an easy road.

He's quiet for a few seconds, his hand lands on my knee, causing me to cease breathing. "I'm really sorry I gave you a hard time. It's just I was pissed having you watch my every move. I live and breathe cars, and your dickhead husband insulted me." He softly laughs, "I didn't expect you to pick the trailer, let alone clean and stay in it. I thought you'd run home to your mansion."

"Believe me, I thought about it, but you were so arrogant, I couldn't let you win." I wink.

"I couldn't have planned the mouse better if I tried. Hilarious."

I backhand his chest. "For you, and then I fell...in my underwear!" I huff, dropping my head into my hands, completely embarrassed thinking of it.

"Don't worry, the girls around town wear far less. Besides, you looked damn good in that Superman shirt." My face heats. "Now quiet, my show's on, they're restoring a '69 Mustang."

I listen and settle in to watch my first car lesson, next to a man who isn't my husband. His hand hasn't left my knee, and somehow I'm more comfortable with it than I should be.

8

—·—

With my eyes still closed, snoring interrupts my dream. "Ugh…David, quiet. I don't want to get up yet." I nudge him beside me. He grumbles.

The snoring is louder and unfamiliar, and then I remember that David hasn't slept with me in months.

I open my eyes, glancing to my left to see a mass of dark curls on my shoulder and a heavy head resting against me. Van.

Did I fall asleep next to him? Searching my memories of last night, I remember watching something about a Mustang and an exhaust, and I must have fallen asleep. So did Van, beside me. The living room is bright with the morning sun shining through the large window over the kitchen sink.

I need to nudge Van awake, but I kind of like him next to me. Moving slightly closer, his hand tightens on my thigh. A swell of excitement sets in; he's touched me all night.

He mumbles again, his head nudging closer to the crook of my neck, and the tickle of his hair against my skin sets my nerves on fire.

I'm not sure what I should do. I know I need to wake him up and start my day, but part of me likes the silence between us, not having to worry about what his reaction is to our touch, or him making a comment that I'm not sure how to answer. Savoring the silence a few more minutes, I listen to the rhythm of his breathing. I find it calming, almost soothing. My mind is telling me to back away, but my heart is beating faster, beat by beat reminding me I'm more alive than I've ever been.

The phone rings beside me, interrupting my inappropriate thoughts. Funny, part of me is pissed for the intrusion. I reach for the phone on the endtable, causing Van's sleepy eyes to open. He wipes at his eye and yawns, moving away from my side. "Morning." I nod, holding my phone against my chest but not ready to answer it.

His innocent gaze has me trapped. His eyes shift back and forth, roaming over my features. "You gonna answer that?" he asks with a husky voice.

I shake my head, glancing down at my phone. David.

"Hello."

"How's my car coming along? Are you looking at it?"

"No, I just got up."

"It's eleven. Why the hell are you still in bed?" His voice rises, stinging my ear.

I can feel Van's eyes on me. I don't want to look up at him. Keeping my eyes trained on my hand fidgeting with the blanket, I answer, "Late night. They were working late into the night."

"As long as they're working and not screwing around. I know how those fuckers work, half the time it's just a big party. Thankfully, I know I don't have to worry about you joining them. You're such a prude when it comes to that shit."

I am, only because he's such a drunk. I want to tell him that so badly, but I refrain. It's not going to help me in the long run.

"I'll be working on next year's budget this afternoon. Any concerns?" I ask, all business, hoping to divert his attention away from any more accusations.

"No. Just make sure my car is done soon." A feminine voice calls his name. I listen harder and hear it again; only this time it's more of a whine.

"Who's with you?" I stand, ripping the blanket off of me. Catching my reaction, I soften my voice, "I mean, are you in a meeting?"

"Meeting? Um…yeah." Liar. A shot of heat runs from my toes to my head. "Look, I have to go. Make sure they do their job."

Turning from Van, I call David's name, but he's already hung up.

I drop my arm with the phone to the side. I look over at Van, shirtless, dark curls in disarray and concerned eyes focused on me. "You okay?"

"No." I don't know why I just admitted that to him.

"What's wrong?"

"He misses me." I lie. I want to tell Van I'm pretty sure David's cheating on me. He bends over, running his hands through his hair, then glides his hands down his face. "I'll get it done soon, Ems." He smiles with his genuine, caring smile, and him calling my new name soothes the sting I usually feel when I think of David and his myriad of affairs.

I want to tell him David doesn't even try to hide it. I check his phone and they talk several times a day. Her name is Daphne. She works at the country club. I don't ever go there because he says that's his place with his friends. I'm not even a member. I want to tell him all of this, scream it, in fact, but I don't. Would he understand or even care?

"I better get to work then." Van shoots off the couch, the blanket falls and he's in black boxer briefs. He stretches, arms high in the air, back arched, a growl deep within his chest accompanies the morning greeting in his pants.

He notices me staring. "Sorry." He adjusts himself, but I can still see it, loud and clear.

I laugh because I can't be serious with his boner glaring at me. Oh my, I don't think I've ever used that word in my life.

"Stop looking." He grabs the blanket, twisting it around his torso. Acting as if he's embarrassed, a mock look of horror on his face. "It's the morning, that shit happens. I'm a guy." He shrugs.

Turning my head, I cover my mouth, hiding my amusement. And when did he lose his clothes?

As he walks past, making his way in the direction of the stairs, he winks and says in a husky low voice, "That t-shirt and yoga pants ain't hiding that sexy ass, sweetheart."

I bury my head in my hands and fall back on the couch, chuckling, he's so natural. He isn't proper, doesn't try to act like someone he isn't, and is so damn hot. Van doesn't even try to hide the fact that he's turned on by me, or maybe it was just because he woke up. Still, he called me sexy, I can't remember the last time I was called that.

He pads up the stairs, drawers open and close, then he reappears with a towel wrapped around his waist. Grecian god or Adonis? I'm not quite sure yet.

"Whatcha lookin' at?"

I straighten. "Nothing. Why do you ask?"

"You're staring and your mouth is hanging open like a dog waiting for a bone."

"I was not." *Oh, I so was.*

He smiles. "Whatever. I'm taking a shower. You can join me if you want, but it will be a hot one. It won't cool off those hormones, but might take care of the cobwebs down there." He moves his finger in a circle, pointing to my feminine area.

"Jerk." I mutter under my breath.

"No, I'm just honest. Your husband may be missing you, but he hasn't been satisfying you. That I can see written all over your face."

"No, you can't!"

"Offer stills stands about the shower." He nods his head toward the bathroom.

"Jerk!" I say it loud enough for him to hear this time.

"I know." He smirks, raises his eyebrows, and walks into the bathroom.

He's right, I want to jump in that shower with him, rip his towel off and run my hands down his chest, watching as the ripples of water cascade down his body. Shit! I need to stop this now. I'm married.

Standing, I glance around the room, wondering where the best place to go would be other than the bathroom. I decide on the kitchen. My stomach growls in agreement.

Starting with the fridge, a full fridge at that, I have my pick of many breakfast treats: eggs, bacon, sausage, cinnamon rolls. This must be his favorite meal of the day.

Even though he's been awful to me, I do want to thank him for letting me stay here and hope to change his attitude toward me. David would laugh at me for lifting a finger in the kitchen. He'd say we have help for that sort of thing.

I shake the thought away. I may be married to him, but now that I've been away from him a short amount of time, I haven't had any decent thoughts about him. This time without him has been different and challenging in its own way, but it's also been liberating and fun. I can't remember the last time I had fun. I can't help but smile when Van's around.

I rummage through the kitchen for a sheet pan and skillet. Cooking is something I've always loved to do. After separating the bacon on the pan, I move on to the eggs. As I work, I can't help but notice the organization to his kitchen, which makes me smile.

Bending down, I place the bacon in the oven when strong fingers dig into my hip, causing me to drop the pan on the rack, and jump up.

"Did I scare you?"

"Donavan Bradley!"

"Sorry, I was just trying to peek over your shoulder and see what you were doing." His body is dangerously close to me, close enough I can feel his stiffness against my butt, and it's not doing anything other than exciting me.

"Can you please back up?" I say in a throaty voice.

By the grace of God, he listens without a snide comment or sexy innuendo.

"Sorry, I didn't mean to interfere. Nobody's ever stayed to make breakfast before. Then again, no one's ever spent the night next to me and not had sex with me either."

Changing the subject, I say, "I haven't made breakfast in a while, so don't get too excited." I wonder how many women have spent the night with him. The thought makes me jealous.

"Right now, I'd eat just about anything. I'm starving." I spin around as he backs up to the counter, lifts himself up with his forearms, and sits.

"Didn't you have enough Cap'n Crunch last night?"

"As a matter of fact, I didn't, somebody said I was too loud. I would have gone back for another bowl."

I smile. "It should be ready in about ten minutes. Can you get the plates and silverware?"

"Sure." He agrees and jumps down from the counter, looking away from him seems to be the only smart move right now. If I risk a glance in his direction, I might not be able to focus on anything else. He's so casual and graceful in his movements. The men I'm usually around are so rigid and serious. Van is a breath of fresh air.

"What do you have planned for today?" I ask, distracting myself with casual conversation instead of inappropriately comparing Van to David, which needs to stop.

"I'm working on the car, of course." Finally feeling in control of my hormones, I look up at him. He's shirtless, as usual. This time he's wearing dark jeans, black socks, no shoes. It's now that it hits me that I'm in his space, his home, and he's okay with it. Not bossing me around, telling me I'm worthless or berating me. A swell of sadness overcomes me. I'm not happy, I've never been happy. "Hey...you okay?"

I straighten, "Sure."

"You looked like you were somewhere else for a minute. Thinking of something in particular?"

I swallow, "No...I mean, just work deadlines." Pausing for a moment to throw him off, I add, "What specifically are you doing to the Bugatti today?"

Turning my attention to the eggs, I swirl the spatula around to swirl the liquid, careful to not burn them. He comes up behind me with a cup. With his distracting body, I hadn't even realized the brewing pot of coffee. As if he reads my mind, he sets the coffee on the counter. "If I didn't have a timer, I'd never make coffee. Thankfully, I had cereal last night and set it then."

I smile that the simple act of him making coffee makes me happy. "I don't think you have time for much. You seem to have a lot of irons in the fire."

"Yeah, well, I gotta make money somehow. To answer your question, I've got some fabricating of the left side door panel and shoring up the left rear axle. Going to be a busy day." He lifts his coffee, taking a sip. "Speaking of which, can I get that on some bread to go? I'm late and can't seem to stop talking to you. I'm not usually this chatty."

"Chatty?"

"Yeah...I think you ask too many questions."

"I think you like to tease me and that's why you're still here. Let me get your order ready."

Taking another sip, he thanks me, and kisses the top of my head. A flame remains where he's touched. *Why did he do that?*

I shake my head, trying to not read too much into it. Taking the pan of bacon out of the oven, the eggs off the burner, and the bread out of the package, I assemble his sandwich. In what seems like seconds, he reappears in a Bradley Restoration navy blue t-shirt and black boots.

"Look at you." He gleams as I hand him the sandwich wrapped up in a paper towel. "I'm pretty jealous of David, he gets to wake up to this every morning."

I suppress a laugh. If he only knew, and I am exceptionally grateful that he doesn't.

"Believe me, I don't do this often enough."

"He's lucky either way." Van grabs the sandwich from my hand, taking a bite. "Delicious," he says with a mouthful of bacon, eggs, and bread. "The lake party is tonight, I expect you there. No excuses. You're coming."

"I don't think so."

He shakes his head, "Oh...no. Don't even try it. You're coming."

"I'll see," I say to appease him. I've never been to a lake party. Sure, I've been on a lake on a boat, but I'm sure their kind of parties are different. Butterflies descend in my belly.

"Okay. I'll see you later." He stops and turns around. "Not trying to be a dick, but don't visit the shop today. I have a lot to get done, and you're kind of a distraction."

"Don't worry, I won't disrupt you today. I have some work I need to get done as well."

He closes his eyes for a brief moment, then opens them. "I'm sorry, I didn't mean to take it out on you. I'm having a rough time, and having someone watch my work...it pisses me off." He apologizes, I think.

Within seconds, whatever animosity I've been feeling about the whole car-babysitting situation melts away at the adorable smile he gives me.

His eyes flutter down, and I can tell he's assessing me. By me, I mean my body. My face flames.

I'm not sure what to do; I seem to be a mixed bag of emotions when I'm around him, and so does he.

"It's fine, I can stay out of the way. I never wanted to be here in the first place."

His brow furrows. "Do you always do what he asks?"

"Yes. He's my husband." I'm saying it more for my benefit than his at this point, reminding myself once again that I took vows.

Van shakes his head. "I'd never expect the person I love to stand around a complete stranger's workplace and babysit a piece of metal." He shakes his head again. "Can't wait to meet this piece of work," Van grumbles under his breath.

Getting my emotions under control, I stand straighter, noticing he's judging my marriage because I'm giving him more insights on my relationship with David than I should.

"Okay." He starts to walk away. His hand raises to cup the back of his neck, then he suddenly turns around. "Hey, you seem pretty smart..." his hand drops and he looks at the ground. "Andrew said you're pretty good with numbers; accounting and stuff. Would you mind taking a look at some of our records? I mean...since you're hanging around here and all."

I can't help the smile that spreads across my face. "Thank you for the 'pretty smart' remark. To answer your question, yes, I'm very good at accounting and numbers. I help run the finance department for two multi-million-dollar companies."

He steps closer to me and I can smell a manly cologne, a mix of musk and metal that accelerates my heart beat.

"It's just that...well, we're having some financial issues. Record keeping. Violet sucks at paperwork. I was hoping you could give her a hand at sorting through some of that stuff. I'll pay you or knock a couple grand off your bill." He runs his hands through his hair. God, I wish I could do it for him.

I clear my throat in response, "I'm not sure Violet will approve of that."

After another woman makes it her mission to make you as uncomfortable as she can, what else could I think?

"I talked with her already...she'll behave, I promise."

"Will you?" I want to cover my mouth immediately. Instead, I bite my lip. I didn't mean to say that.

A smirk forms on his lips while he tilts his head to the side. "I promise." Van takes his finger over his chest and makes a cross to emphasize his point. I almost whimper in response.

I'm sure I turn a shade of red unavailable on the color wheel. *How can I be so affected by him?*

We stand in silence. His eyes narrow on me, I resist the urge to move closer to him. His beautiful, dark seductive eyes, face dirtied with scruff, long eyelashes, and full lips trap me. I can't yank my eyes away.

I feel like I'm locked in a moment with him. As if he's reading my mind, his eyes fall to my lips. My mind wonders what his lips would feel like against mine. Suddenly a V forms on his forehead, I can only imagine he's questioning what he's doing staring at the likes of me. I'm nuts to think he's checking me out.

I force myself to look away, not liking the look of disapproval on his face.

"I'll get my jacket and be there as soon as possible," I say.

"Violet will show you where to find what you need." He turns to walk away, only to stop himself. "You don't have to get all dressed up. We're not fussy, jeans and t-shirt are fine," he adds.

"Okay, I'll consider it," stating as professional as possible.

Van gives a slight smile and nods.

I watch as he moves out of the apartment, closing the door behind him. I falter back against the counter, catching my breath.

Dear Lord, I'm acting like he's some sort of mystical creature. He's just a man I tell myself, a mechanic working on my husband's vehicle.

Oh, how I wish I could believe my own words.

9

—·—

C After the door shuts behind him and the coast is clear, I get ready for the day. Pulling myself together, I decide to put on my white silk blouse. It's what I'm most comfortable in, and if I'm going to have to deal with Violet, it gives me a little added confidence.

Taking a peek in the mirror, my reflection is acceptable for the day. Face free of makeup, hair in a bun, and clothed in my suit jacket.

I leave Van's apartment, careful not to inspect any of his belongings. I'm not sure I could stop myself from violating his privacy once I've started. In my heels, I descend the stairs and peek into the garage. The rear of the Bugatti is covered under a large cloth, while several of Van's workers are working in the front. I duck out without any interaction and head toward the larger shop.

Reaching the showroom, Violet's at the counter, head down. She doesn't even acknowledge that I've come in. She's looking down at her cell phone, texting away.

I can't help but think she's texting about me to someone. Telling them how she's going to have to deal with the unwanted visitor.

Taking in a deep breath, I begin to speak, "Van asked me to help you regarding entering financial information."

She looks up from under her fake eyelashes. "What? Are you some kind of accountant?"

"Yes, I am," I simply state.

"Figures. Rich bitch and smart," she says under her breath.

This woman is testing my patience. She's infuriating, to say the least.

"Look, we don't have to talk. Let me check and see if anything seems out of place. You don't have to be nice to me, but Van asked if I would help, and since I'm here, I'll do it."

She sighs and grabs the laptop and flips it open. "Here, look for yourself. I'm going to take a break."

Violet whisks out the door leading to the garage.

I feel an unbelievable amount of peace knowing she's gone.

For a second, I think it would be nice of her to show me how she enters in information, but then I realize I would actually have to talk to her. I smile at the notion of her disappearing.

I'm not sure what exactly Van wants me to look for, but I start from today and work my way backward.

Violet comes and goes. Customers come and go.

I check the time on the laptop, and I'm shocked that I've been looking through their financial records for over two hours and have found nothing but horrible accounting mistakes and mismanaged money.

They're losing more money than they're making. But the worst part is it seems as if money is disappearing without accountability.

I can't quite put my finger on it yet, but a red alert sign is flashing in my head.

Violet hasn't said a word to me since she handed over the laptop, but catches me looking over at her. She scowls and asks, "What?"

I would like to ask her a list of questions, like how do you enter the information, how do you know the accounts are balanced, what does end of month closing look like? But I know this will just add fuel to the fire.

"I'm finished. You can have the laptop back." I made notes and questions I want to ask Van, but I don't dare tell her.

"You going to accuse me of anything?"

"I looked over some information, things look fine." I leave it at that and walk away. I don't need to get into anything with her. Especially since she could be the one contributing to the financial issues. When it comes to money, I've learned to trust no one.

As I grab the notebook with the questions I need to ask Van, my phone vibrates. It's *him* again.

"Hello, David," I say as pleasant as I can muster.

"Are they done with my car yet?"

"I just talked to you this morning, of course they aren't done yet, but Van assured me your car will be done in a timely manner. But due to the extent of the damage, he may need extra time."

"You will stay until it's done. He's lucky he's the only prick who can fix it," he orders.

"David, I need to get back to the office. Surely this is a bit ridiculous, it's just a car."

"A car?" His voice raises, sounding appalled at the notion. "I knew you wouldn't understand. I'll be there soon, once my parents leave for England. Whch can't come soon enough. I don't need to hear any more of their shit about my car and the stupid fucking yard. They hire people to take care of it every damn day."

"They are just worried for you. It's scary when you get like that." I can barely get the words out. I don't usually share how his actions affect me.

"Scary? No, scary is waking up with one leg," he retorts. "Call me if anything changes," he says and quickly ends the call. I shove my phone back into my bag, casually turning around to see if anyone overheard. Thank God, no one is around.

I'm used to his reaction. Somehow all we end up talking about is his leg. He has a prosthetic leg, top-of-the-line prosthetic. Best that Dawson money can buy. He has no problem getting around, but prefers to use the accident to garner sympathy or attention.

Being around Van has awakened something inside of me. Sure, he teases me, but he doesn't talk to me with such disrespect and malice. His smile does things to me I can't even explain. Of course, David blames me for the night he lost his leg, but should I really let him treat me like a criminal in jail?

I shake the thought of that night out of my mind as Violet walks by and scowls; at least she can take me from feeling guilty to pissed in a second.

"Who was that?" her snooty voice fills my ears.

"My husband, David."

"He sounds like an ass. I mean, making you camp out here. It's like he loves the car more than you." Violet cackles as she walks away.

She's right, he does love his cars, boats, and basically everything but me. When he looks at me, he sees the life he's lost, while all I can see is the life we both lost.

"David? Where are you?" I called, as I made my way through the chapel. It looks so different. Pink, cream, and peach rose petals scattered all along the aisle between the pews, bouquets of matching roses cover every surface of the small space. As I reached the end of the aisle, he steps out from behind a white pillar and drops to one knee. "Emerson, I have loved you since the day I met you. All I see is you in my future, by my side, helping me with my family business, riding beside me in a sports car of your choice." He smiled, making my heart flutter. "I want to build my

life with you, for richer, not for poorer, hopefully, and sickness and in health. I love you, Emerson, marry me?"

The memory crashes into me. It seems like a dream. Has he ever loved me?

I decide to walk out of the stuffy showroom and get some air, stopping any other memories that want to creep up and remind me how life was at one time.

There's another side door that I haven't been through, but I've seen a few people go out that way and assume it leads to the garage.

The door is behind a rack of t-shirts. I check them out on my way. *Sixty dollars for a t-shirt?* Their bottom line should be much more lucrative. In the few hours I've spent here, a lot of people have come in to buy shirts, jackets, purses, jewelry, and countless other items. Violet hasn't had much time to waste on me or herself with a store full of customers.

As I walk through the door, it leads to a hallway lined with other doors that I assume are offices, and when I reach the last door on my right, I hear Van. I know it's the wrong thing to do, but I stop and lean against the wall after I have passed his office. The blinds belonging to his window are shut, but his voice is loud and agitated.

It is none of my business. He could be mad at anything or anyone, but something won't let me walk past his office. My ear touches the door.

"How can that be? Teddy, listen—I'm not putting him in that fucking home. He's fine in his house!" It's quiet for a moment and then he's yelling again.

I tiptoe a little more down the hall. A crash echoes in my ears. My footsteps halt due to the door flying open. I must not have gone far enough away from the door, because when it whirls open it hits me right in the middle of my back and head.

"Ahh..." I scream.

"Christ, what the hell? Are you okay?" Van's eyes are wide, full of concern.

I rub the area to alleviate the pain. And I can already feel a knot form on the back of my head. "Sorry...I was just walking by."

"Oh jeez, Ems, I'm so sorry." His eyes roam over me, looking to see if I'm hurt. His gaze falls to my hand rubbing my head. "Here, turn around and let me look."

His feather-soft touch glides over my head directly where the pain is. "You have a bump. Do you want to go get checked out?"

"No, I'm more embarrassed than anything." Because I am, only I would get hurt walking by a door.

"Come on." He covers my elbow with his hand, leading me back into his office. I follow without hesitation.

He pulls out his black leather office chair and guides me down to take a seat.

"Stay put, Ems, I'll get you some ice," he says, then rushes out of the room. *Ems?* He called me Ems again. A tingle flies up my neck and I want him to say over and over. A vision of him cradling me in his arms, and whispering my new favorite name, forms. *Stop it!* I scold myself for the millionth time since I've laid eyes on him.

Sitting there rubbing my head, I have a chance to look around his office. It's not what I expected. He has a beat-up oak desk, a laptop, and a cup of pens stamped with his logo. The walls are exactly what I expect though, posters of cars covering every inch of available space. They're the same cars that David covets; only I'm positive Van appreciates them. I did, however, expect him to have awards, trophies, or whatever else to brag about his business, but he doesn't. He has a picture of a woman and man on his desk. The man is tall, lean, and tattooed, and the woman is petite, beautiful, and starry-eyed looking at the love of her life; at least that's how I want to interpret it.

When my eyes meet the wall across from the desk, the drywall has been punctured, and remnants of an iPhone decorate the ground.

"Here." Van hands me an ice pack while running his hand through his mess of curls, layered perfectly so that they fall haphazardly back into place. "Does that even help?"

"Um...yeah, I think so," I answer, swallowing to help clear my obsession with his hair.

His forehead crinkles. "I'm sorry that I hit you with the door. I mean, I'd never hurt you." He bends down and starts picking up the pieces of his cell phone before tossing them in the trashcan next to him. "There goes an easy six-hundred bucks in the trash."

I must look like an idiot with an ice bag on my head and staring at him picking up phone parts. I can't help but watch the way his muscles move, and how the t-shirt clings to his tan skin. His hair is in curls, but they are not tight curls, more like loose waves and it is so dark, not quite black but close. His jaw is straight, and one of his upper arms has some sort of skull tattoo. I know what's under that shirt. It's getting warm in here. I take the ice pack from the back of my neck and place it on my forehead to cool my thoughts.

"Did you get hit there too?" Van asks, his eyebrows raised, crouching down beside me, inspecting my forehead, and placing a hand on my knee.

"No, I just...I'm getting hot. You know...because of the heat in your office." I swallow and feel like a blubbering idiot.

He gives a light laugh and stands up. He holds out his hand. "I'll take you to my place. I'm sure you could use a nap. I know I can use a break from this place."

For a brief second our hands touch, and I don't think there's any force on earth that could make me let go of him. It feels perfect, like it was meant to be. On the rare occasions that I touch David I cringe, but Van's touch just...fits.

His eyes look down at our joined hands, and all I see are his long, full eyelashes. His gaze lingers on our hands for a moment, and his eyes flicker back up to mine.

He swallows loudly. Maybe he felt something too? He instantly lets go of my hand. *I guess not, then.*

I follow him down the hall and out the back entrance. I'm feeling like a foolish girl around him because as a married woman I'm not supposed to be acting like a teenager hoping the new boy likes me.

Van stops while I almost bump into his back. He spins to face me. "You haven't forgotten about tonight, have you?"

"The lake party?"

"Yeah, every Friday night we meet by the lake, drink, reminisce, and have a fire."

I look at him with confusion. "Where's the lake?" Making a point to move my head around looking for this lake that I've missed somehow.

He laughs. Pretty sure it's directed at me. "You haven't been past the garage, huh?"

I shake my head no.

"Well, at about eight forty-five tonight, I'll come get you. Don't walk off without me. I'd hate for you to miss it by getting lost...or backing out."

"Miss what?"

With a quirk of his lips turning into a sexy smile, he says, "You'll see."

10

Having no idea what to wear, I take the only pair of jeans that I've brought. I pair it with another tank top and grab a tailored black jacket with some low-heeled booties.

Straightening my dark hair in its bun in the bathroom mirror, I apply some light makeup. A knock at the bathroom door sends butterflies swooping around my belly. Every time I know Van's around, they take flight.

As I open the door, Van stands in the doorway in a black and red flannel shirt, black t-shirt underneath, dark distressed jeans, and his black boots. When my eyes meet his seductive ones, I can't help the smile that forms on my lips. His hair is slicked back, which shows off the beauty of his facial features: a strong jaw spattered with stubble, big brown eyes surrounded by thick eyelashes, and a long, straight nose. Oh...how I love that dimple on his left cheek. His hair must cover it up most of the time because I'm sure I would have noticed it by now...but maybe not. I always seem so distracted by him.

"Hey," Van says from the doorway, tilting his head with a sexy grin.

"Hi." My cheeks heat and my nerves are kicking in. It seems all he has to do is give me a half smile and the heavens sing.

"You still look like you're going to a meeting." He chuckles.

"I didn't bring my bonfire attire," I spit back, liking how easily we can tease each other.

"Is there such a thing?"

I shrug, having no idea. I don't want to tell him I've never been to a bonfire.

"It just makes me wonder…" He places a finger to his chin, "If you had a choice, why did you agree to come here and watch me work on your husband's car. You're not dressed for hanging out in a shop all day. Didn't anyone tell you there's grease here?"

I can't tell him I had no choice.

"I always dress like this. I like the way I dress." Lies, all lies. I want to dress sexier and wear more makeup, and take my hair out of this damn bun. I'm just not sure how to start.

"Okay, well, I just want you to be comfortable."

"So where is this lake you speak of?" I joke, changing the subject to anything other than my miserable life.

"Ah, right this way, my dear," he speaks with either a British accent, or the voice of a pirate. It's so awful I'm not sure which, but it does put a smile on my face.

Leaving his place, we walk toward the first row of trees behind the small shop, and the farther we walk, the deeper into the woods we seem to be.

"Are you sure there's a lake close by?" All I see are trees, and don't see or hear any signs of water.

"I promise, we just have to walk downhill from here."

He points to my left where it looks like if we take that path, we'll fall off the cliff.

Van must notice the look of fear on my face because he grabs my hand to pull me with him. "We'll go slow, and I won't let go." My hand tingles at his touch. I squeeze his hand harder in response. I can't help myself.

We start our descent, my steps quicken, and I try to stop the momentum, but between my boots and my coordination, I start to stumble, my ankle giving. In one swift, yet graceful, movement, Van's strong arms come to my rescue and he sweeps me up in them. "I got you."

It all happens so fast, he's carrying me as if he's done it a million times. Digging my hands into his chest, clutching his shirt, I hold on for dear life. We're moving at a fast pace down the hill. His boots hit the ground, breaking fallen branches as we go. It takes a mere second for us to reach the bottom. When his feet stop, I see what he's been talking about.

Acting as if he didn't save me from killing myself, he says, out of breath, "And here is the lake I speak of."

Still in his arms, I stare at the sight before me. A dark sandy beach and endless water meets the horizon. It's just before dark, and the sky is a multitude of citrus colors.

"Wow, Van, I had no idea."

"Awesome, huh?"

My boots sink into the sand as he puts me down. He's so gentle with me, almost as if I'm as light as a feather. The memory of his strong muscles under my hands and against me are going to be hard to forget. An overwhelming loss comes over me.

There're a few people milling around...setting up chairs, gathering wood for the firepit, and another small group gathered around a beer keg.

From the look of things, the party hasn't even begun and is only going to get much bigger.

I'm not good around a large group of people, especially these types of people. It's been my experience the faker the people are, the better. I know how to pretend to be social in that kind of atmosphere, but these people are real, not worried by social status. No, these people are not proper or worried about being judged for their job. They just live and have fun. That is something I don't know how to do.

My belly grumbles, alerting my nerves to act up. I try to calm myself by breathing in the lake air. It's so fresh, clean, and calming. The sound of the rippling water is music to my ears.

"Grab a chair," Van orders.

"No, thanks. I'll stand, or I can even help set up. If you want?" I add shyly.

"Nah, I've got enough guys here, just relax. Besides your husband's already paying a shit pile of money to me, I'd feel guilty if I made you do any heavy lifting."

I'm not sure if that's meant to be an insult or a joke. Van's words aren't easy to figure out, but I stay put and watch as everyone does their job.

I notice all the guys from the shop are here.

If I remember correctly, Jake is the one setting up some chairs. He has the most beautiful hair I've ever seen on a man; long, blond, and tied back in a ponytail away from his manly face. The other guy from the shop I recognize is Ben, I think. He's the one who called me empress. Ben is equally as attractive, extremely rude, but is not hard on the eyes with his short, spiked blond hair, wearing a sleeveless shirt revealing his muscular arms and tattoos.

Jake's hovering over the keg, trying to get it to work while talking to Violet. Of course, this party would not be complete without her. I start to plot a way to leave early so I don't have to deal with any of them.

While plotting, a familiar voice whispers into my ear, "Glad to see you here."

I jump out of my skin, not expecting anyone to get that close to me. "You scared me!"

"Sorry, I didn't mean to. I figured you've had your fill of Van by now. How's he on the asshole meter this evening?" Ace doesn't give me a chance to answer. "I know these guys can be rough around the edges, but sometimes they can be decent. Even Violet can be a sweetheart." I want to laugh in his face. I'm sure we're not talking about the same person...besides, he argued with Van earlier.

"If you say so?" It's the nicest thing I can respond with.

"It's true. She feels threatened by you. She has a thing for Van. They dated briefly, and anyone who comes within a foot of him feels her wrath." He takes a sip from his beer can.

"That is just silly. I'm married." It is getting harder and harder to admit the truth. I wish I wasn't. For the first time I don't feel guilty admitting it to myself. I purse my lips shut at the smile that's trying to escape.

"I know, but sometimes that doesn't matter to people, especially our group of friends." He shrugs.

"Oh." What I really want to do is bombard him with questions. Is it Van he's talking about? Van dated Violet! *Oh great, now I'm worrying about something that's none of my business!*

"So, what do you think of the shop? Are we doing a good job on the car?"

"I think so. I don't really know what I'm supposed to be watching, but David wants someone with the car as much as possible. It's a miracle he even trusts me."

"Not to sound ignorant or disrespectful, but your husband sounds like a douche."

I laugh, because he's right. If he only knew the reason he was such an ass.

"He's been spoiled his whole life and expects people to treat him a certain way." It's the best I can come up with in his defense.

"Spoiled is probably an understatement from what I can tell of him. Why would he make you babysit a car?" I can't help but notice how cute Ace is, more of a baby face than the rest of the guys he works with. It's almost distracting how genuinely handsome he is.

I almost forget he's talking to me but shift my thoughts to answer him. "He couldn't be here because of work, so I volunteered." He looks perplexed. I don't think he believes me, so I change the subject. "So, what goes on at these lake parties?"

Ace smiles with excitement like it's the most natural thing in the world for him. He wraps his arm around my shoulder, and his other arm gestures out toward the lake with a beer in hand. "You're going to have so much fun tonight. More people are coming. We drink, swim, drink, talk about cars, drink, and by the end of the night there'll either be a fight, or someone will end up naked. Just depends on the night."

I want to run, right now! This is typically behavior for the type of people I have avoided my whole life. I'm stuffy, uptight, and not an overall cool person to hang out and party with. I can't compete with a girl like Violet. Like one of the guys, but she's beautiful and dresses sexy. I'm sure Van isn't the only guy here she's been with.

Something has caught Ace's attention as he turns away from me. I follow his gaze to Van, who is now talking to Violet. By the body language they're throwing off, it looks intense, but I'm not sure if it's in a bad way. She has her arms locked around his neck and staring starry-eyed at him, but he's not returning the gesture. His arms are tense and locked at his side, his hands fisted, and his head is tilted. I feel myself wanting to invade their conversation, but I don't have the guts for that.

Ace pulls me back into our conversation. "So, are you a wine or beer girl?"

"I'm not much of a drinker." I don't dare tell him my reasons.

"So, you aren't going to have anything to drink?" he asks.

"No, just a Coke or whatever."

"I'll get you a cup. Have a seat and get ready for the show. Buckle up, though, because it might be a little more entertaining if you have a small glass of wine or a shot," he adds.

I don't need to be entertained; I need to be left alone. But for the first time in forever, I don't think that's true. I'd like Van to be standing by me right now. I watch as Ace's thin frame moves through the crowd, which is growing bigger by the second.

The nerves begin kicking in high gear. My life is nothing these people are used to, they are free to come and go. No rules or regulations or expectations. Free to be who they are.

Wallowing in my own self-pity isn't working, so I decide the best course of action is to find a safer location. Somewhere no one will notice me or talk to me, but where I can still keep an eye on the Van and Violet situation.

The row of chairs that are lined up along the beach aren't filled up yet. I have my pick of my safe spot. There are random types of chairs, everything from a wooden bench to a rocking chair to a love seat. I laugh to myself, this is so absurd. If the Dawson's saw this...they would not let Bradley Restoration touch any of their cars.

As I approach the very last lonely wooden chair, I take in the people around me. Most are laughing, relaxed with drink in hand. No one seems to even notice me. Something about that bothers me, but I decide not to linger on the thought.

The women around me are wearing tight clothes, short skirts, or shorts, and cleavage galore. Looking down, I examine my clothes. Compared to these ladies, I'm extremely overdressed. My insecurity level is at an all-time high.

I decide to take in the view of the lake in front of me. The beautiful sunset with all the brilliant pinks and oranges, and the peace that radiates from the glow of the sun reflecting on the water. Focusing my attention on the fact that I had no idea how close this beautiful place is to where I am staying. It also brings to mind how much a person can surprise you.

Van is a mechanic, and in my world that isn't a very prized profession. But Van's made it into a very profitable occupation. He must be excellent at his job for the Dawson's to even consider bringing the Bugatti all the way here.

Speaking of Van, where did he go? Looking around it doesn't take long to spot him, as he seems to be the center of attention in a larger group. A few girls I don't recognize, as well as Violet, surround him. I'm uncomfortable even looking at them. They're beautiful. The one girl who is closest to Van is a beautiful blond, wearing a short jean skirt and low-cut red crop top. Just looking at her makes me blush.

Of course, Violet doesn't let her remain next to Van long, she weasels her way in between them, but he doesn't seem fazed. He grabs the blond around the waist and whispers something in her ear. Violet rolls her eyes to the heavens and starts talking to a guy next to her. I can't see what he looks like because his back is to me.

Knowing that I've been watching them for far too long, I turn my attention back to the lake water. The voices around me are getting louder, and more and more people are coming toward the lake. I'm not sure where everyone is parking, but it looks like people are pouring out of the woods, almost like in a zombie movie.

No one but me is sitting. Out of place and awkward, I try and blend in better by standing. When Ace appears, relief washes over me. "I hate that you're sitting here all alone. Come with me." He holds out his hand.

"I'm fine here. I'll stand, though."

"No, come on, you look lonely. I'll introduce you to some really cool people."

With no one to rescue me, I allow him to yank me out of my safe spot. He begins to introduce me to a group of girls, and one in particular, Callie, makes it her mission to talk to me.

"I hear you're staying in one of those tiny houses...what's it like in there?" Callie asks.

"It really is amazing. I can't believe how beautiful and functional it is. But Van sold it, so I'm staying at his place until my husband's car is finished."

Callie has a bubbly and friendly personality. She has blond hair cut into a cute, angled bob and is wearing more clothes than any girl here. She has on jeans and a black t-shirt. Her perfectly applied lipstick-covered lips pop open. "You're staying at Van's?"

"Yes," I state simply.

"Damn!" she says, eyes wide. "He doesn't let anyone stay with him. Even when he brings girls over, they never stay...ever."

An inner part of me smiles. I shouldn't care that I'm the only one allowed to stay with him, or that he slept beside me on the couch all night long.

"I didn't have anywhere else to stay. He was being a gracious host."

She leans in closer. "I heard he doesn't let anyone ever sleep in his bed, only bangs them on the couch." My smile falters. "He's a catch either way. I mean...damn, he's hot." Callie shakes her head, "Don't you think?"

"I'm married." Answering with the safe response. I'd love to tell her, yes, he is the hottest guy I've ever seen, and I slept with his head on my shoulder and his hand on my thigh and loved every second of it.

"Oh, I wasn't implying anything, but a girl can look, right?" She adds a few seconds later, "Even a married one." Elbowing me with more genuine charm than I've ever seen anyone possess.

I nod, but that's it.

We chat a little longer. She asks me general questions about what little time I spent in the tiny house, and what I do for work, but eventually the subject of why on earth I would be here comes up.

Callie's high bubbly voice turns quiet and serious, "So, why would you come all this way without your husband. I mean, it's his car, isn't it? What's it like to drive it." She sounds so excited.

"Yes, it is, but I've never driven it..."

Before I can explain further, a scream rips through the night air. "Bitch, go fuck yourself!"

When I turn my head, Van's holding Violet around the waist and has her lifted off the ground. She's trying to break free from his grip. "Let me go! I'm going to kill her." She then hits his hand with her fist.

"Stop it, V!" Van yells back.

"He's coming home with me tonight, bitch!" The girl whom Van was snuggled up to earlier adds to the screaming, wearing an all-too-eager sly smile. It's clear she's trying to keep Violet wound up.

Ace comes from behind me somewhere and is at my side. He heads over to help with the chaos, along with Ben and Jake. Ben takes Violet out of Van's grasp and pushes her aside, then Ben picks up the blond and throws her over his shoulder. Lucky for the crowd, we get a nice view of her ass. Big surprise, she's not wearing any underwear. I must make a face because Callie laughs at me. "Ew...some people," she says and laughs again, but it doesn't last long before she's glaring at the blond on Ben's shoulder.

"I agree," I respond

Van and Violet are in a heated conversation, but Jake is close by waiting for round two, I guess. Callie is babbling on about how she thinks Ace is a great guy, ignoring the sheer madness going on around her. But when I hear my name, or at least a version of it, I cringe.

"That Dawson bitch over there, you want in her pants, too, don't you? You'd love to get a rich piece of ass, wouldn't you?" she screams and points at me.

My face flames. *What the hell did I do?*

11

—·—

"**E**nough, Violet! You need to leave! You're wasted!" Van yells back.

"You have to fuck everyone! You won't even give us a chance!" Violet shoves Van, causing him to stumble. But before he can react, Jake comes to her rescue, picking her up, and yanking her away from the group.

Van takes a sip from his red cup and then wings it hard into the fire.

His jaw is tight and pulsating, making him look hot even all the way over here. There's something about the heat in his eyes that's making my body steam. I try not to look, but I can't help myself. I wonder why my name came up. Then a little thrill sparks a question I've been trying to ignore, maybe he thinks I'm attractive.

"That's interesting," Callie muses sarcastically, eyeing me as she sips out of her red cup.

"What's interesting?"

"That you've been here for a day or so and they're already fighting about you. She must be jealous, or Van might be interested." She smiles, raising her eyebrows.

"I'm married. That's ridiculous."

"Well, whatever it is, you've lit a fire in Van. He doesn't get worked up over her comments. She struck a nerve, that's for sure."

"I think I should head out now. I don't think I need to stay any longer," I say.

Callie apologizes, "I didn't mean to upset you. I like Van. And you, it was just an observation."

"You didn't, I'm just not into parties. I'm tired, and looks like everyone would be better off if I weren't here." Callie seems to be listening closely, but her eyes roam above my head at something behind me. She gives me a knowing look just as Van's voice invades our conversation.

"I'm sorry about that. She's just drunk," Van apologizes, stepping beside me with his hands in his pockets.

"No, it's fine, but I was just telling Callie I'm going to head back to your place."

"It's not fine. You're here as a client. A very important client, and you're being treated like one of us, and you're clearly not." He takes one hand out of his pocket and gestures toward me. "You don't have to go."

I feel like he smacked me in the face with reality. A client...that's all he sees me as. How silly to think he might see me as something different. I'm nothing like these people, but I find myself wanting to be accepted into this group, especially seeking his approval.

"I'm tired, really, I'm just going to head back."

Van combs his fingers through his silky dark hair that's fallen in his eyes, causing my hand to jerk in response. I have to stop myself from reaching over and brushing the lonely strand from his eye.

"Don't go yet...I know that was intense, but Violet's drunk. Jake's calming her down over there." He points clear over to the other end of the lake. "She gets jealous easily. Brandy and I hang out sometimes."

I wonder what he means by hanging out?

"You don't have to explain the situation to me. It is none of my business." And it isn't. I'm here to oversee a car restoration, but something in me is sad at the thought.

"Please don't let her ruin our night...your night." He quickly recovers and adds, "Callie is a great girl. She's a good one."

"Yes, she seems nice...plus, she hasn't called me a name yet."

He chuckles and it's so cute and natural

"Yeah, and there's that. Where did she go?" Van looks over his shoulder to find where she disappeared to. "There she is." We spot her a few yards away.

And like nothing had happened in the past few minutes, I walk with him to talk to Callie. Not because he asked, but because I do and I don't want to leave yet. She and Ace are talking. Ace looks animated about something and has a huge grin on his face when we walk over.

Ace spots us. "We were just talking about you. Callie said you never rode in the Bugatti, I can't believe it." If he only knew why, he wouldn't be so surprised.

"I haven't ridden in any of his sports cars, only the SUV or limo."

"You don't like to drive, do you?" Van asks.

How did he know? Could he be seeing through me already?

"No. I'd rather be driven around."

"Do you know how to drive?"

"I can't believe you, if you'd been more responsible, then maybe I'd have my damn leg," David said as a beer bottle whizzed past my head.

The memory makes me take a large sip from the cup in my hand; I don't even remember when I picked it back up. "Yes," I answer quickly, not wanting to say more about my driving history.

Thankfully, Callie stops Ace's interrogation, but starts her own, "You must be loaded. A driver, sports cars, do you live in a mansion?"

"No. It's a nice house, though," I lie. It's a mansion, but it might as well be a state penitentiary.

She looks dreamy-eyed. "I hope to find a rich guy like your husband someday."

If she only knew how horrible he is to be married to, she'd take back that sentence.

I watch as Van leaves us without saying a word, moving toward the blond-haired girl he was talking to earlier. He wraps his arm around her waist, and she squeals. Jealousy washes over me. Damn it, I scold myself. It's ridiculous that I keep focusing on him, feeling the need to see who has his attention.

"I saw that,." Callie fires her accusation.

"What?"

"You were checking out Van."

"No, I wasn't." Finding it impossible to hide the truth.

"It's okay if you were. He's hot and would be a great guy to have a one-night stand with. He does it all the time. Plus, your husband would never know." She leans in, talking in a low tone.

"Callie! I would never do that to my husband."

She bumps my shoulder. "I'm kidding. Jeez, but I wouldn't think any less of you if you did."

Thankfully, Ace wasn't paying attention. He's too busy playing on his phone; at least, I think he isn't paying attention.

I glare at her wistful, innocent smile, but I don't respond. Honestly, what can I say? He isn't hot, he's flat out the sexiest man I've ever seen. David's handsome and well-dressed, but nothing compared to Van.

Callie excuses herself, leaving me for another group of people whom I haven't met yet. I've made the only person who's been nice to me uncomfortable. *Great.*

So here I am, left standing next to Ace, who's still on his phone. I scan the area around me. Everyone looks to be having fun, laughing, talking, and hugging. There are several groups that have clustered together, and I wonder to myself why so many.

Ace notices me standing there at some point. "Sorry, I get caught up in technology." He apologizes, holding up his phone.

"It's fine. So, what's so interesting that you're ignoring a certain cute blond?"

"Callie? Nah, it's not like that, if that's what you're thinking."

I don't quite know what to say. His honesty catches me off guard.

He tucks his phone in his back-jeans pocket and answers, "Don't get me wrong, she's hot, it's just, she isn't my type."

"You can't force a relationship. Believe me, I know." Now I'm shocked at my honesty. I hurry and take a sip of my drink to shut my mouth.

"Girls here aren't like you. They don't understand that you don't have to dress like a slut to get a man's attention, or that getting drunk will make you fun." He looks up at me with doe eyes and a soft smile. "You're nothing like them, and I like that."

Within a split second, I become ridiculously uncomfortable. I'm not sure what to say, so I play it safe. "I was raised in a very strict household, so I didn't really have a choice." I redirect his attention so maybe the awkward feeling will diminish. "So, do you think my husband's car will be as good as new?"

"Better," he says, unable to hide his excitement. "Van and the guys will replace every nut and bolt and there won't be a scratch on it. We'll even modify a few things for performance. I made this great program that we can adjust the car for more torque..." He stops and laughs. "You have no clue what I'm even talking about, do you?"

"I have to admit, no," I say sheepishly.

"Let's just say, once I hook it up to my program, it'll be better than new," he states proudly, then looks down at the ground, but looks up quickly with a shy but hopeful smile. "If you want, I can take you back to the shop and explain it better."

"No...um, that's all right. I believe you. I don't really understand that sort of stuff."

Violet walks up to us just as I answer. My body recoils from her standing beside me. I move several steps back from her. *What the hell is she doing?*

I think she realizes it immediately. "Don't worry, I'm done harassing you; at least that's what Van told me. I'm apologizing for my behavior earlier because I was told to."

Although she's not sincere in her apology, she's visibly upset; her dark makeup is smudged and mascara streaks down her face. "Thank you for the apology," I reply as my ingrained manners kick in.

Her hands start to flail around as she talks, the precious liquor spilling from her cup. "He pisses me off. Van's always chasing after some new piece of ass. Like they'll ever love him like I do." I'm shocked and not quite sure what to do or say. Is she trying to be civil by showing she's seeking attention from Van? "I mean, it's not like he'd go after you, you're definitely not his type. I mean, look at you." And she does, eyes me from head to toe.

She has no idea that every word she says is an insulting comment toward me. She must see the look on my face. "No offense." She shrugs. "Ace, you got to get that Brandy girl away from him. Go talk to her," Violet whines.

"You need to calm down and leave him alone. He'll never come around with you acting that way," Ace says, matter of fact.

"You're right," she says taking a calming breath, exhaling directly into my face. Ugh, she doesn't wear whiskey breath well. "I'm going to hang out with you, Mrs. Dawson, and be super nice." She drags out the word super, spitting in my face, "And that way Van will start taking me seriously. You'll help me, won't you?"

Of course, this comment is directed toward me. Ace chimes in, "How's acting like you're friendly with Emerson," he clears his throat, "I mean, Mrs. Dawson, going to help you with Van?"

She rolls her eyes at him, gritting her teeth in between words. "Because he respects her and thinks she's smart. If I can get on her good side..." She thumbs at me, "or at least pretend to, maybe he'll take me more seriously."

He respects me and takes me seriously? I have to suppress the stupid smile that wants to display proudly.

I've got to hand it to her, she's smart in a stalker-ish kind of way.

Ace laughs a wholehearted, you're crazy kind of laugh. "If you think that's the problem of why you're not married to Van yet, then have at it."

Violet's eyes narrow and her forehead crinkles. I don't know her that well. But it doesn't take a genius to figure out I'm her next target.

She leans in, placing a clammy hand on my arm. "You'll help me, and I'll make sure you won't pay a cent for the car repair."

Anger emerges out of nowhere, "I'm not interested in getting the job done for free. We've hired Mr. Bradley to fix our vehicle and he'll be paid accordingly." I'm appalled at her offering. She's unqualified to propose such an action. A light bulb goes off in my mind. Violet will now be thoroughly evaluated by me.

"It's no big deal. The whole family offers shit for free; especially Van's brother, Teddy," Violet states confidently. "They fight about it sometimes, but Van doesn't really do anything about it."

Once again, I'm dumbfounded at her accusations. I'm sure Van wouldn't want her to go around telling clients their personal business. She's giving me great cause to look into her records further.

I look over at Ace, forgetting that he was there, listening quietly. He's looking down at his phone once again. I hope he's been paying attention to us and not to his stupid phone. Even though I don't know him well, I could use an ally when dealing with Violet. So, I decide to elbow him to get his attention.

"What was that for?" he says while rubbing his elbow.

"Sorry," I apologize, but try to send him a look of pay attention. It must work because his shoulders square and he tucks his phone into his pocket.

Violet stands casually with her hands in her back pockets. I want to tell her it's not her job or her position to hand out free services, but I know it would be like talking to the wall. I'll do what I always do, prove it with numbers.

The air grows cold, and I have no clue what to do or say next. Ace must feel it too; within seconds he proposes to Violet, "Let's go grab a drink." Pulling her by the elbow toward the large group of people gathering around the keg of beer.

I'm relieved to have them both gone, but not sure what to do next. It's not like I know anyone well enough to walk up to them and start a conversation.

The crowd starts getting rowdier. Music is louder, more people are dancing, and the chairs are starting to fill up. Just as I start to plan my next move, which is finding Callie, the phone in my pocket vibrates. It's David.

"Hello," I greet him.

"What the hell is all that noise? It sounds like you're at a party," he correctly accuses.

"I am. Van invited me to meet some of the other employees and clients." There, that sounds believable.

"Don't embarrass me. I can't imagine how ridiculous you must look with those people. You're probably wearing a suit." He gives a throaty laugh.

I cringe. He's half right. "I'm fine. I was just being friendly by going. What do you need?"

"Did I interrupt something? It's not like you to be rude for no reason."

"I'm sorry, I just can't hear you that well," I lie again.

"Whatever...I don't care what you do. It might be good for you to get drunk and have some fun, then you could be some other bastard's problem."

I bite my lip. He's clearly been drinking. David is usually rude no matter what, but the insults that're spewing through the phone tonight are one-hundred-percent alcohol induced.

I look toward the fire and see Van on the other side, staring at me, distracting me from David. He has a group of people around him, but he isn't focused on them. Our eyes are locked, and I'm not sure if I can look away.

"Emerson? Are you there? Are you even listening to me?"

"What?" I finally manage to say to David, but before I can say more, a flashing light pulls me from both men's attention. The music becomes louder, thumping in my ears. Someone has drove their vehicle onto the beach. On top of it is a huge strobe light, and I immediately feel the effects.

Heat filters throughout my body, and not a good kind of heat. All I see is the light. I can't focus, and within seconds, my vision blurs. My last thought is...*fuck!*

12

S omeone's saying my name. I can't tell who and I want them to stop.

"Ems! Wake up!" A frantic voice permeates my ears.

I try and open my eyes, but they're not listening.

"Come on. Wake up. I think you had a seizure. Come on, open your eyes."

The voice is now familiar. It's calm, reassuring, and forceful at the same time.

I can feel something touch my hand. "Let's pick her up and take her back to the house."

I know that voice, but I can't think of his name. His quiet tone forces my eyes open.

I try to open them, but they just won't listen, and I fall back into the soothing darkness.

Something smells delicious. I roll over and open my eyes. The black cloud that surrounds me is so comfy and soft and...where the hell am I?

I dart up off the bed, but my throbbing head stops me, my achy body screams back, and my nauseated stomach recoils. "Ugh." I fall back onto the comforter.

"You're up. Damn, you scared the shit out of everyone." He scrubs his hand down his face. "You had a seizure."

"Ah...jeez." It's all I can manage. I know what happened. I should have known better; it's been a lovely seven months of being seizure free that has now come to an end.

My head turns to the left, and a beautiful, stressed Van greets me. "How are you feeling?"

"I'm fine." My voice is hoarse, and I can barely tell it's me speaking.

"You're at my place, in my bed. I wanted to keep an eye on you."

"What time is it?"

"It's about two in the morning. You've been out for maybe twenty minutes. It only lasted a few minutes, but it felt like an eternity. I haven't seen one of those for a while." Van's strong jaw is pulsing, and he runs his fingers through his hair.

"I'm so sorry. I should have known better than to go to a party."

"What the hell does that have to do with having a seizure?" His brow furrows and he's not happy with me.

"You know, the fire and lights and loud music. Too much stimulation for my brain." I point at my head, trying to laugh it off, but he's not having it.

"You can't help it, and you can't stop living because you have seizures. But you should be wearing a bracelet or necklace or something," he scolds. "Especially when you're away from home with strangers."

This isn't the reaction I was expecting. I know the confusion on my face is showing because he answers my unasked question.

"A friend of mine had them when he was younger; luckily he hasn't had one in a really long time."

"Oh..." It's all I can think to say.

"Just lie down and get some sleep. I want you to get some rest and I'll sleep on the floor in case you have another one."

Callie's words from earlier play in my head, *"He doesn't let anyone stay in his bed."*

"Do you remember who you were on the phone with?"

"Mr. Dawson, I mean...David."

"Okay. I'll give him a call so he isn't worried. I'm sure he thought something happened. I was looking your way when you started wandering toward the fire. Luckily you tripped on a chair leg, and then you dropped to the ground in convulsions. If you hadn't tripped on that chair, you would have fell in the fire." He scrubs his hand down his face, I can almost feel the anxiety radiating from him.

I'm so embarrassed. I hate that so many people saw me that way.

Van doesn't say anything else about what happened and grabs my phone from the small table beside me. "What's your code to unlock it?"

"One, Two, Three, Four."

"Really?" He shakes his head and mumbles under his breath, "Only you," he says. I almost tell him I was going to change it because of Ace's comment but never got around to it.

"Hey, Mr. Dawson, this is Donovan Bradley. I'm sure you're worried sick about Ems...I mean, Mrs. Dawson."

I listen intently, waiting for David's response. Van is quiet listening to him.

His face falls, his forehead crinkles, and his jaw pulsates. "What?"

I'm on pins and needles wondering what David's telling Van.

Van rubs his chin, quietly listening. I can hear David's voice, but can't make out what he's saying.

Van finally responds, "What the hell is wrong with you, man? Are you drunk?"

I sit up, worried what insult David just threw at Van.

Van stands and walks to the opposite end of the room by the stairs, which of course isn't very far away.

"Look, no amount of money is worth dealing with this shit. I'll send the fucking car back and you can find someone else to do it. You should get your ass up here and take care of your wife. She had a fucking seizure, and no one knew about her condition." He listens, and David's voice raises, but I still can't make out what he's saying. After a moment, Van replies, "I'll send your car back and believe me, it'll be in worse shape than it is now! Remember, I'm the only person who can fix it...that's why you sent it here in the first place."

He listens some more and then says seriously and with a hint of fire, "We'll see. Maybe you're a decent person when you're sober."

We'll see, we'll see what? Oh no, what did David say?"

Van pulls the phone away from his ear and stares at it in his hand with a blank look on his face, then he turns to me. "What the fuck is wrong with your husband? He doubled my labor price and asked me to take care of you instead of him coming out here. I think I should call Andrew."

"No...don't! I mean, bother Andrew. David travels quite a bit, so I'm sure he couldn't cancel his plans for me." I don't know how to respond other than making excuses. "Besides, I'm fine. Not the first one I've experienced, and it won't be the last." It doesn't take long for Van to react.

"He apologized for you looking like the exorcist, told me that I should have left you there and to not bother with you...that you would eventually wake up on your own," he says it slowly like he's still trying to digest the meaning of the words.

I watch as he makes his way back over to the small black chair and sits. His eyes are still locked on my phone. Part of me wants to chuckle, the other half is embarrassed that he has to even deal with this situation.

"Ems, he said that I should have let you lie there and walk away. That you weren't worth my trouble." He rubs his forehead, "You have no idea how many people at that party were concerned about you. Or how many people sprang into action to make sure you were safe and didn't hurt yourself. Does he treat you like this every time you have a seizure?"

Van finally looks up at me, and I don't like the looks he's giving me. It's a look of pity, and I don't want any part of it.

I rip the comforter off and stand, but of course my head disagrees again, and I stumble back onto the bed. Only this time, Van's arms are there to catch me. "Careful," he scolds.

My head falls into my hands. I brush the hair out of my face, inwardly cringing at the thought of what it looks like. My neat bun is probably a disheveled mess, but I guess that's the least of my worries regarding my appearance. I'm sure I resemble more of a zombie than anything.

"He isn't usually around when I have them," I answer. It's the truth because he's never around me unless he has to be.

Van stands, walks quickly to the other side, then paces back to me. I'm not quite sure what's going on, but he looks mad. *Mad at me?*

He shakes his head and opens his mouth, but quickly closes it. "I have something to take care of, don't get up or anything. I'll be back soon."

Van doesn't even let me answer before he whisks down the steps, and a loud thud of a door echoes through the loft.

So here I am wondering what the hell just happened. Van went from concerned to pissed in a few seconds. What the hell kind of situation did he have to take care of at this time of night? Probably something because he has to deal with me.

A few confusing seconds drift by and my phone rings. I grab my phone off the corner of the bed and see David's name staring back at me. I answer even though every bone in my body is telling me not to.

"Hello, Ems," his voice smug. "I like your new nickname. Sounds like you're getting cozy with the mechanic. He even wants me to pick you up and take care of you. If he only knew about you, what you do to people. I don't think he'd give two shits about you having a seizure." David's voice is vile, the venom spouting from his lips.

My head hurts from listening to him. I hate the way he talks to me. I have every reason in the world to leave him except one; I'm responsible for why he's such a miserable person.

"Please stop. The car will be fixed soon, and I'll be home," I respond, trying to sway him from the thought of coming here.

"I'm coming in a few days. Not because of you, but because of the way that stupid mechanic spoke to me and threatened to hurt my car. I'll make sure I ruin him and his stupid car business. I'll be there by the end of the week, to make sure he did the job right. I expect you to let me know if he does anything to screw it up."

The call ends, and I'm left with a pit in my stomach. Of all the stupid things to happen. Why would Van risk his business for me? He threatened my husband, and part of me is confused, but the rest is thrilled. It's been so long since someone has stood up for me.

As quick as Van whisked out of the loft, he whisks back in, slamming the door behind him. He stands in front of me with his hands on his hips, ready to unleash his thoughts on me. My teeth are clenched waiting to hear what he has to say.

I can't help but be distracted by how handsome he is. There's so much more to him than what's in front of me.

I love the way his wavy dark hair falls carelessly around his face. I'm not used to a man having hair that meets his chin. Granted, it's not long at all, but to me, I've not been around a man whose hair I could grab.

A chill jumps through me, and an unfamiliar feeling tingles between my thighs. A flash of me grabbing his hair in both my hands and smashing my mouth to his play in my mind. Heat pulses through my body. Not the kind of heat I experienced earlier...this is passionate heat. I've never felt this until now.

"Are you okay? Your face is bright red," he asks, concerned.

The last thing he should feel is concern. I'm swooning over a man who's not my husband, but every moment I spend with Van makes me regret every second of being married to David.

I swallow and find a way to reply, "Yes...I'm just a little hot for some reason."

"Here, take the comforter off and leave the sheet." He helps me, but slowly and carefully, almost as if I'm going to bite. I'm lying here with just a sheet. I realize my jacket is off, and my tank top is visible. My boots are also off, and I notice them laying on the chair beside his bed.

"I took your jacket off when we got back here. Ace took it home with him. His parents are dry cleaners, so it'll be here first thing in the morning. It was covered in dirt and ashes from the fire. You fell so close to the fire, and it was hard to move you until the seizure stopped."

"Sorry, people say I start to wander off before I drop to the ground. I don't remember doing it." I bite my lip in order to stop myself from talking and sounding ridiculous.

"Stop apologizing. You can't help it. I am sorry, though."

"For what?" What could he possibly be sorry for?

"The way I talked to your husband. I'm sure he loves you. I guess people have their own way of dealing with difficult situations. I'm sure he'll be better once he's sober. Besides, your marriage is none of my business, so I apologize."

He's too sweet for my own good. "Don't worry about it." I decide I've had enough swooning for one night and want to relax away far away from Van. He makes my body feel things I haven't ever felt. In no way should I spend the night next to another man. This internal dialogue, arguing, and convincing myself that I'm making the right decisions, is more tiring than the damn seizure.

"Lie back and settle in. I'll be right over here." Van gets up and pulls a blanket and pillow from the chair where my shoes are and throws them on the ground.

"I appreciate everything. I mean, you carried me all the way here from the lake and took care of me." I inwardly smile at the thought of how wonderful it felt to be taken care of by him. I remove the sheet and plant my feet on the floor. "I can't kick you out of your bed, let alone make you sleep on the floor. I'll be fine on the couch."

"I've slept on worse. I don't think it's a good idea for you to be alone right now."

"I'll be fine. The worst part is over, I just need some sleep."

I stand, and for the first time since waking, I don't feel dizzy. I go to grab my boots, and Van's hand comes up and blocks my arm. "Please don't go. I'll be worried all night, and then it won't matter if I'll be in my bed or on the floor."

I look down into his deep dark eyes, narrowed in on me and pleading for me to stay.

How can I resist? I lean back and his hand breaks free from my skin. Sitting back, I watch him watching me. We don't say another word. In silence and in some sort of dance, we both settle into our respective beds and cover ourselves. My head hits the pillow while Van reaches above his head where the lamp resides, and with a click, I'm now watching Van by moonlight.

"Goodnight," he says quietly, lowering himself down to the floor on his thin blanket, breaking our dance.

13

I feel like all I've done the past few days is wake up in confusion. I'm sitting here on Van's bed staring at where Van fell asleep. The blankets and pillow have been put away with no sign that he was here last night. He slept on the floor just to make sure I was comfortable and safe.

But I know he was here. I watched him for far too long, but I couldn't fight sleep no matter how long I wanted to stare at him. Seizures wipe your body out, and mine is destroyed.

My whole body feels like I fought a room of one-hundred grown men, and my legs feel as if I've run five marathons in a row.

Stumbling out of bed, I feel a bit dizzy. The palm of my hand automatically goes to my forehead. "Ow."

Opening my eyes again, my jacket is neatly laid across the small chair up against the desk. It doesn't have a speck of dirt on it and is neatly pressed. Ace's family dry cleaners come to mind.

I wonder what time it is? Reaching for my phone, I see that it is two p.m. Crap, I slept the entire day away. I never sleep this late, but I guess my body needed it.

Slipping on my jacket, I make the bed. The black comforter was soft and smelled heavenly. I want to slip back in bed and continue sleeping the day away, but I do have work to do, and I need to thank Van for his help.

Just as I slip on my booties to begin my trip down the stairs, Ace slips through the door. He's wearing dark sunglasses, and his lean frame is dressed in a stylish leather jacket and black skinny jeans. He looks like he could be on the cover of a magazine. I scold myself because I shouldn't be having these thoughts.

"Good afternoon, how are you feeling? I didn't want to wake you," he asks brightly.

"I've been better, and I've been worse."

Ace is holding two Styrofoam coffee cups in his hands, holding one out for me as I reach him.

"Thanks."

I expect him to make small talk and leave, but it doesn't look like that's his plan because he sits down on the couch. "Where are you going? I can't believe you're up and about. You scared us to death. Van is usually very calm, but you had him...concerned." It takes him a few moments to come up with the word, and I can't help but wonder what it could mean.

"I'm fine. It's so embarrassing. I've only been here a short time, and already I'm causing problems. The lights probably triggered it. That's the whole reason why I don't drive any of my husband's fancy cars. The Department of Motor Vehicles is not a fan of mine, and won't renew my license."

"I'm just glad we were there. If that happened when you were by yourself, you could have walked right into the fire. Van stopped you and helped you to the ground. Luckily, he knew what was going on because the rest of us were confused as to why the hell you were walking into the fire." He chuckles to himself.

I cover my face with my hands, embarrassed. "I hate that I have them. For some reason, I decide to walk into walls, or through doors to the outside, or in this case, toward a ring of flames."

Ace laughs lightly and takes a drink from his cup. "You can't help it. Van said your husband isn't coming. Isn't he concerned for your health being in a strange place? I mean, what if we were all assholes and treated you badly. Somehow, you've grown on us, though." He swallows harshly and his eyes meet mine. "You're more than a client."

My face flames at his compliment. Everyone has been so welcoming—well, not Violet—unlike my life at home. I'm used to covering up David's behavior. He used to be quite nice to me before the accident, but since then he's become awful, along with his parents. His parents are the definition of enablers, and I'm caught in their web.

"I think he has a problem. He needs help, Mrs. Dawson."

She stared at me like I was speaking in a different language. "He doesn't need help. If you were a better person, he wouldn't have lost his leg. We need to give him time to recover, and that means being a devoted wife, willing to do whatever makes him happy, even if that means giving up your own happiness."

I can remember her words as if she'd said them only a few minutes ago. Shaking the memory off, I concentrate on Ace.

"Anyway, I told him that he had nothing to worry about. The hard part was over. There really isn't anything he can do for me now. I'll call my doctor and see if maybe they can increase my medication, or start me on a new one."

"I wanted to take you to the hospital last night or call an ambulance, but Van wouldn't let me. He said he knew how to take care of you, and I guess he was right. I can take you to get your medicine after you talk with your doctor," he suggests, taking a sip from his cup.

"Thank you, I may take you up on that offer."

"We can go to lunch...if you feel up to it?" he offers, a hopeful expression crosses his face.

"That's all right, but I think I'll run down to the shop so everyone doesn't think I'm dead," I chuckle, trying to make light of the situation. As I move to reach for the doorknob, it opens, startling us both, and from behind it, gorgeous Donovan Bradley appears in front of me.

Van greets me with a smile and peeks behind me to see Ace. His smile fades but recovers when he looks back at me. "How are you this morning?"

"You mean this afternoon. Sorry, I slept in so late. You should have woken me up."

I look down to see that Van is also carrying two of the same cups that Ace was carrying when he greeted me earlier.

I catch him looking down, lifting up the cups. "I guess we were thinking the same thing, huh, Ace?"

"I was looking for you on my way here. I need you to hook up the Bugatti to the computer and determine if we need to boost the power. Ben's working on the hand controls, and I've finished the passenger door panel. It's coming along faster than expected, ahead of schedule." He directs the last sentence at me.

Ace smiles in my direction too. I don't like being the center of attention. "He's the boss, I got to go. Hope you feel better, and if you need a ride to the pharmacy, I'm your guy." His lips turn up to one side. He winks and places his cup on the counter as he exits. I'm not sure what to make of him.

As he leaves, Van takes his place.

"I need to ask you a few questions regarding some accounting stuff, if you don't mind, or if you're not up for it yet, it can wait." His head tilts, and his eyes soften, which does nothing but accelerate my heart.

I saw a glimpse last night. A man with a past and present full of women. The typical playboy, but the way he's been treating me is so sweet and sincere, I can't help but think this is the true Donovan Bradley...and not the womanizer Van Bradley.

"I'm fine, really. What do you have questions about?" I focus my attention back on the task instead of focusing on the beautiful man in front of me who happens to have a huge following of admirers.

"Okay, well..." He sighs. "Violet doesn't seem to be charging the right price on some t-shirts and stuff. I ordered a shit pile of them, and there are only a few left on the racks. But I can't find the sales receipts for any of them." He stops, looking everywhere but at me. He adds another sigh and then continues, "My brother, Teddy, usually handles the money stuff, but...I want to make sure he isn't missing something."

I think I may know what's been going on. I can see the price points are high so the profit should match, but I need more time. After I leave, I can send Van a professional report of my findings.

If she's stealing and his brother isn't catching her, I'll give him all the evidence he needs. Thieves not only steal money, but they steal dreams. Dreams are worth more than any amount of money. Someone has put their talent, heart, soul, and life into their vision, and in one swoop it can be stolen. David tells me I robbed him of his dream, but I'm beginning to see, he's the one who robbed me.

"Give me the inventory records and I'll check into it. I've used that particular system before in our stores. It'll tell me everything I need to know. I should have the answer in a week or so. I'll be back home by then, but I'll make sure you get the report."

Van's silent and listening intently to my rambling. I can't even look him in the eyes, my attention is on the stubble lightly dusting his square chin and chiseled jaw. Catching myself again, I shake my head and clear my throat.

"Okay, I'll do that. Thanks for your help."

"Of course."

He points to the door., "I better get back to work. I just wanted to make sure you were up and moving around okay."

My heart melts at his small, sweet gesture. "Thank you, I'm fine."

Once he's gone, I take the flash drive I downloaded off of Violet's computer. I would never have done it had I felt things were being handled correctly, but there are some things that aren't adding up. Thankfully, they are the same concerns Van mentioned. Opening up the records, I dive in and find out what the documents show.

A large amount was transferred from the business checking to Theodore Bradley, Van's brother. The description states bonus, but forty-thousand dollars for a bonus without taxes deducted seems worth mentioning to Van—along with several other deductions that aren't adding up.

After looking through all the paperwork, I'm wiped out. I still have a headache from yesterday. It's nearly nine o'clock when I finish making notes. The couch is getting a bit uncomfortable.

I glance longingly toward the upstairs loft. His bed was so comfortable. I'm sure he won't mind me taking a little nap. If he comes home, I'm sure he'll kick me out. Without any more hesitation, I take the steps more eagerly than I should.

Snuggling under the covers, I inhale the scent of his comforter. It has an earthy scent, very masculine with a hint of something...maybe gasoline or some type of fuel. I chuckle to myself at the odd revelation. Whatever it is, I take a deep breath and allow the smell to permeate my senses.

I find myself covering my head with the blanket and feeling very safe in this cocoon, my very own Donovan Bradley cocoon.

Realizing the effect of just the smell of his blanket should not make my hormones, or any other part of my body, react this way, I flip the covers off of my head.

I let out a deep breath. I need to get it together.

What am I going to do when I have to go home? Or worse, what am I going to do if David comes here and I'm fantasizing about Van's bed.

Even though I'm cold, the best thing to do is lie on top of the covers. So, I make the bed and find a comfy spot on the mattress. I nuzzle my head in the pillow. It's no use, he's encompassing me. Letting myself succumb to him, I quickly drift off to sleep while inhaling my new favorite scent, Donovan Bradley.

14

I awake from my sleep to hear voices coming from outside the door.

Scanning the room to make sure no one's here, I then look behind the bed and out the large A-frame window. Rolling over on to my belly, I peek out the corner of the window. To my disappointment Van's making out with the girl from the bonfire party.

I try not to react, but it's near impossible. All types of emotions flood my mind. I'm sad, mad, and annoyed. It shocks me back to the realization, Van's nothing but a womanizer—a player who wants in every girl's pants. Just as Violet said and Callie alluded to. I can see it clear as day. I already have a relationship like that, but worse, why would I do it again?

The girl is exactly who I would expect him to bring home even if I'd never spoken to him. I would have picked her out of the crowd for him. As a matter of fact, I already had at the party. Moving back from the window, I try to persuade myself not to care. I'm not with him. He's a single, handsome guy. He should have lots of girls fawning over him. Van isn't mine.

It's wrong for me to have feelings for this man who's a business associate. Except in a short time, he's affected me in a way no one else has done.

I lie there listening to muffled voices and a girl laughing...no, cackling is more like it. My legs start to twitch; nervous energy runs rampant through my body. I'm not sure what to do with myself. I can't help but want to take another peek out the window. Of course, his damn bed just happens to overlook the porch, with a fresh breeze blowing in from an open window letting me in on their date.

Closing my eyes, I force myself to think of anything else but Van having that girl's body pressed up against his. I think of David's mother, I think of her telling me I'm a horrible wife, a bad businesswoman, everything is my fault. She's a subject that can always erase any good thoughts, except it isn't working, because Van's laugh flutters into my ears. That sound voids any dark feelings I have for Mrs. Dawson.

What has the slut done to make him laugh?

Jealousy rages as I sit up, but again I stop myself, gaining a minuscule amount of control. Maybe it's all part of his plan to get in her pants. He sweet talks them, seems like he's genuinely listening and thoughtful, then bam...he's got his tongue shoved down your throat with his hand up your shirt.

That's it! I can't take it anymore. Trying to be as quiet as a ninja, I gingerly ease myself up on my knees and slink over to the window. My head slowly bobs up, stretching my neck as high as I can go without making too much of myself visible.

My nose is below the window frame, but I can see all that I need to. The blond's back is to me, she's smashed up against the porch. My view is high enough that I can see the top of their heads, and the entire spectacle is visible. Her outfit's exactly as expected, tight red dress with matching stripper heels and tits up to her chin.

Van's hands are locked on her hips while they're engaged in a heady kiss. It's rushed and sloppy, lacking any emotion or passion. As if they're simply going through the motions to get to the final destination of the evening.

My eyes grow wide at the vision of Van's hands roaming up her sides, yanking the bottom of her dress up with them. He exposes her behind to reveal a black thong strangling her ass crack. Leaving me trying not to wish mine looked half as good.

I'm waiting for the window to fog up from the heat steaming off them.

My eyes make their way over to Van. I try to only concentrate on her, but I need to see the way he kisses. *No, I have to see it for myself...maybe I'll be repulsed and stop ogling?* I spot her hands entwined in Van's dark, long locks. She's doing what I haven't been able to stop thinking about since I first laid eyes on him. She's feverishly pulling his face to hers. A flash of his tongue swipes across, and I'm getting hot and can't pull away from the show. Somehow, they've managed to switch positions to the side. Now I have a glimpse of the perfect vantage point of roaming hands, moans, and wrestling tongues. The way he's holding her, so manly and strong. Another flash of his tongue, he moves it methodically, tilting her head in a position that makes her moan even louder. I have to move away from the window, stop watching them like a peeping Tom or an obsessed stalker, but I'm having a hard time listening to myself. Something about them, they are so sexy, rushed. It's hot and I want to be the blond so badly.

They start to move awkwardly toward the door, trying to stay connected. The blond takes her hand out of his hair to find the doorknob. The sound of the door jiggling snaps me out of my sex haze. I clumsily fall back onto the bed, trying to jump and hide under the comforter before the blond can figure out the door. Only my foot gets caught and tangled up in the process. The door finally clicks, and I freeze, tangled in the sheets.

Closing my eyes, I pretend to be asleep.

Oh God, did he forget I was here? Does he even care that I'm in his bed? Maybe he fucks them right where I'm lying. I cringe at the thought.

I'm sure she doesn't care where they do it or who's watching.

Van shushes the girl.

In the most seductive voice, she pleads, "Donovan, let me come in. I'm a great fuck. You've never had a girl like me. I can make all your dreams come true," she purrs.

I gag.

I hear the laugh in his voice, as if he thinks it's fake too. "I'm sure you can, but I told you it wouldn't be happening tonight. Ems is inside, and I'm not disturbing her. Thanks for the ride home."

I'm hiding under the covers while they continue to whisper, trying not to wake me up.

"Ems?" she questions with a high-pitched whisper. "The girl who looked like the exorcist at the bonfire?"

The blond laughs at her brilliant joke.

Van surprises me as his voice is stern and void of humor, "That isn't fucking funny. I think it's about time for you to get out."

"Come on, baby." She whines. "It was just a joke." Her voice suddenly jumping a few decibels higher.

"Quiet!" he commands, no longer whispering.

"Ugh, quit being such a dick!"

I can almost hear his eyes roll, prompting me to move part of the comforter from my eye and spy. The slits in the railing give me the perfect view of him taking her by the arm, more forceful than I would have expected from the way they were in the throes of lust a few moments ago.

"Okay. Time to go." He pushes her through the door, slamming it behind her.

I dip back under the covers. The room becomes silent. Wondering what he's doing, I force myself to remain still. I contemplate pretending to wake up, but then decide it's best just to act as if nothing happened and go about my night. After all, it's not my concern...only, I'm so damn jealous of that blond.

Loud footsteps tromp along the wood laminate floor and up the stairs. "You can stop hiding. I saw the top of your head at the window," Van accuses. I can hear the amusement in his voice.

Damn it!

The covers slowly glide down my face, stopping at my chest. Van stands before me, wearing a sexy smirk. His eyes glance for a second at where the blanket haunts, quickly moving back to my face.

"You would suck at being a spy. Do you always watch people on their private dates?" he asks with a knowing grin.

"No, and I wasn't spying. I heard noises, weird noises," I spit the last words.

"You weren't spying?"

"No, I wasn't."

Van lowers himself to sit at the side of my bed. His hand reaches for my hair, smoothing down a few stray strands that have gone awry. In the process, his finger lightly brushes against my cheek, making my eyes automatically close in response, savoring the fire he ignites inside me.

As my eyes open, they meet his hooded eyes, looking intently at mine. His hand stills on my cheek, his thumb, however, glides along my bottom lip. I have to stop my tongue from jutting out to taste him. I can't make myself turn from him, his eyes concentrate on my lip, and he bites his lower lip in return.

Closing his eyes with some newfound power, he abruptly removes his fingers, and himself, away from me, backing as if I'm some sort of disease. Standing and shoving his hand in his pocket, he stammers, "I…I…let's get some sleep.

"Okay," I say quietly.

Van pads over to the dresser, grabbing some clothes from it, moves past me with his jaw clenched, and heads down the steps. A door slams, and I assume he's gone to take a shower or change.

I take a moment to catch my breath. *What the hell just happened?* My body reacts to his touch in a way it has never done before. Certainly, never like that with David.

David—oh God! I am not thinking clearly around him at all. It is as if my brain forgets to mention to me that I'm married, but maybe he's forgetting too. The way he looks at me and touches me. He shouldn't be touching me at all.

The water starts to run in the shower, giving me extra time to figure out what to do next. *Should I pretend to be asleep again? No, that didn't work. Go to the couch? No…he's down there. With my luck he'll sleep down there with me again. Do I grab my iPad and pretend to work and ignore him? Oh jeez, what have I gotten myself into?*

I roll over to face the wall. My hand automatically touches my bottom lip where his thumb traced. I can still feel it.

The bathroom door opens, prompting me to roll back over, and a glorious Donovan Bradley walks up the steps like a Grecian god. His hair's wet, slicked back, with water dripping from the dark strands. I watch it dance down his perfectly sculpted pecs. His chest is shaped like the Adonis he is, not too large and Hulk-like but strong and chiseled. Speaking of chiseled, my eyes roam down to his six-pack glistening with water droplets. His abs are nothing short of sublime.

But that is not what makes my face flame...no, it is that itty-bitty towel wrapped around his waist.

The sexy V that women are always going crazy for in romance novels, is a real-life occurrence, making me want to reach out and run my fingers along the top of his towel, tracing his skin.

Van's physique is nothing short of perfect. I have to stop the urge from going over to the other side of the room to touch his chest like he's some sort of mythical creature.

Tearing my eyes from his body, I look up at the sexy smirk on his face. "Like what you see?" he asks, alluring me further with just his voice.

In his trance, I answer, "Yes." A twinkle dances in his eyes. Catching what I've said, I quickly say, "I mean, no." My voice is a high-pitched squeal. "What I'm trying to say is that you shocked me by only wearing a towel. Didn't you just grab some clothes?" His playful grin brings me back to reality. *Cocky bastard.*

I'm rambling. I have to shut my trap now. Luckily, he saves us both. "I grabbed a shirt instead of shorts."

He walks over to the dresser and pulls open a drawer, grabbing a pair of black and gray camouflage shorts. I fully expect him to go back in the bathroom to change, but of course, he doesn't. No, he steps into them, hikes them up under his towel, and the towel drops carelessly to the floor. Van picks it up, throwing it into an empty basket near the bed.

I must look like the biggest weirdo. If I didn't know better, I'd think I was a brace-faced teenage girl looking at a boy for the first time.

Thankfully, Van ignores my teenage gawking. Flopping himself on the bed, he covers himself, but only from the waist down. I freeze, unsure of what the hell he's doing. His smooth chest is visible, and I catch myself staring, again. He blinks and looks at me, "Do you mind if I watch some TV?"

"No...but there's another TV downstairs."

"And you're in my bed."

"Sorry. I'll go to the couch." Starting to stand, he touches my arm.

"Stay. We're adults. Besides, the bed's more comfortable. Why should we both suffer if we don't have to."

I nod and relax.

"Good, I need to unwind after a night like tonight. Girls can be a real handful," he says after he gives a knowing wink, ignoring my comment about the other TV. "Do you like action movies?" he asks, moving the conversation in a different direction.

"I don't watch TV or movies." I want to scream at him, "what do you think you're doing lying next to me in your bed," but he questions me before I can ask.

"So, what do you do then? You have to do something to unwind." He rolls over on his side to face me, the cover falling down a smidgen to reveal more skin, giving me his full attention.

"I read or research makeup trends. I find it fascinating." The words flow freely from my lips, forgetting myself. I never really discuss what I like to do with anyone. In this moment, I think he has to be the only one to ask me something so personal in a long time.

"Really, makeup? Huh? Never would have picked that for you. I mean that I can see you doing it as a job, but not actually enjoying it." Van's genuinely surprised. He continues, "You barely wear any. Violet piles that shit on by the gallon, and in every color of the rainbow. I'd expect that answer from her, but not you. So, do you just watch those makeup YouTube videos, or do you actually put makeup on people?"

Van settles in a more comfortable position, with one arm resting leisurely above his head, and the other at his side, holding onto the remote. I follow his lead by settling into a more comfortable spot myself. Resting on my side, bending my elbow while leaning my head against it.

"I do watch those videos, too, but I'm more interested in making the cosmetics, the chemistry of it. The Dawson's own a cosmetic firm, but it's not as profitable as their jewelry company. So, I can't focus the attention on it like I would like, but I do get to visit the lab, learn, and even help in the developmental stages. I'm starting my own line soon."

Van's dark eyes are trained on me. The light from the TV glistens off them, but it's the undivided attention he's giving me that has me overcome with emotions. He's genuinely listening to me with interest. I've divulged information about myself that I've never told anyone. The employees at the cosmetics firm just think I'm checking up on them.

"You're full of surprises. You get smarter by the minute."

I laugh. "I guess when you grow up the way I did, you don't have a choice."

Van turns down the volume on the TV, rolling more onto his side he mirrors my position by resting his head in his hand, elbow supporting the weight. I realize how much he's concentrating on my words, giving me his full attention by ignoring the TV, and I'm loving every second of it.

"How did you grow up?" His concern is apparent in his tone.

"I guess a little different from most people. I was adopted by a wealthy family. With very traditional values. I was expected to be perfect. So, when I make a mistake, I take it very personally."

"Adopted? Wow, that must have been tough?"

"Not really. My real mother was fifteen when I was born, and she wasn't sure who my father was—at least, that's what I've been told."

"You never wanted to find her?"

"No. My life is complicated enough, I don't need to add to it."

He bites his lip and stares off over my head. He must be thinking of something else.

"What's your adoptive family like?"

"Good parents in everyone's eyes...strict, but good providers."

He's not satisfied with my answer. "How about to you, in your eyes? Good providers seems like an odd way to answer the question."

I'm not sure why his response triggers me to feel annoyed, and the sudden need to defend myself, but I do.

"How do you want me to answer it?" I say with a haughty attitude. "I had food, designer clothes, great schools, extravagant parties, everything a young girl could ever want."

"Except?"

"Except what?" I spit back at him.

He sits up, raising an eyebrow. "I'm sorry, I didn't mean to hit a nerve or insult you."

"You didn't." I sigh, calming a bit. "I had a very privileged childhood, and now marriage." I accentuate the word marriage, not for him, but for me. Reminding myself that my marriage is none of his business.

Van flips onto his back, turning the volume up to where it was prior to our uncomfortable conversation. I blew it. He was just being nice, trying to get to know me, and I was a complete bitch to him.

My eyes glance over to Van. He's concentrating on the TV in front of us, so I take his lead and do the same. I'm not sure what else to do or say. Idly, I watch as well, noticing it's about race cars. A movie like this is exactly what I would expect him to be watching.

He lightens the tension in the room by asking if I've ever watched a race in person.

"No, I'm usually working when David attends a NASCAR event."

"David goes to NASCAR? I bet he's not camping out." He chuckles.

I giggle back, "No, he usually sits in an owner's box. His father owns two cars."

"Oh, so he owns Dawson Motors? I never put it together. Probably because I never liked the team."

"Guilty...we do, actually."

"I was right, you get more interesting by the second. You own a NASCAR team, and you don't even go to races?"

"Guilty, again."

He shakes his head, giving a hearty laugh. Van sits up, throws off the covers, twists, facing me. "We're going to a race. There's one an hour away from here in two weeks. I can say we've run into a problem, and you can stay longer."

"No! Don't do that. I mean, David will come here if it takes too long. I'd like to avoid that at all costs." I'm hoping David was just threatening me about coming at the end of the week. I doubt he would waste his time.

Van narrows his eyes, and that spark of excitement in his gaze vanishes. He doesn't question my reaction. "All right, but I'll find a way for you to see a race. If you don't want to go see a NASCAR one, I'll take you to a local one. There is a street race Ben runs. You'll have a good time."

I nod and smile. "Okay." I'm relieved that I've diverted his original idea. I cannot have Van and David in the same room. David's already accusing me of having a thing for Van, and he's going to cause him a problem somehow, I just know it. It's what he does, what he lives for. The less attention I bring to Van, the better.

We grow quiet, continuing to watch the movie, cars racing and crashing into each other. I have wanted to go to one of our NASCAR races, but it's David's hobby, and he doesn't allow me to go. Although, I usually look forward to when he goes away for a race. I don't have to deal with him.

Van lies beside me, not close, but close enough that I'm very aware that he's there. I wonder how I'll be able to sleep all night with him inches away. What if I snore, or kick him, or cuddle up beside him? I won't be able to help myself in my sleep.

We don't make it long through the movie when Van's cell phone rings.

"Granddad? Are you all right?" His voice is thick with worry. Listening carefully, he then answers, "I'll be there in a second. Don't move."

15

Van jumps up, looking around the room for his boots. He hops on one foot while trying to get on the other. He rummages through his pants pocket. "What's wrong?" I ask, knowing that his grandfather's in some type of danger. He looks frantic, unable to find what he's looking for. "Can I help?" I'll do anything to calm him down in this moment.

"My granddad is having pain in his chest. It's probably heartburn, but I need to check on him. I'll probably stay the rest of the night with him."

I don't know what makes me ask, but I do. "Do you need me to go with you?"

He pauses, not in a million years would I expect him to take me up on my offer, but to my surprise, he does, "Yeah. You might be a good distraction. He can be difficult. He'll listen to a beautiful woman before he listens to me. Found it."

Van snags a key out of a jeans pocket and then slips them on while grabbing a shirt out of the hamper. I grab my robe that's hanging up on a hook beside the bed and head out the door with him. We walk hurriedly to a red brick tiny house with a large, matching brick porch, white doors, white window frames, and wooden rocking chairs with a small table in the middle.

Van rushes through the door. An older, balding man sits in a blue La-Z-Boy chair with his hand clutching his chest. Van's at his side before I even step a foot through the door. He kneels beside his grandfather. "What's going on?"

"Damn heartburn," the large man grumbles beside him.

"You look pale, let's check your vitals," Van says while grabbing a container beside the chair.

"Who's that?" The gray-haired man dressed in red boxer shorts and a white t-shirt says from the chair.

As I watch his grandfather, his breathing is labored, and the crinkle in Van's forehead has me concerned. Van rummages through multiple items until he grabs a cord that's linked to a blood pressure cuff, wrapping it around his grandfather's upper arm.

"Damn it, Donovan! Get that fucking thing off my arm. I'm fine!" he says, trying to rip it from his arm.

"Let me just check it!" Van bites back.

To defuse the situation, I intrude while Van grabs some other medical test. "Donovan's done a wonderful job restoring my family's car." A glint in his eye appears and he stops struggling against Van.

"Oh yeah, what kind of car?"

Van answers for me, "One-off, Bugatti."

"No shit!" Mr. Bradley mumbles.

"A beauty, that's what that car is. Only ever seen one like that, remember Joe Wilders?" Van asks, turning toward me with a relieved smile on his face.

They ramble on and on about Joe Wilders's Bugatti. I only catch a few words because I'm distracted by the methodical way Van goes about checking his grandfather's vitals. It's as if he's done it a thousand times. Then he is testing his sugar. His grandfather is so intrigued that he doesn't even notice when Van pricks his skin with a needle, placing a testing strip to soak up the blood for the monitor to read.

Van shakes his head, "Over two hundred?" Then he finally checks his blood pressure.

"Blood pressure two-hundred and twenty over ninety-nine. Christ, Granddad!" He drops his hands to his sides, pausing to think for a moment. "We need to get you to a hospital. I'll call an ambulance."

"You will not! I'm fine. If you want to drive me there, I'll go to make you feel better, but I'm not riding in no ambulance!"

Van looks in my direction, letting out a sigh.

"You go pull the car around and I'll keep Mr. Bradley company."

He nods and agrees with my suggestion. "Just sit with him. If he tries to talk you into anything...ignore him. I'm going to load his wheelchair in my truck." His voice is so hurried, I can barely make out the words.

I decide it's more productive to distract Mr. Bradley. Feeling like he might try to fight any commands I give him, I suggest a glass of water. My voice comes out shaky, I don't like being in charge of an uncertain situation, or a man who weighs two-hundred pounds more than me.

He waves his hand, "Oh hell, Donovan gets worked up over everything. I told him to just let me die in a nursing home, but that son of a bitch won't let me. He'es the only good kid in the whole damn family."

"He's been very...accommodating. My family sent me here to oversee the car restoration." I have no idea why I keep saying my family, it's not my family, it's my husband.

"Your family sent you here to watch over a car?" he grumbles.

I shrug, then say, "Yes."

His eyebrow raises. "I may be old, but something about that don't seem right. Sending a beautiful young lady to hang around a shop with filthy boys. Are you staying in one of the houses?"

"No...I mean, I was, but Van sold it. Let me grab you that glass of water." Hurrying past him to the sink, I grab a small glass from the dish drainer, fill it up, and contemplate taking a sip myself. What an interrogation? I walk back over, kneeling to give Mr. Bradley his water. His forehead's cascading with droplets of sweat, and his breathing is more labored than before.

He takes the glass from my hand but drops it as his hand automatically grips his chest. "Granddad!" Van yells from behind me as he slumps over to the right.

Van moves to grab his granddad, but he's too heavy for Van to even budge. Without a second thought, I yank the cell phone that Van's holding and dial nine-one-one. Van's eyes widen with fear as I begin talking to the dispatcher about what's going on. He's holding on to his granddad's hand, the fear written all over his face.

I ask Van for the address and relay the information. The dispatcher tells me that there's an ambulance a block away. I head outside the door to greet the ambulance. Biting my nails, I pace back and forth, waiting and saying a prayer that Mr. Bradley will be fine. It couldn't be more than a few minutes when I see a car approach. I feel a second of relief until it dawns on me that it isn't an ambulance. Instead, Ben and Ace greet me. Ben races out of the car and approaches me.

"We heard your call over the radio. I'm a fireman," Ben explains rapidly, then pushes me aside and rushes to Mr. Bradley. Ace grabs my hand as we walk outside to give Ben room to do whatever he needs to do. Ace blows out a breath. "You okay?"

"I hope Mr. Bradley is going to be okay."

"You sounded so scared. But you did a good job. I'm sure Van was happy to have you there." Before I know what's going on, he steps closer and pulls me toward his body, hugging me tighter than necessary, softly rubbing my back. I stand there awkwardly, wondering how I went from lying next to Van to having Ace so close to me.

"I'm fine," I mutter while trying to break from his hold. He relents but still slings his arm around my shoulder, not completely letting me go. We stand for a few moments longer, then Van stands in the doorway. His eyes rake over mine, but narrow when he sees Ace's arm around me.

"Ambulance isn't here yet?" he asks with aggravation.

Ace answers, "No, we're looking out for it."

Van huffs, "Yeah, I'm sure you were." Then he turns to go back in the house.

I manage to escape Ace's clutches, or maybe he let go because of the glare Van shot him.

Ace looks my way. "He's upset. Just ignore him." He gives me a small smile.

After what seems like an eternity, but probably only a few minutes more, the ambulance arrives. Flashing red lights fill the white porch. I move out of the way onto the rocking chair while Ace ushers them inside. I can hear the sound of Van's voice but can't quite make out what he's saying.

Within ten minutes, the paramedics load Mr. Bradley into the ambulance. The guys hover around the ambulance until it pulls away. Van has his hands in his pockets, trotting up the steps with his head trained down. He's visibly upset, and I want to comfort him in some way, but quickly understand that it's not my place. Although, I do wonder why he didn't ride along with his granddad.

Ace steps behind him while Ben lights up a cigarette. "We're going to head to the hospital. I'll call you with an update." Ace directs his comment toward me.

"No, you won't. You guys aren't coming. You have to finish that damn car," Van interrupts from behind me, pointing at the shop. "Besides, Ems can keep me company."

"No. I don't want to be in the way," I reply, shocked that he wants me with him.

"Not my idea, Granddad asked for you to come," he says casually while walking toward the black car parked along the front yard.

"I need to change."

"Hurry up then."

I don't respond, only nod, put my head down, and race back to his apartment. I could say no and tell him it isn't any of my concern...but I feel the need to be there with Van.

16

V an opens the passenger side of the door. It is a rusty older car, mostly black, except for a few green panels that must have belonged to another vehicle. My guess is a Ford Mustang judging by the horse logo on the side of the car.

Once I'm sitting on the ripped leather black seat, he slides in on the driver's side, shutting the door, and the car rumbles to life. After a few revs of the engine, he doesn't back up like I expect him to. Instead, he chooses to whip the vehicle in a complete backward circle until he straightens the wheels. I feel like I'm in a cop movie, or possibly a *Dukes of Hazzard* scene.

"Sorry, I'm just in a hurry." He glances over, probably to see my eyes wide with fear.

"It's fine," I assure him, I understand why he's driving so fast, but I hope he doesn't mind if I lose my dinner in his car.

The streets are dark, and not many lights brighten our way to the hospital. The town must be smaller than I initially realized because within a few blocks we're there. The hospital is smaller than any I've ever seen, with only one entrance and one floor.

He sits still instead of leaving the car. I wait for his move before I decide to get out. And yet, he sits.

"He's going to be fine. Right?" he asks quietly, looking at me with sad brown eyes.

I swallow. "We got him here fast. They'll do everything they can."

"He didn't ask for you to come. You can leave if you want. I'm sorry to drag you here. I know he isn't your family or your granddad, but I...I'm afraid he's going to die." His honesty steals the wind out of me.

I reach for his hand that's resting on the shifter. I whisper with conviction, "He's not going to die." Van squeezes my hand, our eyes lock on each other, and with unspoken words I know he needs me. "Let's go inside and let him know we're here."

He lets go of my hand, but not before bringing it to his lips. Not quite touching them, only letting my hand hover, resting it there for a brief second, contemplating for a moment, then dropping it.

We get out of the car and I'm shaking, not because we have to go in a hospital, but because of the way he held my hand, the way I felt safe and at home with him touching me, and how badly I wanted him to touch his lips to other parts of my body. He wants *me* with him, not his friends, but me.

As we enter through the hospital doors, he reaches for my hand. There it is again, home. I don't protest or remind him I'm married. No, he needs me, and I need him, only I don't know exactly why.

We get to the nurses' station, and the beautiful, dark-haired nurse greets him. "Donovan Bradley, I haven't seen you in forever. What brings you here?"

"My granddad was brought here by ambulance. Can you tell me where he's at?"

Her eyes widen, and she looks down at her computer screen, clicking the keyboard. "He was transferred to ICU, but you can go back to the waiting area. I'll take you," she says, getting up, but then turns around to add, "I'm sorry, but only family can go back. She'll have to wait out here." I don't miss the insult or the way she looks at Van because it's the same way I do.

"No, Dolly, she's with me. She's family," he answers without hesitation.

"Oh, how's she related? I don't remember meeting her." She stops us from entering the doorway, waiting for an answer.

"Long-lost cousin," he states, but she doesn't move. "Can we go in, please?"

She scowls and shakes her head. "Fine, Van. But I didn't let her back here."

We follow Dolly as she navigates through the maze of hallways. I'm surprised, for such a small hospital, the length we have to walk to get to Mr. Bradley. When we reach the room, Dolly tells us that we can only visit for a few minutes.

"What's his condition?"

"I don't have the authority or the information. You'll have to speak to his nurse." She faces Van, stands up on her toes to reach his cheek with her lips, and holds them there much longer than necessary. "If you need anything, you know where to find me." Even in Van's time of need, I can't stop but think of how someone's still willing to let him in her pants.

He clears his throat. "Thanks." She turns and gives him a wave. "We went out a few times," he explains.

"No need. Although, I hope I don't get her in trouble." Not true, that's a bold-faced lie. I hope she gets canned for letting me back here.

"I'm going to find a nurse or doctor. Will you...would you go in there?" he asks with hopeful eyes.

"Okay." I want to protest, but it occurs to me that this strong man isn't so strong when it comes to his granddad. He's a scared little boy in this moment.

"Okay, then. Thanks," he says quickly and moves to find someone.

I step through the glass doors; Granddad's eyes are closed and he's resting comfortably. Thankfully, he doesn't wake since I'm the last person on earth who should be in here. I take a few steps toward him. I'm not sure what to do next, so I whisper, "Van's here. He's gone to talk to the doctor." I wait but no answer. Feeling relieved, I sit in the chair beside his bed.

After a few long minutes, Granddad says, "I knew he couldn't come here by himself," he grumbles. "He hates hospitals."

"I offered."

He coughs. "I'm glad."

"Just relax and get some rest," I say. I stand and hold his hand. I'm not sure what this family is doing to me, but for the first time in my life, I feel needed.

Granddad thankfully listens to me and shuts his eyes. After about ten minutes, Van still hasn't come in. I'm ready for Dolly to break in the room with the police. I decide to step out and go looking for him. I don't make it very far...he's sitting on the floor with his arms hugging his knees and his head down.

I close the door behind me and walk to the left of him and sit down on the cold white floor. "He's okay. He was talking and joking."

"They think he's had a heart attack. They're taking him in for surgery. What if he doesn't make it?"

"I can't lie to you and tell you he'll be fine because I don't know, but I have faith that he'll be in God's hands."

Van finally looks at me, "How did I know you'd tell me that?"

"If you mean that I believe in God...yes, I do."

"Come on, let's go visit the old man." The scared look in his eyes fades a little as he walks into his granddad's room with a stronger presence.

***

The surgery started over fifteen minutes ago. His grandfather was in good spirits and alert before he went in. Van's been restless since we've been sitting in the waiting area. For such a small hospital, I'm amazed at their abilities. I thought for sure he'd need to be transferred to a city hospital.

It's now early morning, around six, and I am exhausted. This has been one of the longest nights of my life. I've taken root on a bench, playing on my phone. Van brings a cup of coffee and hands it to me while he takes a seat next to me.

"Here, I thought you could use this."

"Thanks."

"I've held you captive long enough, I'll call Ace to come and get you."

A little part of me just died. "No, don't bother him, I'll wait till Mr. Bradley gets out of surgery."

"You're too nice for your own good. This isn't your problem, and I made you sit with me because I didn't want to be alone." He lets out a slight chuckle, "You're a wife of a client who's paying me a lot of money. I'm treating you as if you are a gir...friend. You're clearly off limits."

I'm not sure how to take his words. They do strike a nerve, though. I retaliate, "I can leave any time I like. I'm a big girl, but I choose to stay here because I'm your friend and care about you and your granddad."

His eyes grow wide. "Thank you. I appreciate that."

I sit back, wanting to pat myself on the back for standing up to him. Instead, I close my eyes and calm my racing heart. I haven't felt this alive in forever. Van brings out so many emotions in me; I'm not sure what to do with myself.

After a few minutes, I feel Van get up beside me. I decide not to open my eyes. I've had enough awkward conversations to last a while. Just as I'm starting to relax and think that Van has gone to pace the hospital floors, he returns.

"Ems, here...I got you a pillow." I open my eyes to Van's hopeful smile. I look down to the pillow on his lap. He answers my unasked question. "More comfortable, lie down. I won't bite, promise."

He looks so tempting; sexy smirk, careless hair, and sad eyes. I can't say no. I bend down, placing my head on his lap and adjust my legs to fit the bench.

After a few minutes, I am so thankful for the soft cloud under my head and the smell of Van. His hands are at his sides, I'm sensing he's not sure where to put them. I have mine held hostage between my thighs while lying on my side.

"It's a long surgery, two hours or more. You know, my granddad taught me how to turn my first wrench. He taught me how to rebuild my first engine. He also taught me how to throw my first punch." He chuckles. "He's been in a fight or two in his life."

"He doesn't seem like the kind of man to sit on the sidelines. I think it's wonderful that you take care of him like you do."

Van's lips quirk and cheeks blush while he looks down at me. "I try. I called my dad, he told me to deal with it. He's with his new wife, this is wife number three." Holding up three fingers, he adds, "And she's my age. Okay, a year older than me," he says sarcastically.

"Does anyone else help?"

"My brother Teddy, at times, but he's not reliable either. He usually travels, getting us new business. Sometimes I think he's just in it for his inheritance. He barely ever turns a wrench. Which would be fine, if he didn't act like he was the one restoring all the cars."

"I'm sorry. Family can be hard to handle. All you can do is take care of your grandfather and the rest will work itself out. It's good your grandfather has you," I say.

"Can I ask you something personal?"

"Depends what it is," I answer with a hint of sarcasm.

"Is your husband a good guy? He seems like an ass." He huffs, "I can't believe he sent you here with his car. I get it's valuable...but so are you." Heat rushes over me; I'm valuable...to him?

How can I even begin to answer that?

"He's had a rough couple of years."

"Have you?" I can hear the concern in his voice.

I don't know if it's because I'm tired or it's him, but for the first time I tell the truth. I don't make an excuse. "It's been worse, much worse for me."

I close my eyes at my admission. "I'm sorry," he says, and I feel his hand in my hair, and soon he traces a finger along my hairline. His touch makes me forget all the pain I've been through. Again, I feel safe and at home with him.

"I don't think you should go home to him?" he says quietly.

My eyes open and I turn my head to look up at him. "It's not that easy, I have to go home...to him."

He huffs in frustration, "You're not happy with him. I've only known you a few days and I can see the sadness in you...you're afraid of him, and I don't think you love him. Why do you stay? Has he hurt you, physically?"

He's got it all right. Every. Single. Theory. I close my eyes as he begins to lightly graze my cheek with his finger. I can feel a tear waiting to slip from my eye, but I refuse to let it. I refuse to let this man, whom

I've only known for a few days, have me in such disarray. As much as I want to be here, with him, like this, I can't. I'm married, I made a vow to God to stay for better or worse, in sickness and in health, till death do us part.

I sit up and his hand falls away. "Ems?"

Turning to face him, I say forcefully, "It's Emerson. You can call Ace. I'm going to wait for him in the main lobby. I'll be praying for your granddad." I grab my purse and leave as quick as I can. Racing down the hall, I find a ladies' room. I open the door and find relief from my ever-changing emotions. Van makes me feel things, things I don't want to, things that I can't even begin to comprehend. I'm tired and I just want to run to my chapel and be left alone.

Cold water rushes down my face as I splash myself. The cold wakes me up, helping my breaths come easier. I need to cleanse myself of my feelings for Donavan Bradley before it's too late.

When my emotions settle, I take one last look in the mirror. My eyes are red, makeup is gone, and my brown hair is up in a messy bun. My t-shirt and yoga pants look fine, but I'm not used to wearing them out in public. Ugh, I'm a mess.

I open the door without looking out in front of me and bump into a wall of muscle. A familiar wall of muscle. Donovan Bradley stands before me looking amazingly sexy. His hair is pushed back from his intense face, his stubble sprinkles his square chin, and his dark eyes are focused solely on me.

"I'm sorry," he says solemnly, shoulders slouched in defeat.

"What are you doing here?"

"I needed to apologize, your marriage is none of my business. I'm not good at keeping my opinions to myself."

I want to scream at him, tell him my life is none of his business, but I can't. My voice is silent. My eyes scan the crease in his forehead, the way his eyes dart back and forth over my features, searching for my forgiveness.

"It's fine. I'm going to go, though. You need to be with your family. I'm just in the way."

Van grabs my elbow as I walk past, halting me. "Please, don't go. I don't want to be here by myself. I promise no more questions, no more accusations, and no more intruding."

I swallow. The memory of his fingers brushing my cheek floods my brain and heats my skin. As if he reads my mind, his forehead falls against mine and his arms encircle my waist. "Please, stay."

"Okay."

17

We've waited two hours. Van kept his promise and didn't question me. In fact, we barely spoke. I napped off and on while he paced the room or watched the local news station. A nurse walks into the waiting area, looks around the room, and then nods in recognition. "Mr. Bradley?"

Van stands. "Yes."

"Your granddad's doing well. The surgery couldn't have gone any better. We were able to remove the blockage and add a stint. He's resting comfortably. You can go in and see him now," the elderly nurse says with a smile on her face.

Van's shoulders relax, and he lets out a breath, "Thank God."

When we reach room 217, his granddad dwarfs the hospital bed. He's hooked up to oxygen, beeping monitors and random machines, but is sleeping peacefully. Van moves to stand beside him. "He looks good. Color is back, I wasn't expecting that."

"He does," I say and Van smiles a wholehearted smile in response. He brightens up the room as if he were the sun himself.

He takes me by surprise; he can stop my heart or set my world on fire with one quirk of his lips. I shake my head to calm my thoughts. I need to get out of here. "I'm going to get something to drink, would you like anything?"

"No, thanks. Do you want me to call Ace now? You've got to be exhausted."

"Yeah, that'll be good. I need to get some sleep." He nods and digs in his pocket for his cell phone.

I head to the door, and on my way, I pass the general waiting area. It's full of people. Pausing for a moment, I take in the audience in the chairs and those standing up in conversation. Some people I recognize, and some I don't. But the one thing I can't deny is they're all here for Mr. Bradley. Ben, Jake, Violet, and Ace. I can't help but notice the glare Violet's sending my way.

Before I can vanish, Ace comes rushing over, while shoving his cell phone in his pocket. His slender frame envelops me in a tight, too-close hug. "How is he?"

"He's out of surgery and in a room. They said he's doing well. How long have you been here?" My voice is breathy, since he's squeezing the lungs out of me.

"A few hours," he shrugs.

"A few hours? Why didn't you come back?"

"We weren't allowed. We were told Van didn't want anyone back there with him," he says, cocking his head to the side.

"I didn't know. Surely, he didn't know you were here, or he would've let some of you back there."

"Well, he had you." He gives me a small smile.

"Has everyone else also been here for a couple of hours?"

"Pretty much. I just got off the phone with Van, he wants me to take you back to the house. Is that what you want?" I'm not sure how to take his comment, where else would I go?

"Yes, thank you. I'm pretty tired."

As we leave the full room, I can feel eyes staring daggers into my back along with some hushed whispers. Are they talking about me? How I shouldn't be here?

Ace moves his hand to the small of my back, ushering me out of the hospital. I'm not happy he's put his hand on me, but the faster I get out of here, the better.

I spot a bench and sit while Ace goes to find his car. I told him I would go with him, but he said he parked too far. It's weird how he's treating me, how all of them are treating me. The lines between client and something more are becoming visibly blurred.

I take a moment to breathe in the warm air. The weather's beautiful. After all, I'm in the South. The sun is bright in the sky, it's a different sun than I'm used to. Somehow it feels much closer. A few clouds dot the skyline, and a subtle breeze sweeps across my skin.

I inhale, gaining a sense of peace. It's been overwhelming and crazy being here, but I don't ever recall feeling this vibrantly alive in a long time, if ever.

Glancing around the parking lot, trying to find Ace, an elderly couple comes into view. They're smiling, holding hands, and walking in my direction. As they move closer, it strikes me how much in love they are; glowing as they walk together hand in hand. The older gentleman is walking with a limp and wearing oxygen, rolling the cart for it in front of him.

I'm drawn to his limp. My eyes slide down to the bottom of his pant leg and I spot the exposed prosthetic.

In this moment, I realize that David will never wear a bright smile with me by his side. We'll never be like the couple walking past me. I should feel sad, but I don't. Something inside me flourishes realizing that I don't want to grow old with David.

Ace pops into my line of view, "Hey! Ready?"

"More than ever."

Ace opens the door to an expensive car. I've seen this one before; in fact, before the accident I had one, an Audi A6. It looks different than mine. He's added a few new parts. I'm not even sure what to call them, but I can tell he has much more chrome than I did. The inside is very tidy, and the stereo is so loud that my seat is vibrating so much I feel the music in my chest.

He starts to speak but I can't hear a word he's saying. Finally, when he takes his eyes off the road, I point to my ears.

Ace gets my gesture, then touches the knob to turn down the volume. "Sorry about that, I'm used to having it loud. I forget you're not like that."

"It's fine. I just couldn't hear you."

"I was saying, you could stay at my place tonight. I'm sure Van's going to want to be alone, and let's be honest, sleeping on his couch has to be miserable. I know he brought Brandy to his place last night. That had to be awkward."

"It was fine. She didn't come in. I don't want to be in the way anymore than I already am. After all, I've had a seizure, been in the way of a very *intimate* moment, and have been an overall inconvenience. This trip has not gone as expected."

He laughs. "Yeah, I don't think anyone expected you."

I'm not sure if I should be appalled or accept it as a compliment. "Thanks?"

"I just mean, we all expected you to be this bitchy rich older lady, but instead you're sweet, intelligent, and beautiful." My face floods with heat at his words.

Glancing over, I peek from under my eyelashes. He's giving me a sexy smirk, and for the first time, I notice that Ace is not only attractive, but his eyes are full of lust.

I'm not sure what the heck to do or say next. I'm trapped in this car with him. So, I just smile and stare out the window as if he didn't just call me beautiful and give me a panty-dropping smile.

We don't say anything else on the way to the house. Luckily, it was only a few blocks more. This is all new to me, spending my time with different men, both of whom are paying attention to me. Ace makes me feel uncomfortable but Van...he's so different. He wanted me with him all night, not his friends or Violet...me. My heart swells, and I'm not sure I've ever felt this way before.

The car pulls up outside Van's apartment and I step out. Ace gets out and jogs to my side. "If you need anything, call or text. I'll be at the shop, trying to get some work done." He winks and jumps back in. The music blasting from his car tears into my ears as I turn away to walk up the steps.

Once inside, I fall back onto the bed. What an emotional roller-coaster? Then it hits me for the first time, I forgot about Andrew.

I can't believe I haven't thought about him even once. He's been my rock through my marriage. He knows better than anyone who David is and what a monster he can be.

Picking up my phone, I dial him but get his voicemail. Odd, but I leave a message letting him know I'm all right and not to worry. I'll try calling him again later. A yawn escapes and I can barely keep my eyes open. I also know that being awake for this long with the stress of the night will be the perfect storm for another seizure.

It takes me less than a few minutes to cuddle under the covers, and the smell of Van invades my nose, but I don't fight it, I welcome his scent, it soothes me. Within moments I'm fast asleep.

18

—·—

"Ems, wake up," someone says, shaking my shoulder. A woman? "Come on, Ems, wake up." I moan, "No."

"Yes, get up!"

Now I recognize the voice, Callie. I open my eyes to a bright-eyed, long blond-haired girl. "Did you grow your hair since the last time I saw you?"

She laughs. "No, silly, I was wearing a wig last night."

I sit up. "Why would you do that?"

"I like to mix it up a little. I'm in school now for cosmetology. Hoping to open my own salon soon."

"That's wonderful." I'm happy for her but I can't help the tinge of jealousy I feel.

"No. What's wonderful is I'm in Van's place without sleeping with him. I've always wondered what it was like in here." She glances around, taking in his room. She purses her lips. "Damn, he's super clean. I would never have expected it. And look at you all cozy in his bed."

"It's not like that. I was exhausted, and he wasn't here. That couch is not comfortable at all," I lie, I didn't even lay on it by myself because Van kept me company that night. Just thinking of our night next to each other sends tingles through my body.

She kicks off her flats, sits beside me, and lifts the comforter to snuggle in the bed. "So, here is the deal. Everyone's talking about how you stayed with Van all night in the hospital. We were all there most of the night. He came out a few times to update us, but never mentioned you at all. Ace kept asking where you were, and he would never give him a straight answer. It's quite the scandal in our little social circle. I'm not trying to pry but...is everything...good?" She takes longer than necessary to finish the last word.

"Yes. I don't know why he didn't want anyone else back there. Maybe because he was pretty emotional and that he hates hospitals. I'm sure it's easier to let a stranger see you upset than friends."

She bites her lip, "Well...whatever the reason, I'm glad you were there to help him out. He's a good guy. A little on the womanizing side, but maybe he just hasn't found the right one. Ace, on the other hand, thinks he has found his unicorn, and all he can talk about is you, young lady."

"Me?" I act as if this is a huge shock but really, he hasn't been hiding it well, I've noticed he pays more attention to me than necessary.

"Yes...you." Callie rolls over on her back, looking up at the ceiling. "These guys have never seen anyone like you. Successful, reserved, so...put together. Most of us are hometown girls who have never left this town other than to go on vacation. You are the big leagues, my dear."

I give a somber smile. "You make it sound much more appealing to be me than it really is."

"Do you ever just want to be someone else?" Callie asks, not taking her eyes off the ceiling. The ache in her voice is palpable and one I can relate to.

"Yes," I answer as an overwhelming sense of relief overtakes me as I admit my deepest secret. "All the time."

"Who would you be?" she asks, finally turning to face me.

I roll on to my side to meet her inquisitive stare. "Someone who doesn't have to be all those things that the guys haven't seen. Someone who doesn't have to be perfect all the time. I hate having to be put together and responsible."

She rolls back, pursing her lips, and then jumps up with excitement. "I've got it!"

"What?" I ask, with hesitation.

Sitting on her knees facing me, she says, "I was coming over here anyway to see if you wanted to go shopping. Let's give you a southern girl makeover." Callie grabs my hand and squeezes it. "Come on, say you'll let me."

"I don't know about that?"

She squeezes harder. "Please. I'll make you look sexier than you can ever imagine."

"Tasteful, though, right?" Excitement and nervousness begin twisting together, inside of me.

"Of course, I wouldn't make you look like Violet." We laugh.

"Okay, then." I jump up from the bed, ripping the covers off me. "Let's go."

****

I finish dressing in black linen capris, a black-and-white-striped blouse, and black pumps with metal studs garnishing the heels. These are the most edgy pair of shoes I own. For the first time, I don't feel uncomfortable wearing them. Callie's relentless swooning over them also helped.

We arrive at a tiny boutique on the small-town main street. Little shops decorate the brick sidewalk. People politely smile and say good morning as we pass by and enter the store.

"Morning, Nancy." Callie waves at the woman hanging up a blue satin shirt.

"This is Emerson Dawson." She gestures to me, as if I'm a showcase item on a game show.

"Well...hello there. I've heard about the fancy woman from the city staying over at the Bradley's place. What can I help you with?" She's an older lady, wearing jeans, a pink and green flannel shirt, and cowboy boots. As I take in her appearance, I'm surprised that this is where Callie has chosen to take me to for a makeover.

"She needs a make-under," Carrie answers. "Sorry." She apologizes, probably noticing the expression of annoyance on my face.

"I just mean, no suits or buns. Do you ever do anything else with your hair?"

"Of course, I do." Callie cocks her head.

"Okay, no," I say as my shoulders slump at the realization that I'm not only uptight but boring as well.

Within moments the saleswoman has jeans, t-shirts, tops, and shoes scattered on the counter. Picking up the jeans and flowery top, she shoves them in my direction. "Here, we'll start out slow. Flowers are still feminine but not boring."

Callie whisks me away into a dressing room. I begin to try on jeans. I can't remember the last time I tried on a pair so I settle into the dark denim, twirling around to see how my bum looks in the mirror. "Huh, not half bad."

"Did you say something?" Callie calls over the curtain.

"No," I reply, catching my smirk in the mirror.

A new pile of clothes spills over the curtain rod. I pick from the mass chaos of clothes a black tank top with a low-cut V, leather and metal accents. It's not anything I would have ever picked out for myself, but I'm intrigued to see how it looks on me.

After I build my courage, I open my eyes to the sight of myself in the dark, tight jeans, my boobs pressed together in the tank top creating an ample amount of cleavage that I didn't know I had.

"Here," Callie calls, passing a pair of black leather stiletto-heeled boots under the curtain.

"These are gorgeous." I pick them up, marveling at the craftsmanship.

"They're like shoe porn, aren't they?"

I rip the curtain back, "They really are!" I can't wipe the smile from my face.

"Wow! Girl. Look at you!"

I take a step out of the safety of my dressing room. "You think?" I ask, pulling up the cloth to cover my exposed chest.

Callie glances at my hand, "Quit it." Reaching out to stop me. "You look hot. Too bad your hubby won't be around to see you, he'd go wild."

"No, he wouldn't," I slip, forgetting she doesn't know David.

Her eyes soften. "I know I have no business asking, I've only just met you, but is everything okay at home? I mean, you and your husband get along, right?"

I want to lie, to tell her that we are the happiest married couple in the world, but something in me can't lie to Callie as much as I can't lie to Van. She's been so sweet and welcoming. She's quickly become a friend. Besides Andrew and Shelly, I don't have any friends to count on.

I sigh, taking a few steps back into the dressing room, sitting on the bench. She kneels in front of me, placing a comforting hand on my knee. I've never wanted to let anyone know the pain I've felt through the years, but there's something about Callie...tears start to sting my eyes.

"My marriage is horrible," I confess, "You can't even imagine," I whisper.

"Oh...Ems, I'm so sorry. Is there anything I can do?"

"No...there isn't anything anyone could do."

She shakes her head, "Don't say that. Of course, there is...just leave him."

I huff. "I can't."

"Why? You don't have to stay with him if you're unhappy."

My head falls into my hand, "You wouldn't understand."

Callie leans in closer. "Tell me."

I pat her hand. "Another time. Let's finish shopping."

She stands and squints, surveying me. "Don't do that. Tell me what's going on. Is he hurting you? I know something isn't right, anyone can see it. He made you come here, a strange place with strange people, to watch a damn car. It doesn't take a genius to figure out something's wrong."

It's as if someone has thrown cold water on me. I haven't fooled anyone.

"His family is very powerful."

She ignores my answer and asks me, "Does he hurt you? Physically?"

And just like that, the memory resurfaces. *The whiskey was so strong, the scent of it wafting off of him burned my eyes. His breath was so close I could almost taste it. "Don't." I pleaded.*

"Or what?"

"I'm so sorry. If I could take it back, I would." Before I could say anything else, a sharp pain exploded against my cheek.

Tears stung my eyes. I stumbled but his arms came around me. He gasped and wrapped me tight. "I'm so sorry, Emerson. I didn't mean to do that."

He loosened his grasp and I pulled away. The pain in his eyes, the terror of what he'd just done, was written all over his face, but the shame was most evident. "I didn't mean to do that. I had too much to drink. Forgive me. Please. I'm so sorry. I'll never do that again. Forgive me." And I did because that's what I was raised to do. Put on a false façade and move on.

"Once, after his accident, the one I caused." The tears fall, I haven't admitted that to anyone. Andrew doesn't even know. If he did, there is no telling what he would do to David. I've lied to him to protect all of us.

Her soft frame envelops me. I'm not sure how I've let this happen. I told her my secret. Panic shuts down the tears. "I'm sorry." I pull away from her, wiping at my eyes.

"It's okay, Ems. You don't have to talk about it. Do you want to keep shopping, or head back to Van's?"

"Let's go back, but I'll take whatever you picked out. I'm sure they'll fit fine."

Callie smiles. "You don't have to talk about it anymore today, but I hope you'll tell me more when you're ready."

I give her a small smile with no promises. "Thanks."

19

—·—

When we return to Van's, the apartment's empty but the garage is in full chaos. The humming of tools takes over any chance of nature making a sound.

Callie decided to hang out with me a little longer. I think she might be trying to get more information out of me about my marriage, or maybe even more about Van. But I'm not about to crack on either topic. Looking over at her on the couch, she's out like a light. Her mouth is wide open with her head resting against the back. She has to be extremely uncomfortable; I am just looking at her. I chuckle to myself.

As I sit on the sofa, I try to relax and take a little nap too. But I can't seem to settle my thoughts. I'm not sure if I should check on Van. I'm still concerned about his grandfather, but I'm more concerned for Van. He was a mess last night.

Unable to turn off my brain, I wander around the house and settle in the kitchen. Rummaging through the cupboards, there is definitely some OCD taking over this apartment. I chuckle to myself at the rainbow of cans that are arranged by color.

My phone chimes in my pocket. So I don't wake Callie, I grab it as quick as I can manage without checking to see who it is first, all while shutting the cupboard.

"Hello," I whisper.

"Emerson, dear. How are you, my love?" Her fake façade filters into my ear.

I sigh. "I'm fine, Mrs. Dawson. How are you?"

"Do we have a final completion date?"

"I'm sorry, but Mr. Bradley is still working steadily to fix the Bugatti. There was substantial damage, and it seems it's going to take a few days longer than originally estimated," I lie. Van only alluded that it might take longer. I'm not sure why I just lied to her, but the thought of seeing her brings on a migraine.

"They aren't incompetent, are they?" She doesn't give me a chance to answer before adding, "We can't have idiots working on this car. This is David's prize possession we're talking about."

"I know," I agree with an eye roll.

"And what exactly have you been doing all this time?" Her voice rises in suspicion.

"Monitoring their progress, taking notes. It's been fairly dull. I did experience a medical...situation."

"I know all about it. You shouldn't have been associating with the riffraff. What on God's green earth were you thinking mingling with those kinds of people?" She accentuates the word those. I don't miss her insinuation. I know exactly what she thinks of "those" people.

"I was trying to be polite by accepting their invitation. But I've learned my lesson and will keep to myself." I find it painful to spit out the words. With each moment of speaking with her, I hate myself and who I've become—their puppet. As I defend myself, I'm ashamed. Ashamed that I feel the need to, and I've allowed this woman to treat me this way for so long. It's as if a light switch has turned on illuminating my whole view on how I've been manipulated by her, by David, by them all, but mostly horrified how I've treated myself.

"I'll call you if and when I have a confirmation on date of completion. Until then there's no need to contact me." I end the call without a chance for her rebuttal with a smile on my face. Pride fills me, I want to jump, and fist bump the air. My chest expands in excitement. It may have been an insignificant defiance on my part, and she may not have even noticed, but I would've never spoken to her like that before, and I'm glad I finally did.

As if on cue, the one person I want to share my victory with opens the door.

"You're all smiles. Happy to see me?" Van asks with a wink.

"I am."

"Plotting my death?" he asks with a worried expression.

I laugh. "No. How are you? I'm sure you're exhausted."

He holds up his hands. "That's it, you're not going to tell me why the most serious person I know has a huge smile on her face?"

"Just a nice day with Callie." I shrug, pointing over to where Callie sleeps on the couch. "She's all tuckered out from shopping," I say, lowering my voice. "How about you, did you get some sleep? How's Granddad?"

"Some. I had some fabricating to do on the Bugatti. The left door panel was destroyed. What a dumb fuck!" He shakes his head and then shoots an apologetic glance in my direction. "Sorry," he adds. "I came to grab a snack and then get back at it."

"I can make you something," I offer, opening the fridge.

"Naw, I'll just grab an apple or something." I bend down to the bottom drawer and grab an apple for him. I glance back at him and catch his gaze on my backside.

"Ahh...you know." He clears his throat. "I was thinking, would you like to help me fix up your husband's car? I bet he'd be stoked to know that you helped fix it. I don't think there's anything sexier than a girl wearing a little grease."

Shaking my head, I tell him, "I know he wouldn't find it appealing at all. In fact, he'd think it was very unattractive."

He takes the apple from my hand and takes a bite. With a mouthful of apple, he mumbles, "You know this guy is a bigger ass than I thought." Van sets the apple on the counter and steps closer, brushing up against me, and rummaging through the cupboard to my left. "Ah...there it is."

"SpaghettiOs?" I ask, suppressing the chuckle that's ready to explode into full-blown laughter. He opens the tab on the can, grabs a spoon from a drawer, and sinks into it, scooping a heaping portion into his mouth.

"Gross. You're kidding me?"

His eyes widen., "What?"

"You're not going to heat that up?"

"Nope." He shovels another spoonful.

I cringe. "That's disgusting."

With a wicked gleam in his eyes, he shoves the spoon toward my mouth. I move, but not enough because I feel something wet on the tip of my nose. I manage to push his hands away, but fling some at him in the process.

"Now you've done it." He sends the spoon back down into the can, and before I can react, a glob of noodles hits me in the face, smack on my right cheek.

"Ew..." I swipe my hand over the goo and fling it back in his direction. Before I know it, his body is flush up against mine, and his rough face is rubbing up against my cheek, smearing his food on me. The warmth of his skin sets mine on fire.

Something happens, and the playfulness turns serious as he backs away, and his eyes focus on mine. They dart back and forth, causing my heart to race at the intensity he's looking at me with. His head is inches from mine, and the sudden impulse for his lips to press to mine is urgent. I want his lips on mine. I've never wanted anything so badly.

He reaches his hand up, swipes his thumb across my lips, causing me to dart my tongue out. I catch a quick taste of his thumb and my legs tremble.

"What the hell is going on?" Callie calls from across the room.

Van jumps back, causing a cold flash of air between us.

"Nothing. She doesn't like my SpaghettiOs dinner," he says casually with a shrug as if I just didn't melt under his touch. "This is a first."

"What is?" Callie asks as she enters the kitchen. Suddenly, I feel there is one too many in the room.

He rips a towel off the counter and swipes it down his face. "I'm usually kicking chicks out of my apartment. Now, I come home to two. Different. But kinda hot," he says with a smirk, returning to the womanizing smartass I've come to know and become fascinated with.

"You wish," Callie retorts.

He ignores her comment. "Betcha you've never had a food fight with SpaghettiOs.

Wiping the slime from my face, I reply, "Never had a food fight ever."

"Food fight virgin?" His eyebrows rise up dramatically.

"Guilty." I shrug.

"Huh?" He tilts his head. "Maybe we'll try something sweeter next time." He smirks and winks in my direction. My heart jumps in my throat at the thought of him drizzling chocolate over my breasts. My face flames at my daydream. "I'm going to clean up. I suggest you do the same, Ems. He peeks past me and speaks to Callie, "Bring her to the shop later. The race is in two days, and we need all the help we can get."

"What race?"

Callie frowns. "Ben's," Van adds, "Don't worry, Callie. There'll be beer there, that way you won't have to talk to him."

I glance over at her sad expression. "Thank God for alcohol." And just like that she smiles.

20

—•—

Ten minutes after Van leaves, Callie suggests we start the make-under.

"Are you sure I don't look stupid? I don't feel like this'll help me fit in here," I whine. I know I shouldn't, I'm a grown woman, but I feel like a teenager going to her first dance or something.

I yank up the tank top that is cut way too low, revealing cleavage that I'm not ready to put on display.

"Stop tugging at it. Besides, the more you tug it up, the more your belly button shows." Callie cocks her head to one side. "Although, why you don't show off those abs are beyond me." She taps my stomach. "What do you do…a million sit ups a day?"

"Yoga."

She huffs, "Of course, you do." Callie rolls her eyes but giggles.

"You can cover up with this if your heart desires, but it does get hot in there between the cars and the sexy guys." She wiggles her eyebrows. "If ya' know what I mean." And hands me a flannel shirt. I laugh. I can't remember the last time I laughed with a friend. "You can wrap it around your waist."

I take the red flannel shirt and slip it on.

Catching a glimpse of myself in the mirror, Callie has done it—a tasteful make-under.

My dark hair is styled in loose waves, makeup is brown and pink hues to highlight my brown eyes, slight cat eye eyeliner, and black mascara to finish.

"Pucker," she commands. I push my lips together and out. She swipes a pink gloss over them. "Press." I do as she says.

"Damn, girl. You look H.O.T." She shoves the makeup back into her bag. "Did you think I'd make you look like a clown?"

"I wasn't sure."

She grabs her other bag. "Come on. Let's go show these boys what sexy and sophisticated really looks like."

We head down the steps, but don't make it far because Violet stares back at us, eyes blaring. Briefly, I wonder how long she's been here.

"Can I speak with you a moment, Emerson. Alone," she says my name like it is a curse word.

"I'm not going anywhere. I'd like to hear what stupid words are going to come from your mouth," Callie snaps from beside me, ready to have my back, and that alone makes me ready to face whatever the night holds.

I place my hand on Callie's shoulder and nod at her. She backs away a little.

"Sure, Violet. Let's talk," I say in a high-pitched octave. *Settle down, Ems,* bracing myself for her attack.

Violet lifts a cigarette up to her lips, taking a drag, and blows out a puff of smoke at my face.

The vulgar air burns my throat, causing me to cough. I brush the air away from me.

"It's just a little smoke. Jeez." She scoffs, dropping her cigarette butt to the ground, and stomps on it with pink hooker heels. "Where'd you get those clothes?"

I gather the flannel and overlap the fabric to cover my body. Callie glares, subtly knocking my hand away.

"We went shopping. What do you care? Jealous?" Callie informs.

Her lips curl to the side. "She looks ridiculous. Did you tell her she looks good?" Violet gestures over to Callie, laughing at the both of us.

Callie takes a step toward her, causing Violet to take a step back.

"She looks a hell of a lot better than your skanky ass could ever pull off."

"Fuck you, Callie."

"Never. Even if I was into chicks, I wouldn't fuck your nasty ass."

My stomach jumps into my throat. I'm not sure what to do or say. Thankfully, Callie grabs me by the shirt, yanking me away from the confrontation.

When I turn to walk past her, Violet grabs a handful of fabric covering my arm to stop me, causing me to spin and face her. "What's going on with you and Van?"

"What do you mean?" I snap back. The sound of her saying Van's name irks me.

"You. Staying at his place. You spend the night with him at the hospital and his apartment. Nobody ever stays there. It's his rule."

"Rule? Nothing is going on," I tell her.

"You stayed with him and his granddad. We were all told no one was allowed back there." She takes a step toward me and I don't back away. "How the hell weren't you kicked out?"

"There is nothing going on. He asked me to stay...Granddad did, not Van," I emphasize. "Besides, he's being polite, making sure I'm not in a dump since I'm paying him tens of thousands of dollars to fix my husband's car. Don't forget, I'm married."

Violet's staring at me with hatred in her eyes.

"You should start acting like it, then."

Callie steps in between me and Violet and I realize I'm inches from her face, standing up to her, meeting her word for word. Not backing down at all.

"Let's go to the garage. Van's waiting for us," Callie says, pushing me backward.

I turn, feeling heat radiating up my neck. She's right, though, I'm not acting like I should.

"Damn, girl. I thought you were going to start throwing punches soon." Callie laughs.

"I don't know what got into me. She was making me so mad. I just look at that ugly scowl and it automatically pushes every button in me."

"God. She's such a bitch!" she yells, gritting her teeth, spinning to face Violet. She sends Callie the middle finger.

"I can't believe we were once best friends." My eyes bulge at her admission.

"You were?" I can't hide the shock in my voice.

She purses her lips, "It's a small town...not many choices." She winks and pulls me by the fabric of my shirt. "Let's go before she starts with us again."

I giggle. It's great to have someone on my side for a change, sticking up for me. Even though it's over something silly, it still means the world to me.

"I don't know how I've managed to walk all this way on rocks in these heeled boots?"

"You don't get any sexier than lace-up, black, stiletto boots," she says, flipping her blond hair over her shoulder. "You're welcome for the introduction to them."

I laugh at her. It seems that's all I've been doing around her. Always keeping the mood light and fun. As we get closer to the main garage, we see the lights illuminating the darkness, music blaring, and tools roaring. Callie raises her voice, cupping her mouth with her hands. "Let's get drunk, Woo-hoo!" she shouts, running toward the large crowd huddled around a race car.

I walk behind her, fidgeting with my shirt. Unsure if I should let it fall open or button it all the way up to my neck. I roll my eyes at myself. *Loosen up, Ems.*

The garage is filled with familiar faces. Ben, Jake, Ace...I cringe at the sight of him. It's not as if he's not friendly, but his over-friendliness is becoming uncomfortable to be around. I don't have to wonder or search long for Van. He's bent over the hood of a race car. A bright yellow vehicle with stickers of companies and logos scattered about.

As I put my hand in the air to give a wave, a black-haired girl wearing the shortest shorts I've ever seen comes up to him with a drink in hand. Over the noise, I can still hear her say, "Just for you, babe." He takes it from her hands, takes a sip, and stares in my direction.

He nods, then leans over to give her a kiss on the cheek.

I know my eyes bulge from their sockets. *Who the hell is this one?*

Callie steps in front of me, blocking my view. "Come on, let's get you drunk. I have a feeling you're going to need something to help you survive this night."

I trail behind her. "What's that supposed to mean?"

She lets out a breath. "Ems, I know you can't take your eyes off of Van." She places her hands on her hips.

"You're ridiculous." I shake my head.

She quirks up her mouth. "If you say so...just so you know, he can't take his eyes off you either."

"No, he wasn't looking at me. He was focused on his *babe*."

Callie laughs. "See...you like him."

"I'm just concerned. He seems to have a lot of women surrounding him. Who was this girl anyway? Her hair was down to her butt, and she sort of looks like a witch, if you ask me." I can't help but roll my eyes.

Callie laughs. "They're nothing. We call them garage sluts. They hang around, bring food, beer, and anything else they can think of to entice the boys. The sluts dote over the guys in hopes of becoming one of the guys' girlfriend. It'll never happen with these guys, though. Those aren't the kind of girls you bring home to the family—you only fuck those." She nods in the dark-haired slut's direction.

I follow her like a lost puppy and whisper, "Do they?"

She spins to face me with a playful grin. "Do they, or does Van?"

I swallow. I've been caught and she thinks it's funny, but I don't. I'm not sure how I feel other than I want to yank that slut away from Van. Looking over, she's leaning against the car, pushing her tits closer to his face.

"Yeah, they all pretty much fuck those girls, but not for long. There seems to be a steady rotation of them. They start with Van first, because let's face it, he's the hottest, and he isn't commitment material, if you know what I mean?"

She grabs a red cup by the keg and pours a beer for herself. "Do you want one?"

I don't drink...ever. But my nerves are on edge, between Violet unleashing on me, and my new look, and knowing Van's fooling around with that slut...a beer doesn't seem like a bad idea. *How much can one beer hurt?*

I take the cup from Callie. "Cheers!" We clink cups. "Let's have some fun."

Callie takes me by the hand and we practically skip over to her brother, Jake. Ben's standing beside him and speaks first. "Don't you think you've had enough?" Ben asks with a scowl.

"No." She looks at me and rolls her eyes. "This is our first one, and besides...Ems and I are going to have fun tonight. Unlike you, the party pooper. You act like that car is your girl or something. You need to get a life."

Ben's tall frame rises up from the stool, standing toe to toe with Callie. She doesn't back away from his intimidating gaze, unlike me, who wants to curl under the car and hide.

"I don't need a girl. You're all a pain in the ass, especially you!" He pushes his finger into her shoulder. She doesn't even budge at his strength.

"Enough, you two. You guys fight like you're her brother." Jake nods, directing his frustration toward Ben.

Ben huffs. "I'm going to take her outside for some fresh air. Sober her up a bit." Ben grabs Callie by her arm, leading her toward the door.

"Christ," Jake says, shaking his head.

"When are those two going to fuck?" A guy whom I haven't seen around the shop before yells from under the car.

"Fuck you!" Jake yells back. "They're not like that. I'd kill him if he ever touched her."

A few chuckles filter through. Even though Jake's her brother, I've noticed Ben is more protective. Always watching her, telling her what she should and shouldn't do. I'll have to remember to ask Callie what's going on with Ben.

Breaking up the chuckles, the sound of Van's drill drowns out the voices.

Now that Callie has left and I'm on my own, I'm not sure what to do? Do I talk to Van? I mean, I'm staying with him. No...he's busy, not only with his car, but the almost naked girl beside him. She hasn't left his side for one second.

The green monster is becoming louder in my head. The voice is telling me to go over there and interrupt them, tell the whore to find somebody else to hang all over.

I decide to fill up my cup with more beer instead.

Reaching the keg, I spot Ace in front of it. I should have paid more attention because his face lights up like a Christmas tree as he spots me.

"Hey," he says, kissing me on the cheek. Like we've been friends forever, ignoring the cute brunette beside him scowling in my direction. "Look at you." His eyes widen as he scans my body. "Wow, you look great tonight. And your hair is down. It's beautiful."

The girl beside him huffs and walks in the other direction.

"Thanks." My face flames at his reaction to my new look. He runs his hands through his hair and clears his throat. "You're drinking tonight? Should you be...with your condition and all?" He gestures toward my cup.

"A little bit is all right. Plus, this is it for me, my drinking partner was dragged off by Ben."

"Those two." Ace shakes his head.

"What do you mean?" I ask, tilting my head to learn more.

"They just always have some sort of...I don't know, drama."

"I'm beginning to get that from them too."

He laughs softly. I scan the crowd, unsure of what to say next, but Ace eases into conversation.

"How's it going staying with Van? Is he treating you okay?"

"Yeah. I mean, it can be awkward at times, living in some single guy's place. He's practically a stranger to me." I find the words flowing freely from my lips, so I take another gulp of beer to stop the word vomit.

We both stand quietly while I take more sips from my cup. The bitter liquid is starting to taste delicious. I'm sweating, so I carelessly remove my flannel and toss it back on the chair. Ace smiles.

Jake walks up beside Ace. "We got everything done we wanted to tonight. So you can work your magic tomorrow." Jake leans past Ace, his eyes roam over my features.

"Damn, Ems. I didn't realize what you were hiding under those suits. You always look good, but that…" He moves his hand to mimic the curves of my body, then purses his lips together and whistles.

Instead of blushing or hiding, I proudly smile.

"Come on, Ace, let's go mess with Van. I'll tell him that his fender is messed up or some shit."

"Nah. I'm going to hang here with Ems for a while. I don't want to leave her alone."

Jake makes a face. "Your funeral, man."

21

— ⁘ —

I 'm feeling a bit more relaxed. The music's getting louder and my body sways to the beat. The car's no longer the center of attention. People are talking, dancing, grinding, and overall coupling up.

"What did Jake mean?" I ask.

He shakes his head. "Nothing." Leaning in closer to my ear, he says, "He's had too much to drink. But it looks like you haven't had enough yet. Here, try this." Ace hands me another cup.

I stare down at the amber liquid. "What's this?"

"Whiskey."

The pungent smell burns my nostrils as I lower my face to the cup. I scrunch up my nose, but decide to ignore the strong odor that reminds me so much of David, and why I shouldn't be drinking this. Taking a big gulp, I cough and choke.

Ace laughs as he slings his arm around my shoulder. "Careful, killer. Not such big sips or you'll get wrecked...quick."

Over the next hour, or hours, who knows, Ace, Jake, and I talk about everything and anything, but nothing personal, just random car facts and old stories. I'm enjoying myself, only I can't stop taking the occasional peek in Van's direction. That slut is never far from his side. Although, he doesn't seem to be paying much attention to her. The car has his interest.

Our little group hasn't left the corner by the keg. I'm glad; I don't think my legs can function properly. I can't recall ever feeling this...fun. It's nice to laugh at nothing and everything.

"So, what do you think of our little town? Not like the big city, huh?" Ace asks, raising his eyebrows.

"It's nothing like where I'm from. Although, I don't go out much."

I know I should shut my mouth, but I can't stop the words from flowing.

"That's okay, you're here now with me. We're going to have a blast." He slings his arm over my shoulder, bringing me closer to his side.

A few people whom I've never met before chat with us. Ace hasn't lifted his arm. It seems as if he's gotten even closer and now, he's a little more daring because his arm is resting on my lower back, hand wrapped around my waist.

I take another sip out of my red cup, the whiskey keeps getting sweeter on my lips. Glancing around the large garage, that earlier included a large, raucous group of people fixing the car, is now a room full of bodies rocking against each other, swaying to the music.

Leaning close to Ace's ear so he can hear me over the music, I ask, "I didn't know this place turns into a strip club after midnight?"

He pulls me close against his chest and kisses the top of my head. Laughing, he replies, "Yeah. I guess that's what it looks like."

A country song about a girl shaking her ass blares through the mass of people. Hoots and hollers become louder. Ace releases his hold on me to spin me around. "Wooh..." As I'm released from Ace's firm grasp, I come to a stop and see what has caught his attention.

The yellow race car that held everyone's attention earlier, now holds it for a different reason. I can hardly believe what's playing out in front of me. *How much did I drink?*

The garage slut who hasn't left Van's side all night is now dancing on top of the car. Standing on the hood wearing only her cowboy boots, daisy duke's complete with visible ass cheeks, and a bra. *Wait, when did she lose her shirt?*

Her ass jiggles, and the screams of her admirers becomes almost deafening.

She gets on her knees when Van walks to the front of the car. It's like a horrific car wreck that I can't turn away from. Taking a few steps, I inch closer as she slides down from the roof to the windshield, Van bites his bottom lip, reaching for the top rim of her shorts, yanking her down the glass to the hood of the car.

He brings her closer. She settles in front of him, then wraps her naked legs around his waist, tilting her head back. It's absolutely the sexiest gesture I've ever seen a man make. In this moment, I wish I could trade places with her and have my legs wrapped around him.

His tongue delves into her mouth, his hand under her ass, digging in, gripping her closer to him. Ace says something from beside me, but I don't care to listen. I'm not pulling my eyes from this show.

Van's eyes open with passion raging inside, hooded, dark, and mysterious, locking with mine. His mouth on hers but his eyes focused on me. My inner thighs tingle at the heat directed toward me.

Ace stands in front of me, effectively dousing the fire. "I asked if you want to get out of here because I think you've had too much to drink. I've been calling your name and you're not answering. Are you okay?"

I swallow and nod, "Yeah...fine." Peeking over his shoulder, Van and the girl I wish was me have disappeared.

"I think you're right. I need some air." Because I definitely need something to take me away from this chaos. Even in my drunken state,

I know that the look in Van's eyes affected me more than it should have.

Stepping outside in the cool air is heaven on earth. I take in a deep breath, closing my eyes to inhale, but as I do, a spinning sensation takes over. I open my eyes, thankfully it works, but my stomach starts to protest. "I've definitely drank too much."

Ace's blue eyes glimmer under the low lights in the parking lot. His eyes flicker back and forth, taking every inch of my face in. A slow song leaks outside, reaching us. "Do you want to dance?"

We're all alone out here. The pounding has stopped and I'm feeling a bit unsteady. I wobble a bit, and his arms find my waist.

"You could have just said yes," he says, as a playful smile graces his lips.

"Sorry. I mean, thanks for catching me."

"I'll always catch you."

Triggering David's face, his response makes me uncomfortable.

Sobering, I say, "I don't think that...that's appropriate. I'm married."

Ace leans in, his whiskey-laced breath tickles my face as he's within inches of my cheek. "I know you're not happy with him, Ems," he says softly, inching closer to my lips. "Everyone can see it." Closer, softer, he whispers, "Let me show you what..." Closing my eyes, I brace myself for...what, I'm not sure. "How a real man treats the woman he loves." As his lips touch mine, they're yanked away, replaced by a waft of cool night air and a roar.

"What the fuck do you think you're doing?" My eyes fly open to Van slamming Ace into a parked car beside us. The thud of Ace's body against the metal makes me cringe. "She's married, fucker!"

"So?"

"She's not yours. Have some goddamn respect, for fuck's sake!" He lets go of Ace's shirt, but Ace fires back.

"Is that what you show her? Respect? Fuck you, Van! You wouldn't know how to show respect to a woman. You were practically fucking Katie on the hood of the car in there," he shouts, pointing to the garage.

Van shoves a handful of hair off of his face and screams, "Fuck!" He bends over, breathing hard.

I'm not sure what just happened. I thought they were friends. Why are these two friends fighting over me? Really?

I somehow manage to get in between the two of them. "It's fine, I've had too much to drink," I tell them, finding my voice.

"You don't need to apologize to him, Ems. He just wants you for himself. Just to say he's fucked a rich bitch and get some money from you. He's a greedy bastard. Ask his family, they'll tell you all about it," Ace yells, a single vein in his forehead protruding.

"You son of a bitch!" Van shoves against him, slamming him against the car. Again, his body thuds against the metal, then he rears his fist back to meet it with Ace's face.

Swarms of people come rushing beside us. Jake grabs Van and manages to pull him off of Ace. Somehow, I get pushed to the side. Ace spits a red stream of blood from his mouth to the ground toward Van. "Fuck you, Van! You know it's true!"

Van shrugs off Jake, walks past me, meeting my eyes, glaring...and stops, pausing for a moment. He stares down to the ground...then comes at me like a raging bull, hoisting me in the air and over his shoulder.

"Van! Put me down!" I flail around, screaming and banging with my fists on his back.

"No!"

I keep yelling and banging, but he's not returning words. We're heading for his apartment. "Put me down, please."

Finally, he says, "You drank too much. You can't even fucking walk straight. Ace shouldn't have taken advantage of you like that. He's not who he seems." He mumbles something else, but I can't make it out.

The dizziness I felt earlier is nothing compared to what's circling now. "Put me down, I'm going to be sick." My stomach roils as he lowers me to the ground. As my feet touch the ground, I'm barely able to stand, I fall to my knees, and my stomach heaves the alcohol from my body.

When I stop throwing up. I find the flannel wrapped around my waist, untie it, and wipe my mouth.

"Ugh." I moan, falling back on my butt, and resting my head in my hands.

After a few moments, Van says, "Come on. You can throw up the rest of your whiskey in the bathroom. Let's get you off the rocks."

Van's hand rubs my shoulders, then guides me up by my elbow. He steadies me, touching the small of my back, instantly soothing my upset stomach. We slowly head up the stairs, and he carefully guides me one step at a time, as if I'm going to break.

We step through the door and immediately he directs me toward the bathroom. Ducking down to my knees, I heave once more, but thankfully the toilet's in front of me.

The water runs behind me as I moan. "I feel awful."

"That's what happens when you mix beer and liquor." A cool cloth touches my neck. "Here, this should help."

"Is that from heaven?" He chuckles from beside me. "Sorry. I've never drank like that before."

"Ace knows better. I'm not sure what he was doing," he says under his breath. Van crouches down to sit beside me.

"Please, you don't need to sit here. I'll be fine. I'm already a mess. You don't need to stay and rub it in."

He rolls his eyes. "First, I don't like to see you a mess, and second, I want to make sure you don't pass out and choke on your own vomit." He hands me a toothbrush with some toothpaste on it. "Here, spit in the toilet."

As I brush, the mint tastes awful, but at least the disgusting taste is gone. "Thanks." I lean back against the wall, weak and needing its support.

Van gets up from beside me and walks out of the bathroom. Thank God. I know he just came in to harass me about being such a light-weight. Does he really think I believe that he cares about me? What was all that about Ace? A flash of Van, punching him in the face re-enters my thoughts. The alcohol must be wearing off, my mind seems to be clearing.

Closing my eyes, I take in a few deep breaths My stomach has calmed. Van hasn't returned, and I couldn't be happier. I think of moving to the couch, but I'm too tired to get up.

I must have dozed off because my eyes open and I'm floating. Alarm washes over me, and I try to move from someone's grasp. "It's okay. I got you." Van's voice calms my fear.

We reach the couch and he sets me down and slides a blanket over me. I can't help but smile at the thought of Van tucking me in. Oh God, I'm all over the place.

"Here," he says, handing me a glass of water. "You'll get dehydrated if you don't start now."

Taking a sip, I indulge in the coolness of the liquid.

"Scoot," Van orders.

"What?" He takes the glass from my hand.

"Scoot over so I can lie down too. I drank too much and punched one of my friends. Not one of my better nights." He tilts his head, "Please?"

How can I refuse his pouting? I slide over as he slips in beside me. Covering himself up to his waist, it strikes me that he's not wearing a shirt. My face flames as I can't take my eyes off of his abs. Perfectly sculpted, roaming up to his chest. Forgetting myself, I touch his rippled stomach. He reaches over, stopping my roaming fingers. "You're still drunk."

I try to pull my hand away, but he holds it in place.

"What a night, huh? Aren't you glad you came to our fun little town?" The sarcasm drips from his words.

"It wasn't my choice, believe me. You have no idea what it's like to be married to him," I say, forgetting who I'm talking to, the alcohol's still in control.

"What do you mean?" Van sits up. "Tell me."

"I shouldn't have said anything."

"Yes, you should. And everyone can see that something isn't right."

"They do, don't they? That is becoming apparent."

He moves closer, with intensity in his eyes. "Tell me...tell me you love him. That he isn't as horrible as he seems, that you love him and you have this great life. Tell me you're happy with him and love him, because seeing Ace trying to kiss you fucking wrecked me. I know it shouldn't have, you're married, but..."

"But you and that girl tonight?"

"I'm sorry about that. I knew I couldn't have you, and she was there, paying attention to me and you were with...Ace. He had his fucking hands all over you. You were giggling at his jokes, looking up at him with those big, beautiful brown eyes. I didn't know what else to do."

"Van..." He looks so sad and hopeful at the same time.

"Give me a reason not to take you in my arms and show you how a man should treat you. Not in a fucking parking lot, or send you to some strangers to watch over a fucking car. Let me show you how a man should worship you, in his home, in his bed, in his world."

His eyes search mine for an answer. Van's tongue swipes over his lip. Such a subtle movement, but I want to know what they taste like. I don't want to pretend any longer. I've been attracted to this man from the moment we met. I wrecked him, and me? Well, he's wrecked me too.

"I don't love David. I hate him. He's horrible to me. He blames me for his ruining his life. I hate being married to him and being a part of his family." The words flow freely and without guilt. "I hate my life. I..."

His lips press against mine, stopping my thoughts. His hands entangle in my hair with a yank, bringing me farther into his mouth. Our tongues tangle and I can't seem to get close enough to him.

His taste is pure heaven, fueling my passion for him. I reach up and savor the moment when my hands meet his silky curls. I can't help the moan that escapes.

Van groans, managing to roll us on to our sides until he settles on top of me. His lips haven't moved from mine. Van is kissing me. Me. His erection rubbing against my my sensitive area, causing me to rock back against him. A growl comes from deep within him.

He stops, jumping back, breaking us apart. His hands are gone, and grief overwhelms me. Van is on his knees, straddling me.

"What?" I ask, breathing heavily. I barely recognize my own voice. He turns away from me, running his hands through his hair. "Van?" I call, almost begging him to face me. "Van!"

He spins, coming at me again, only this time, our foreheads touch. He swallows, "Do you want this? Us...me...to happen?" His heavy whiskey breath dances against my skin.

"Yes," I whisper. "I've never wanted anything more."

His lips tilt up in a slight smile. "Fuck...I've never wanted anyone more than I want you right now." His hand swipes along the top of my jeans, against my exposed stomach, bringing my skin to life. "I like this new look. And the hair..." He reaches up, touching the strands as if they're precious to him. "You look sexy as hell."

I don't blush, I don't disagree, and I don't hesitate to pull his head close to mine for our lips to touch again. We continue getting to know every inch of our lips. He reaches around to my ass, and I wrap my legs around him. "Fuck." He moans, bringing me closer, while he stands with me in his arms. He carries me over to the steps. "You can tell me to stop. I won't take this any farther if you don't want me to. You're married." He chokes out the last word.

His words should douse the fire inside me, but they don't. In this moment, those vows I've tried so desperately to uphold mean absolutely nothing to me. David means nothing, Van means everything to me.

"He doesn't touch me. He ignores me. He hates me," I confess.

Van's eyes close as if he's trying to calm himself. "Ems..."

Taking a deep breath, I notice his unsure expression. "I want you more than anything, but you're hurting, and you've had too much to drink. I want to do this when you're sober and when you've left him."

The heat has left my body and is replaced with the cold, hard truth. I belong to another. I turn away from him and take each step slowly until I reach his bed. He slips in beside me, pulls the covers over our bodies, leaving enough space in between us for another person. I focus my attention ahead of me at the blank TV, anywhere but on him because I still want his lips on mine, his hands in my hair, and his body wrapped around me.

"Is your stomach better?"

"Yes." My voice is hoarse, so I clear my throat. "Yes, much better."

The glow of the TV interrupts my thoughts as Van surfs through the channels. "I'm not tired, but I need something else to concentrate on."

"Van?"

"Babe...we don't need to talk about it right now. Tomorrow. There's always tomorrow."

22

— · —

I need some time to myself. Stepping out of the shower, I'm relieved Van hasn't been here all morning. Toweling off and getting dressed, I still can't shake the look on Van's face, his confession of how I wrecked him. Doesn't he know he's done the same to me? I've never wanted anyone, including David, to kiss me as much as I wanted him to.

I can't wipe the smile off my face as I finish applying lip gloss in the mirror. My brown eyes are bright, my cheeks pink, and the excitement level inside me is through the roof at the thought of seeing Van today.

I finish getting ready by applying a dab of lotion to my hands, the large rock on my finger mocks me, taunts the happy butterflies, and makes them run from the swarm of bees invading my belly. "I'm married," I say to the girl in the mirror as if she's forgotten. Because she has, I have. Van makes me feel alive and happy, and I desperately want to be happy.

David's face weasels its way into my thoughts, and so does the guilt he brings with him. I've kissed another man. Another man's hands have touched my body. It goes against everything I believe. I took my marriage vows seriously, stayed loyal to David through his accident, his abuse, and the cheating and lying, and I've never been more myself than I am right now.

What do I do now? Do I tell David? Do I leave David?

I know what the answer is…yes, I'm done with living a life I hate.

Slamming my makeup back into its bag, and zipping it up with more force than necessary, I head out of the bathroom, rolling my eyes at the situation. I may be getting all worked up over nothing. We were both drunk and I wasn't the only girl whose mouth his tongue visited last night.

"Ugh."

The apartment is quiet, and I have nothing to do but let my thoughts run wild. Maybe I should go find Van? No, I'll just wait here until he comes back.

I wander around the kitchen, imagining Van cooking a frozen pizza or arranging his cupboards. A smile comes with my thoughts.

Running a finger along the immaculately cleaned counter, I laugh at the rodent-infested trailer he made me stay in just a few days ago. It seems like I've been here much longer than I have.

My phone vibrates in the back pocket of my jeans. Speak of the devil himself, David's number lights up the screen. I better answer it, or he'll just keep calling, or worse, call Van.

"Hello, David."

"I need an update on the car. Mom and Dad are heading to Europe, and I need to squeeze some extra cash out of them for the upgrades I told Van to make this morning. I told him to add some more power to it." His voice is odd to me, excited, maybe? "Well?"

"I haven't talked to him today. What did he say to you about it?" I should already have an answer for David, but it hasn't been on my mind.

"He's still got some work to do, but it's coming along. I told him I need it to be faster than I originally planned. Deacon's got a Bugatti, too, and I need mine faster than his. So, it better be. Don't you think you should have found this out already? What the fuck have you been doing all morning?"

"Working on next year's budget. Just because I'm not in the office doesn't mean I'm not working." The confidence somehow rolls off my tongue.

"Good. That needs to be finished along with my car. I can't wait to have it home, and I'm not too thrilled with you being there. I don't like the thought of those low-lifes looking at what's mine...and I'm not talking about the car."

In complete and utter shock, I have no idea how to respond. *He's not happy with me being here?*

Saving myself from overthinking, I reply, "Van and his staff are working diligently to get it finished as we speak."

He huffs, "Good. He is. I just want to make sure he's actually working on it before I fork over another hundred grand."

I swallow, almost choking. "That seems excessive."

"Well, the fucker didn't want to do it. He said it would take more time. He didn't want to prolong your stay. I don't either, but you went there to do a job, and I made him an offer he couldn't refuse."

"He doesn't want me to stay?" I whisper. He doesn't hear and keeps talking over me.

"Money talks to these types of people. You should get that by now."

"David, we need to talk, and I think I should come home." I can barely get the last word out, but if Van doesn't want me here, then all these crazy feelings bubbling inside me need to stop. I need to end things with David and figure out the rest of my life.

"What? No. Finish this project. Take care of my girl."

"Huh?"

"The car." He hangs up with not another word.

My girl, I should have known he wasn't talking to me. I'm all confused. Van doesn't want me to stay, but I can't live the way I have been. I need to get out of here and breathe in some fresh air.

The southern air is stifling hot, hitting me like a brick wall. Van's attached garage is empty, so I head toward the main garage. Maybe I shouldn't, but I can't help myself as the sound of tools working pulls me in.

As usual, the main garage is busy, loud and full of people as I approach. The yellow car from last night is now gone and replaced by the Bugatti, but the same two people are under the hood, Van and the slut from last night. She's rubbing his back while he's leaning over, working on something.

How could I be so stupid? He was drunk, I was drunk. It was all a mistake. He didn't mean those words he said to me last night. I didn't wreck his world, but he wrecked mine.

Straightening my shoulders, I focus on the crowd in front of me and trudge forward. I'll act as if I don't notice them. I won't notice how she's leaning against the car with her tits hanging out. Taking a quick peek from the corner of my eye, I notice he's not paying attention to her, he's watching me. *What kind of sick game is he playing?*

I move forward, leaving the chaos and broken heart behind me. I head into the hallway that leads into the showroom. I pass by the *Hook-Up King's* office and open the door to the showroom. I glance over to the desk and see bright purple hair mocking me. *Nope. Not today.* I can't deal with her shit.

Instead of facing her, I turn back around, closing the door, and decide that Van's office will work. He's never in there anyway.

He hasn't locked his door, so I walk in and put my laptop on his desk. Turning the computer on, the screen flashes Dawson Cosmetics. Who cares about Van or David? I'm successful on my own; I don't need them or the Dawson family. Only I do need the Dawson family. They own my career. They can squash all that I've worked for, and my cosmetic line will vanish along with my hard-working reputation.

I immerse myself in the new formula for the new lipstick line I created.

Moments later, the door opens and Van stands in the doorway, looking glorious with his arms crossed and a smirk on his face.

"Can I help you?" I ask, already annoyed at myself for wanting him to touch me.

"I think you have that wrong. The last time I checked, this is my office."

"Last time I checked, I don't care," I throw back at him.

He smirks again, only this time he steps closer, pushing himself casually from the doorway, the smell of fuel and Van mixed together assaults me. Uncrossing his hands, he places them on the desk and leans down, at eye level with me. "Really? You don't care? I find that hard to believe." He's squinting, appraising me.

God, he looks hot. Those dark eyes are burning into me. It's almost as if he's looking into my soul. The stray curly strand dangles down beside his eye. I can't help myself, I reach up and brush it from his face. His breath hitches at my touch, his eyes widen, causing him to release his hold on me. Van backs away, swallowing loudly.

"About last night..." he starts.

"It was a mistake," I spit out before he can.

He frowns. "You really think that was a mistake?" His eyes narrow, making me unsure of what to say.

"Obviously, it was because that slut is all over you. Again. Did you tell her you kissed me last night before bed?" Unable to control my emotions, my hands are on my hips, and my jaw's so tight not even a crowbar could yank it open.

"I didn't." Van walks around the desk to stand beside me. I swivel my chair to face him as he leans in, holding onto the arm of the chair. "It wasn't a mistake. In fact, it was... fucking amazing. I've wanted you from the moment you screamed at the damn mouse, in that fucking Superman t-shirt, with your ass playing peek-a-boo with my cock. But you're married and I can't break up a marriage."

"What?" His words take me by surprise.

"Emerson, I don't want to be the reason you leave your husband. I want you to leave him because you want to, and you want to find what makes you happy, not who." I'm a tangled, frustrated mess. He wants me, and every inch of me wants him, but he's right. I can't cheat on David no matter how horrible he is to me. I've lived with this guilt for so long, and I've got too much to lose if I leave David for another man, and not for my own reasons.

He tips up my chin, his lips close enough to kiss. "I want you, Ems. Not Katie out there, but right now, she isn't married and she's only a distraction. A distraction because all I can think of is you in my bed, waking up beside you, cooking me breakfast, and your arms around me." He pauses, "But I want you when you're not married to David. I want to know you're mine and that you don't have to go home to him. I won't share you."

"Van, I won't share you with her. Not now, not ever."

"I promise there's nothing between Katie and me. I won't sleep with her if you don't want me to."

"I don't."

He smiles. "Nothing will happen between Katie and me, then. You have my word. I don't want anyone but you, so I think we should end this..." He gestures with his hand between the two of us.

"Do you want me to leave?"

"No, that's the last thing I want. We can be...I don't know...maybe not a client and a guy who's fixing your car...friends. Let's just hang out and get to know each other, but nothing more can happen."

I'm utterly shocked at his admission. His words are soothing, hopeful, but sadden me all at the same time.

"What are we now?" I ask, hardly recognizing my low voice.

He leans in closer to my lips, almost touching them. "Right now, I'm not sure, somewhere in between. I guess we'll be friends who hang out and you can spend your time with me."

"Friends?" I whisper.

"Only if you want to be." Van backs away, leaving me breathless and wanting more from him.

His voice changes from soft and sexy to louder with an edge, "I'm going to pick up Granddad from the hospital and you're coming with me."

"I am."

"Yep, let's go...friend."

23

—·—

"Quit fussing over me." Granddad's voice booms through his tiny house. "You and that pretty girl need to go find something better to do than sit around and watch an old man."

He sits down in his chair, wrestling with his blanket.

"We're good, Granddad. We can hang out and watch a movie. Besides, I'm making us dinner." Van holds up a can. "Chicken soup and some crackers."

"Oh, hogwash. How about some fried chicken and mashed potatoes?" He nudges my shoulder with his.

I nudge him back. "Sorry, he's the boss," Thumbing my finger in Van's direction.

"I'll eat it but I ain't going to like it."

"At least you're home and can rest in your own place," I say, hoping to ease the tension.

"I'm just glad you're feeling better," Van adds.

I smile at the way Van talks with his granddad. He's so happy to be with him.

As Van finishes the dishes and the movie is reaching its climax, Granddad snores like a freight train. Getting up from the couch, I cover him with the crochet blanket that's fallen off of his shoulders.

"I've got some work to do out in the shop, he should be fine by himself. Do you want to help me?"

Shaking my head, I say, "I don't think I'll be much help. I don't even drive. I couldn't tell you what's even under that hood." If he only knew the reason why I don't drive.

He tosses the towel on the counter, "Come on." Van opens an app on his phone. "We can watch him from out there." He turns the phone so I can see, his granddad sleeping appears on the screen. It's then I notice a small camera above the TV.

"That's brilliant."

"I feel kind of bad treating him like a toddler, but it's better than something happening to him. Plus, I don't have to sit here and babysit him." He extends his hand, waiting for me to take it. "Come on, I got a lot to finish if we're going to make the Bugatti faster and get ready for the race tomorrow."

I take his hand. It's rough and comforting at the same time. He doesn't say anything on the way to the garage. As the lights from the main garage illuminate our path, I start to feel anxious. I don't know the first thing about cars. The last time I was behind the wheel, I wrecked it and hurt someone I cared for at the time.

"You okay?" Van asks.

"Yeah...why?"

"You squeezed my hand. I promise not to make you do any of the hard labor."

Van opens the main door of the garage. Still holding my hand, he guides us over to the rack of shirts against the wall. "Here, put this on." I want to tell him this has nothing to do with hard labor, only him, always him.

I let go of his hand and push my arms through the shirtsleeves. I spin to face him. "How do I look?" I say, posing like a mannequin.

"Like a grease monkey." He gives me a knowing wink.

"I'm so sorry about saying that to you. I didn't mean it, I was mad."

"I'm just messing with you. It's no big deal."

"I didn't mean it, you made me…"

Van interrupts, "I said don't worry about it. Now, let's show you how to change a spark plug."

"A spark plug? I don't think a spark plug costs over a hundred grand."

"So, your husband told you about his phone call to me?" He opens up the hood and twists on something, pulling out what I can only guess is the spark plug.

"Only to emphasize the fact that his friend, or more of an associate, has a faster car than he does, and he can't have that on his conscience."

He shakes his head. "Oh, how the other half live. So, is he going to race his friend?"

Tilting my head, I say, "Race each other…no. Pay someone else to race, yes."

He stops what he's doing and looks up at me with wide eyes and open mouth. "That fucker pays someone else to race? What a prick."

"He would wreck it in five seconds." I gesture to the car in front of us. "Obviously."

Van chuckles. "Yeah, I wouldn't let him race on our team."

Ben is the one with the talent. He'd put David in his place. If he could just get his life straight, he'd go somewhere."

"What's wrong with his life?"

"Let's just say he's got some things going on and he doesn't always make the best decisions off the track."

"I got some of that last night when he dragged Callie out of the party. What's going on between them?" I ask, curiosity rearing its ugly head.

"I'm not sure, but if it isn't an innocent relationship, Jake's going to kill him." My mouth drops open. I can't wait to get more details from Callie. It strikes me now that I don't remember her coming back.

"Did she ever come back to the party? I don't remember with all the...chaos that occurred."

"Yeah, I wasn't paying attention either. Between keeping an eye on you and dealing with Ace, she wasn't on my radar."

Before I can respond, I need to know the answer to another question. "You told David you didn't want to do more to the car, why?" I shouldn't be asking, it's only going to cause me more pain, but I have to know.

"He's your husband. I don't have the right to keep you here."

Silence fills the room. His honesty is unnerving and refreshing.

Unsure of what to do with myself, I look around the garage for something, anything, to do. Casually leaning up against the tool bench, I place my elbow on the table, but instead the bench slides, rolling away from me as tools crash to the floor, clanging and banging around me as I tumble to the ground.

"Christ, Ems. You okay?"

I sigh. Great, this is the second time I've landed on my knees. Freeing my hands from the ground, I try to stand, but Van is crouched down in front of me suppressing a smile.

"Don't you dare laugh," I snap.

"Come on," he tells me as he reaches for my hands. "Sorry, but you're the clumsiest person I know." His façade breaks and his chuckle makes me smile back.

"Stop it," I whine.

Van bites his lip, I'm sure to hide his smile. "I can't help it." He clears his throat. "Okay..." He tries to take on a serious face, only it makes me laugh too.

"Fine. You win, I'm a klutz."

"Thank God you're wearing that shirt. Grease monkey." He ruffles the hair on my head like I'm a five-year-old.

"Again, I'm so sorry about that."

"I told you it was okay. I was just teasing you."

As we stand eye to eye, an overwhelming feeling comes over me, I need to explain it to him.

My lips begin before I can reason with myself to stop. "I come from a well-educated family. A family that only paid attention to me when I graduated college or married into a hugely wealthy family." He sucks in his bottom lip, holding it between his teeth; cautiously waiting for me to stop, then Van puts up his hand to stop me.

"Your so-called family is paying five-hundred grand to fix a car that hadn't even left the driveway. I'm well aware of where you come from."

"First of all, its eight-hundred grand, and that's the reason I'm still looking over your books. But it's not just the Dawson's, it's my family too. I was raised by people who saw others who did manual labor as less than, and I've come to see that..." I swallow, not wanting to confess. "I did too. That was until I came here."

Van huffs, "You think that's news to me? That's why I made you clean my trailer. You came here an entitled princess, you've..." He pauses, opens his mouth and closes it again. After a brief second, he finishes his thought, "That's not you. I've had my fill of you explaining the obvious to me. Back to the car."

Van pulls my arm, bringing me against his chest. His whole demeanor softens, taking me by surprise. "I'm well aware of where you came from, who you're married to, but I want to show you a different way of life, a better way to live." He doesn't elaborate, and I'm not sure I'm ready for him to.

Van backs away, turning to grab the board from against the wall. "I need to get under the car a bit...do you think you can clean up your mess?" He winks, gesturing to the floor.

"Yes, smartass."

He chuckles, leans back on the board, and slides under the car.

Thankfully I've been tasked with something other than insulting Van or him touching me in a way that only serves to increase my fascination with him.

It takes me longer than I thought to pick up the mess. Silently I thank my clumsiness. It gives me something to do other than concentrate on him.

Van slides from under the car, his hands covered in black oil, and a kohl-colored streak on his face.

"Grab that flashlight on the cart..." he says all bossy. I raise my eyebrows in warning. He adds, "Please" with a twinkle in his eyes.

"No problem, I think I know what that looks like."

"Grab another creeper and slide under here with me. I need your help."

"A what?"

He rolls his eyes at me. "Okay," he speaks slowly as if I'm not going to understand. "See this thing I've been lying on—get the other one, tip it over until the wheels hit the ground, and slide it over."

Rolling my eyes, I bend down, pushing the creeper near him.

I kneel in front of it, not sure how to get on the thing.

He taps the seat. "Sit here, lie down, and rest your head here." He points to the padded pillow.

"It's like a bed while you're working." He chuckles. "I guess it's better than being on an oil-soaked floor."

I sit, then do as he instructed. Feeling like I'm in gym class on a scooter, I slide my creeper next to his.

He's under the car while I'm waiting for his direction.

"Turn on the light, shine it to the left of my hand on this bolt."

"You mean, you want me, under there, with you?"

"Yes, come on, don't be a wuss. I need your help. I can't see that little bolt."

I slide under, brushing his shoulder with mine. I shine where he's pointed while he struggles loosening the bolt.

"Shine it closer. Over here." He points, grunting. I do as he asks. Van grunts again, shaking his head. "I need another hand." Dropping both hands to his sides, he says, "I need your help."

"Aren't I already doing that?"

"Yes, smartass, but I need you closer."

"If I get any closer, I'd be on you." I snort, laughing at my little joke, only he's not laughing back. "What?"

"I need you to hold this bolt in place while I try to get this pin out. Normally, the car is on a lift and it's easy to get to, but I can't risk having this car off the ground."

Scanning the little space, I can't fathom what he's talking about. "Can we fit?"

"Barely." I notice a glint in his eyes. "Slide out."

I listen to him and sit up, but he's still lying flat on the creeper. He pats his chest.

"You want me? On you?" I can barely choke out the words.

"How else are we both going to fit under there?"

My heart catapults into my throat. He wants me to lie on him?

"Come on, we're running out of time. You need to put your back to my front."

Taking a deep, calming breath, I steel my nerves. Not sure how to go about it, I freeze, hesitating, but Van doesn't. He sits up, yanks me on his lap like I'm light as a feather. My body wilts under his touch, obeying his commands and ignoring mine. He guides my body down so that I'm flush with his. He hardens underneath me.

"Lie down," he says with a hoarse voice.

I do as he asks, my back resting against his front. He takes my hand, putting it up on the car where he needs my help. His chest rises against my front, his heart hammering as rapidly as mine. He nestles his face against my neck, rubbing his nose against my skin, melting any chance of me leaving this damn creeper. "I like being this close to you," he breathes, making my skin tingle. "You smell like vanilla." His voice even more husky than before, he kisses the surface of my neck. "And your perfume," another kiss, "and the sexiest scent of all," he bites my earlobe, unleashing a moan from my throat, "Emerson."

I melt, literally coming apart in his arms. My eyes close, my nerves tingle and spark, aching for his touch. Van's free hand travels up my thigh, across my stomach, caressing every inch of skin along his path to the side of my breast. Another moan escapes. As I turn my head, his tongue darts out and grazes my earlobe. "Mmm…"

With a whoosh, Van slides us out from the car, as if it's about to explode from above us.

He sits up. My body's so limp from his touch that it has yet to recover and get with the program. It obeys his, moving with him. Van grabs my ass and pushes me off of him.

"You can't do that shit to me!" he yells, tugging his hair back away from his face.

I find my voice. "What did I do? You just kissed my neck!"

"You came here. You brought that stupid car—all in a sexy suit, high fucking heels, long legs that I want wrapped around me all the fucking time, and that knot above your head…and when you let it out, silk falls around your shoulders…smells like fucking heaven. Shit!" His hands find his hips and he looks to the ground. Biting his lips to stop himself, I think.

I'm not sure what to say to that, so I say, "I'm…sorry."

"Sorry…you're fucking sorry." Van drops his hands to his side, gritting his teeth. He glances up from the ground with an intensity I've only seen one other time—the time he threw me over his shoulder. Only this time, he doesn't throw me over his shoulder. He charges across the room, picks me up by my ass cheeks, and just like before, I easily straddle him, wrapping my legs around his waist as he backs us up against the workbench.

He sits me on top, his eyes narrow; he swallows hard but doesn't say anything or touch me. A tool clanks to the ground, and his lips are on mine. His hands run down the side of my head, holding it in place as his tongue takes charge. Tasting every inch of me. And dear God, does he taste like heaven. I moan into his mouth, and it only spurs him on.

One hand leaves my face, only to land on the button of the work shirt he put on me earlier. Torturously slow, he unfastens each one, exposing my tank top. He palms my breast, his lips never leaving mine, his finger dips the top of my tank, my skin excites at the contact. He bites down on my lip, and I move my hands from his back to his butt and pull him against me. His hard cock presses against me, igniting the spark. This man can have me. I don't care, I'm ready for him, I want him. I…I…shit!

Van jumps away, pulling me down off the bench. The garage door opens. I didn't even hear it in my haze. Thankfully, he did. Catching my breath, I overlap the shirt to cover myself. Glancing at Van, he's wearing a small, knowing smile, but acting as if he's working on some-thing and he didn't just have me ready to fuck him a second ago. Heat reaches my cheeks.

Ben and Jake enter a few seconds after the door goes all the way up. "What's she doing here? More babysitting?" Jake asks in his natural cocky tone.

Van says calmly from beside me without missing a beat, "Yep. Isn't that what she's here for?"

"What's with that? I hope she bought it," he counters, pointing at my shirt.

"Do you think she wants oil all over those expensive clothes?" he asks, fumbling with some metal thing as he walks over to the car and slides under it on the creeper.

"Yeah, I guess that would be awful." He feigns. To my relief, changing the subject away from me. "What the fuck was that about with you ready to bash Ace's skull in last night?"

He doesn't answer, but metal clangs to the ground. He says finally, "He was an ass last night, I'll clear it up later."

"You better—the race is tomorrow, and we need a big win against Rex," Jake says, ducking under the hood.

After a few minutes of only the familiar sounds of these guys working, I take off the work shirt and put it back on the hanger. No one's paying attention to me, so I start to walk away from them, but Ben stops me. "Where are you going?"

"I don't really know anything about race cars or this car," I gesture to the Bugatti. "I'll just get out of your way."

His blue eyes dazzle and he winks. "If you haven't guessed, nothing gets in our way. Besides, we have a few more people stopping by to help," Ben adds, stopping his work to look at me.

Van stays buried under the car, not offering a comment. I'm uncomfortable, I want him to acknowledge me in some way, but I know he won't. Not in front of these guys.

He acts as if he didn't just have me pressed up against him, as if we weren't glued to each other, exchanging sparks of our own a few moments ago.

"Really, I'm tired. I'm going to head up to bed. I'll see you at home." I slip, forgetting it isn't my home at all. As I say the words I can't take back, Van yelps, "Shit!" from behind me.

I'm not sure if it was in response to my comment or something he did under that car. Regardless, I wasn't sticking around to find out.

24

—•—

There it is, the mistake I've been looking for: five-hundred thousand thirty-three dollars and eighty-five cents transferred to an unidentified account. Because the bank it was transferred to is out of state, it's been difficult to narrow down the branch location. I have contacts across the country, and one, in particular, is brilliant at this kind of thing. It took him no time at all to track down the information. Of course, I cannot get the account holder's name, but I was able to narrow it down to a specific city and state. If Van has an idea of where the money was transferred to, then maybe he can give me the why.

I've been working all day on Bradley Restoration's books. I'm tired and hungry and unsure how to approach Van about possible embezzlement.

Violet sits outside on the curb, smoking a cigarette, as I leave the showroom.

"He's getting ready for the race tonight. Setting up and stuff."

"Who?" I question against my better judgment.

"Van. He's at the spot, doing a test pass."

No idea what that entails and I'm not about to have her elaborate. I don't want to give her a chance to insult me. "What are you looking for?"

I stop. "Excuse me?"

"The books, You finding anything?" she asks as her purple hair blows in the wind, looking more vibrant in the sunlight.

"I can't discuss this with you."

"I just want you to know if you try and accuse anyone in the Bradley family of doing something..." Her eyes glance up to the sky, "bad."

"Why would I accuse anyone in the family of doing something...bad?"

She tosses her cigarette to the ground and stands. "Teddy's on his way in tonight for the race. He's not like Van or anyone else in the family. The dude's unstable, if you know what I mean?"

I sigh, tired of her veiled comments. "No, Violet, I don't know what you mean, and I don't care at this point. I did Van a favor because I felt bad about being here, overseeing his work. I'm starving and I'm headed back to his apartment to sleep on his couch. I have no idea what you're insinuating or why. I've tried to be nothing but nice to you and at this point, I'm finished."

I don't stay to see her expression or wait for another comment. But I can't help thinking she might know more than she's letting on, after all, she did say Teddy was unstable, and that's exactly who the numbers are pointing to.

Arriving at the apartment, relief sweeps over me. I close the door, sag against it, and immediately relax. After dealing with Violet and knowing that Van isn't coming home for a while at least, it's time to be alone. But I can't help thinking about Van not coming home last night that keeps nagging at me. I'm worried that he stayed away because he didn't want to have to face me.

Spying the couch, I kick my shoes off and a chill washes over me. Pulling the blanket off the back of the couch, I cover myself and savor the thought of calling it a night, going to bed at...I look over at the clock on the cable box seven fifteen, perfect. Cuddling on the couch seems a better solution than facing Van. He won't be back here since the big race is tonight.

Before giving into sleep, I check my phone, Andrew left a text message.

Give me a call!

"You have no idea how excited I am to hear from you."

"Me too," he says, with little excitement.

"Everything okay?"

"Yeah. No. I've been stuck with Dawson senior. He's been relentless. I've been in and out of cell phone service. Shelly hates that I'm gone. I need to cheer up. Tell me about the South. You are having fun?"

"Andrew." I let out a sigh. Should I tell him about Van? Would he judge me? No, I can easily answer.

"It's wonderful." It's the truth.

"Wonderful? Emmy, what am I missing?"

"Everything...I think I'm..."

"Yes, Mrs. Dawson. I'll make sure you have a dress for the charity event in a few weeks." His tone changes, and I know exactly what he's up to. Mr. Dawson has entered the room. "I'll call later with the report."

And hangs up, but before he does, he says, "You better tell me everything."

I smile. I can't wait to tell him...well, maybe not everything. Closing my eyes, I settle back against the couch. My stomach growls, reminding me I haven't eaten all day.

I huff, opening my eyes. "How did I forget to eat?"

Stomping over to the fridge, the door opens and the ice cream shines like a diamond in front of me. "Mm...that's just what I need."

Spooning a heaping scoop of chocolatey goodness in my mouth, I loudly groan, "Mhmm."

"Damn, can I have some?"

Spinning around to Callie with her hands on her hips, I reply some garbled version of you scared the crap out of me.

She reaches out her hand. "Seriously, hand it over." Ripping the carton from my hand, she shovels some into her mouth. "That's some high-quality stuff. Van has good taste." She winks playfully.

Her expression is priceless. Laughing at her with a mouthful, some of it drips down my chin. "Argh."

"You better clean up. Van sent me here to get you."

"For what?"

She scowls like I've lost my mind. "The race...tonight." Callie sets down the carton and jumps up on the counter as if it's her own kitchen.

"I'm not going to watch a race." Turning away from her, I start the process of getting my cozy on.

She jumps down and approaches the couch. "Yes, you are. Van said I absolutely could not leave without you," she tells me with her hands on her hips.

"He doesn't want me there."

Callie eyes me suspiciously. "What's going on between you two? After I left the other night, you caused a brawl, girlie."

"I didn't cause it. Van did. And nothing is going on."

"I call your bluff. He punched his good friend because he tried to kiss you—or did, I hear that part of the story wrong?"

I shrug, "There's nothing to tell."

Callie shakes her head. "Nope. I don't buy it. I've never seen Van so...involved with another girl as he is with you. He's always watching you, includes you in his day, and the whole Granddad thing...there's something going on there...now spill."

She is relentless. "Ugh!" I cover my face with the blanket. "We kissed." I confess.

"What?" she screams, rips the blanket off of my face, jumps on the couch next to me, and says, "Details now."

"I don't know," I sigh loudly. "We kissed the night he punched Ace, and then again last night. He told me he doesn't believe in ruining marriages, but he wants us to be friends while I'm here. One minute he's distant, and the next he's holding me in his arms, kissing me."

Callie's visibly shocked, her mouth hangs open, then she recovers with, "What do you want?"

"I don't know." I sit up. "Last night it was the hottest experience I've ever had, and then Ben and Jake interrupted us. Van didn't even acknowledge me when I left."

"Did the guys see you two?"

"No. They were oblivious. He jumped away from me like I was about to sting him or something."

"Do you want to be more than friends?" she asks, and I can sense the caution in her voice.

"Yes...no...I'm married." I drop my head in my hands. "Callie, what am I doing?"

She grabs my hand and places hers on top of mine. "Listen, I know you don't want to talk about your husband and marriage, but I know you're not happy. I know for a fact he treats you poorly. I think you need to put yourself first. Figure out what you want. Don't be swayed because of vows or because some hot guy makes you feel good for a few days. Pick you, Ems." Her speech puts a lump in my throat.

"I haven't felt this alive in...well, ever. Van's so sweet when we are alone. He makes me feel important to him, but then when he's with his friends and in a crowd, he has some random girl hanging all over him, ignoring me completely. I just don't know what to think."

Callie scoots closer and wraps me up in a hug. I can't remember the last time a friend authentically consoled me.

"Thanks."

"Your happiness first, everybody else...whenever and whoever you choose. But above all, you need to have a little fun." She pulls away from me. "Racing is exhilarating and fun and loud and crazy. Just what you need as a distraction from your problems."

"Won't I be walking directly into the path of my problems?"

"Yep. If he's going to ignore you when he's in a group or let some garage slut grovel all over him, then we'll show him what he's missing."

****

An hour later my plans to wallow have ceased and I'm getting out of Callie's truck, walking toward a large crowd of people.

"I didn't expect you to drive a truck." She's so petite, but come to think of it, I can't remember seeing any woman I know drive a truck. "I don't even have a license."

"I'd die if I couldn't drive. When people piss me off, a long drive is the best medicine."

"Are people...Ben?" I ask.

She stops in her tracks and faces me. Her usual bubbly personality morphs into bitterness. "He's exactly the people I'm talking about. He treats me like a child who needs protecting. It's ridiculous." She throws her hands in the air but starts walking.

I don't follow. I'm going to get an answer out of her. Crossing my arms, I say, "You need to tell me what's going on with you two. I confessed all my secrets to you, now spill."

Callie spins around and stomps back to me. "First, you didn't tell me all your secrets. And I slept with Ben. Once. But if my brother found out...well, he can't. Besides, it didn't mean anything."

I narrow my eyes to gauge her honesty. Nope. I don't believe her, but I don't want to push her either, so I let it slide. "If you say so."

"I do."

I calmly say, "Okay." She nods back and we walk a few feet in silence.

To lighten the mood, I tell her that my husband's family owns a professional race car team. "Isn't it crazy this is my first race, and that it's a street race?"

Callie's eyes widen. "Damn, you can go to a race anytime you want, and you choose this dirty street drag race." She laughs. "Ben told me about your husband owning the Dawson Racing Team. He's secretly excited to have you here. It's the closest he thinks he'll ever come to professional racing."

Glancing around, two Bobby Houston t-shirts walk past me. "I never paid attention, but here I am in the midst of Dawson Racing fans."

"Yeah, and we haven't even passed through the gates yet." I giggle with her. It's true, Bobby's doing a great job for Dawson Racing. He's bringing in huge profits since he joined the team a year ago. Of course, that's the only thing I have to do with the racing, the books.

"Come on." Callie grabs my arm and speeds up to get through the gates. She winks at the guy holding a stamp, and he gives a sheepish grin.

"Hey, Callie. Are you watching Rex tonight?" he asks in a deep southern drawl.

"Now, Jimmy, you know I never tell who I'm rooting for. How much do I owe ya for us two?" Callie flirts like no other, brushing her finger down his face. Jimmy's face flames in response.

"You know as long as I'm manning the gate, you'll get in for free, and so will this pretty thing too."

"Thanks, Jimmy." Callie holds out her hand and he can barely keep his hands from shaking to press the stamp on her skin.

I reach out my hand, he stamps it, but his eyes are still on Callie.

Callie pats his cheek and sways her hips past him.

"I need to learn that trick."

"What?"

"You had that guy falling all over himself."

"And you'll have Van falling all over himself, too, if you already don't."

The car to my left catches my attention with its shiny black paint, skull graphics, and the gleaming chrome engine shining under the lights. The track isn't what I expected either. I guess I was expecting an oval racetrack, and this is a regular straight, paved road. On either side of the road are trailers and cars.

Engines rev all around me, one beside me sounds as if it's charging toward me, causing me to jump.

"Easy," she commands. "It only gets louder as the night wears on." Callie puts her hands in the air. "Welcome to street racing." Her eyes are alive with excitement. I can tell she's in her element, loving every second of it.

I follow the road as Callie greets people along the way. It seems to me that everyone knows her.

"Come on. I see it."

"What?"

"Ben's car. Look, the yellow one that was in the garage the night when you had your little...thing with Van."

I roll my eyes at her. *Brat!*

As we approach, the car is being backed out of a trailer. Callie thankfully tells me where to stand and be out of their way. "Things get crazy so close to the drivers' meeting. You have to have your car ready to go."

Once it's completely out of the trailer, the engine cuts off. Van emerges from the driver's seat. My mouth dries. He's the sexiest man I've ever seen. He's wearing a worn ball cap backward with a few stray hairs poking from the front, his white t-shirt is stuck to him like it's been painted on and stained with grease, and his jeans are slung low on his waist revealing his V as his arms go up above his head while he's talking to Ben. He hasn't seen me yet.

Callie nudges me to follow her. "Hey, guys," she says cheerfully. "Ready to go?"

Van turns and his eyes widen when he looks in my direction. I give him a small wave.

He swallows and then gives me a brief nod. Good Lord, this whole situation is infuriating. I turn away from him. I just can't...I'm really wishing I stayed on the couch tonight.

Callie grabs my hand. "Let's go sit in the trailer. It'll just be a few minutes, and then we'll go stand at the starting line."

"We don't have seats?"

She laughs at me. "No, silly. You can't see anything over there." She points to three rows of homemade wooden bleachers. Not exactly the type of seating I expected anyway.

There are no chairs in the trailer, only a few stools. I sit on one and Callie the other. Ben's starting to get dressed in his race suit. Of course, he's equally as attractive as Van, but in a different way. His short blond hair is darting every which way, his eyes are intense, and I can tell he's getting focused for the race. I glance over at Callie who's watching him carefully. I wish she'd confess more about him to me.

Jake steps into the trailer with us. "Looks like we're ready, man."

"Good," Ben says. "Callie, can I talk to you for a minute?"

"About what?" Jake pipes up, confusion written all over his face.

"She said she had some news about Dawson Racing?" Ben says, looking at me to agree with him.

I nod. What else can I do?

"Um...yeah. Thanks for the info, Ems." Callie stands and walks out of the trailer with Ben.

Jake turns to me, waiting for me to explain. "Why don't you just tell him then?"

"Nothing important, Ben will tell you later," Callie explains as she passes her brother.

"Oh. Okay." He shakes his head and walks out of the trailer. I'm beginning to think Jake isn't the brightest out of the bunch, or maybe he doesn't want to see what's right in front of him.

I can hear Callie and Ben talking, but I can't make out what they're saying. They're standing within earshot of the window beside me.

I scoot my wheeled stool closer, straining to listen. "Are you eavesdropping?"

Van stands in front of me, wiping his hand on a rag.

"No," I swallow, lying to him.

"I think I've seen you do this before," he says, walking closer to me.

"Obviously, you have a bad memory."

"I didn't think you'd come."

"I didn't want to. But Callie wouldn't take no for an answer."

"I'm glad you're here."

"Are you?" I don't recognize my own voice, cold and stern.

He sits down beside me on the other stool. "Yes. I am. I'm sorry for last night. I shouldn't have...well, you know."

"Yeah, I know." He can't even say the word. "Look, just forget about it. I'll be going home soon enough, and you won't have to worry about me. I assume there should be some rooms opening up in the hotel after tonight's race, so I'll just move myself over there tomorrow," I lie. He looks at me suspiciously.

"I've got to go and help Ben. I'll talk to you later."

I nod. When his back is to me, I let out the breath that I was holding.

****

Callie and I have watched at least ten races waiting for Ben's turn. These cars are regular, everyday cars, modified and tweaked to become fast machines. Callie explained how they are hooked up to computers, they run numbers and stats telling them how fast they're going, how much boost they're putting out, and how much nitrous they need.

Most of it means nothing to me, but it's exhilarating watching them race by me, two by two. Both cars drive up to the line and the guy shines the flashlight for them to go, adrenaline fills the air. A hush falls over the crowd, and all you can hear are the roar of the engines until the final call is made over the radio, and there are cheers for the winner, and cussing from the losing side. Next up, Ben drives his yellow Mustang up to the line. Van's behind him, dumping something on to the road, and then Ben does a burnout. "What's that for?" I yell over to her.

"Helps the car stick to the road." She cups her hand, yelling back. I have to remember to ask Callie about it later. It's just too loud for any more questions.

Van directs Ben back to the starting line and runs over to the side to get out of the way. The guy with the flashlight nudges each car up a little more and then flash, they're gone. A yellow streak flies past me. Rex's car, the red Camaro, is neck and neck with Ben's. I hold my breath until I can't see them anymore, a hush falls over the crowd along with screeching tires, clanging metal, smoke, and people running.

Callie screams, "Ben!" taking off into a dead sprint.

I don't know what to do, or what's happened, but I'm getting pushed around by people trying to see. Thankfully, I'm able to jump to the side, out of the way.

"He's okay!" I hear someone scream. "He's good!" Giving a thumbs up.

People start to walk back, no one in a hurry anymore. As the crowds give way to the street, I see Ben, Jake, and Van pushing Ben's pristine car in front of us with a mixture of relief and triumph.

Rex's car is nowhere to be seen.

"That fucker Rex intentionally swerved into his lane," some guy says beside me.

"Yeah, that was some badass driving on Ben's part," another says.

I'm relieved to see that Ben's all right, but not sure why he's pushing his car instead of driving it.

It seems like an eternity until they pass by me and head straight into the pits. Callie hurries back over to my side. "He's fine. Thank God." She practically sings, the relief written all over her smile.

"What happened?"

She leans near my ear so I can hear her. "Rex lost control and swerved into Ben's lane. Intentionally tried to wreck him, I heard. But Ben kept the car straight and won."

"Why's he pushing his car if he won?" I don't understand any of this.

"He broke something, and we're done for the night, but they'll be able to fix it for the next race."

An unexpected wave of disappointment comes over me as I realize that I won't be around for the next race.

25

— · —

Two hours after the race, we're back at the main garage. The guys are far from race mode, and heavily into party mode. I've overheard talk of everyone headed to the lake. I'm ready to head to bed.

Callie and I walk over to where Ben and Jake are standing, recounting the tale of how Ben avoided Rex. "I saw him head in my lane with a smile on his face. He was close enough to my door that I could see him close up."

A chill hit my spine. Creepy. Why would he intentionally wreck into Ben?

Callie pipes up, "He's an ass."

"You would know," Ben says under his breath.

"Fuck you, Ben," Callie says and turns, grabbing my arm. "Come on, let's head to the lake. Anywhere away from him." She glares back at Ben.

"What the hell was that about?"

"Nothing. I told you he treats me like a child." We're arm in arm, heading in the direction of the lake before I can protest. "He hates that Rex and I dated for a little while."

I stop, halting us mid stride. "How could you not tell me this?"

She releases my elbow and drops her hands to her side in defeat. "I had a huge thing for Rex, he finally went out with me, and then he cheated on me. It was over before it began. But he's been trying to get me back for months now, but I'm never going back to him."

"And I thought I had some drama with Van, I think I may have some competition," I joke, finally able to laugh at my situation.

"Come on. Let's party and forget about these guys...actually, all guys." We walk down to the lake party, causing a knot to form in my belly. I should just turn around now, but I don't.

Ignoring my problems and having fun is going to be hard to do since I see Van and Ace are standing at opposite ends of the party. I haven't seen Ace since the other night. I put my head down, hoping that he'll ignore me.

No such luck as he strides toward me. "Hey," he says, forcing me to raise my head. Ugh.

"Hi." I give him a small wave. Callie speaks up, "Why weren't you at the race? You've never missed a race."

He shrugs. "They didn't need me."

"Of course, they did. Who told you that?"

"Don't worry about it." He waves his hand. "Would you mind if I talk to Ems for a minute?"

"No," she says quietly, but looks to me for an answer.

"It's fine."

He takes me by the elbow, and we head away from the crowd near a tree that hides us from the others.

The uncertainty that fills me every time I'm around him is present, but I plan on this being a quick conversation.

"I wanted to make sure things were okay between us."

"Yeah...sure."

"I was drunk, and I pushed too far. I'm sorry for that, but I can't deny I find you attractive. And you're married. I'm going to respect that."

"I appreciate that."

He nods, then, and turns to walk away, but turns back to face me with a more determined look on his face.

"Nothing's going on between you and Van, right?"

"No. Why would you ask me that?"

"Because he may seem like a good guy, but he's not. I've known him for far too long. He's cheated on everyone he's ever been in a relationship with. I mean, you've seen him, all the girls he lets hang all over him."

I nod in return. I've seen all his women, but something in Ace's eyes makes me uneasy. If he really was Van's friend, would he be breaking their trust.

"Do you want to hang here for a bit? Away from that?" He points to the chaos off in the distance.

"No, I think I'll head back."

"Ems, I think you should stay away from Van."

"I don't think that's any of your business."

"I do think it's your husband's, though."

"Are you threatening me?" I ask, unsure of the turn this conversation has taken.

"Maybe he should know that Van has more plans than just fixing his car."

I'm speechless, why is he being so hurtful. Staring at him, something catches my attention.

Van's here and relief floods my nerves immediately.

"Ems. I was looking for you." He hasn't looked in my direction, only focused on Ace.

"We've been talking," Ace flatly states, standing up straighter than before.

"Let's head back, Ems," Van suggests.

"She's fine here with me." Ace's voice becomes louder and more assertive.

I watch as their pissing contest continues, and it's time for me to go. I'm not reliving the other night's brawl. "I can answer for myself and I'm going to head back that way." I point to the lake. "If you'll excuse me, I'm going to find Callie."

As I leave them, their voices fade, and I'm relieved I can't make out what they're saying. The amount of stress they induce in me is infuriating. Thinking of the other night and how silly it was, they were fighting over me. I can't recall that ever happening. Oh, wow...how long have I been walking? This doesn't look familiar. Wait, I'm confused. Did I really wander this far from the lake? It seems much farther than I thought.

My head starts to hurt, like really hurt. Oh no...the lights from the fire start to blur, and my legs feel as if bricks are tied to my feet. Oh hell, not again.

A row of trees to my left catches my attention. If I can focus on them, control my breathing, maybe I can stop a seizure from coming on. Taking a few steps, the rough bark is a welcome distraction. Bracing myself against the tree, I lower myself down to the ground.

Relief washes over me. Breathing in and out, I find my head clearing a bit.

"Ems...you okay?" His voice helps me focus. Van.

"Yeah." I can barely hear my own voice.

"Lie down. I'm right here."

I do as he asks, because I always do.

In seconds my head's resting on his lap, cushioned by him. His fingers brush my hair from my face, and he silently soothes the fog away. Van stays silent as he glides his fingers through the strands of my hair over and over again, rhythmically lulling the seizure away.

"I'm sorry. I hope I didn't upset you and brought this on."

"I'm all right. It passed." I sound more like myself. "I think it was an aura, just a warning."

"Do you want to sit up?"

"Yes, please."

I move to sit as Van's hands clutch my arms, helping me to a sitting position. His eyes roam over my face. His hand comes up to brush my hair from my skin but stays to run along my cheeks. "I hate that you have to deal with this. Is it selfish that I'm glad I'm here to help you through it?"

"No. I'm glad you're here."

We sit in silence, but our eyes don't leave each other's. His dart back and forth, consuming and tracking every movement of mine. He's searching for something, just like I am. Although, I don't think either of us know what it is.

He moves his hand from my cheek to my bottom lip. Dipping it down, his face moves closer. My eyes close, and his soft lips touch mine, brushing lightly and then over to my cheek.

"Can I show you something?" he whispers with a huskiness in his voice.

"Yes."

He stands, breaking our moment but not our connection. He helps me to my feet, not letting go. His arm snakes around my waist as he leads me farther into the woods. I glance over in the direction of the fire, but it is long gone.

We walk in silence. My legs feeling a little bit like Jell-O. I know if I was on my own, I wouldn't be able to stand, let alone walk, but Van brings me strength.

"Just a little longer," he says.

"Where are we going?"

"My first house."

We pass a few more trees, the fallen leaves crunching under my feet, and when we stop, a tree house in the middle of two trees awaits us.

"You built this?"

"My dad and I did. When I was ten."

"What are we doing here?"

"I need quiet, I want to be alone with you. Is that all right?" He's so sincere and cautious at the same time. No snarky comments, no teasing.

"Yes." I swallow. Clearing my throat, I ask, "How do we get up there?"

"A ladder." He winks at me.

"Of course. I see a theme to your works of art."

"Work of art? Huh? No one's ever put it that way."

He guides me over to the ladder. "Climb up. I'm right behind you."

I grab on to the first rung, and he's flush up against me. I peek over my shoulder. He smiles. "I don't want you to fall back."

Taking a rung at a time, he's in time with me, only one step behind. I reach the top and step off the ladder with his help. Thankfully, there's a handle there to help me.

Standing in the middle of the tree house, I can't see a thing, only guided by Van's soft commands.

"Hold on a minute, I'll get us some light."

Within seconds, I hear a click, and the room glows with a flicker of light, and an old-time oil lamp is the source.

He's behind me as something scrapes across the wood floor. "Here, have a seat."

A worn green leather beanbag begs to be sat in. Lowering my body, I watch as Van drags a much more worn, duct-taped beanbag. I can't help but ask him how long it's been here.

"I stole it from Granddad's when I was a kid, I think, so forever ago."

I smile at his cute admission. "I'm sorry about earlier. I wanted to see if you were okay, but instead, I made a nuisance of myself."

"Why do you do that?"

"What?" Having no clue what he's referring to.

"Quit apologizing for being sick. Needing help is not a weakness. It means you're strong to live with this every day, that takes strength, not weakness."

Van leans in closer, the beans in the chair rustle under him as he moves. His hand finds a place under my ear, while his thumb rests against my lips.

"What has he done to you, Ems?" he asks so quietly, I have to strain to hear him.

"Nothing." I can't look at him, keeping my eyes trained on the wooden floorboards is the only way to keep my secrets.

He drags his thumb across my lips. "Look at me...please."

The softness of his voice filters through my skin. I look up because my body listens on its own. Glancing up, his eyes dart back and forth, searching mine.

"Van...I can't."

I try to pull away, but he forces me closer to him. "Tell me, please." He begs once more, I want to tell him so badly. Do I? Do I let him know what I did? I search his eyes this time and know that I can trust him. Even if he thinks I'm the worst person in the world, I know I can trust him, so I let the words free. "I almost killed him."

Van lets out a slight gasp, but he doesn't move away or let go of my face. Still assuring me that he's here for me. He leans against my forehead to reassure me it's okay and says, "Tell me."

"We were leaving a fundraiser at the country club. I had one drink, and he was wasted." I allow my mind to drift back to that night. Something I try to avoid at all costs. The last few years I've tried to forget that awful night ever happened. "I told him in the beginning of the night I wasn't feeling well, but he didn't care. Then when it was time to go home, he couldn't even stand up straight."

"Come on, David, the valet's going to help you into the car."

His body's limp; he's mumbling something as the young man drags him from the front door of the country club to the passenger seat. He tucks in his legs and closes the door. I give the valet a hundred-dollar bill, hoping this will keep him from spreading gossip about David's condition.

Climbing into the driver's seat, I start the engine and drive the few miles home. We brought the Ferrari tonight and wanted to show it off. Unfortunately for me, it's a standard. I know how to drive it, just not well.

All I have to do is get through one last intersection and I'll be home, then I can unload his drunk ass on the couch and crawl into my bed. Moving the shifter to first, then to second and...headlights, screeching, banging, clanking, and...screaming until the car stops, and David's bloodied head lies on my lap with his eyes closed.

I shudder at the memory.

"I never saw the red light, and a car slammed into David's door. I was too busy trying to shift that I wasn't paying attention."

"Accidents happen, Ems. You can't blame yourself. He got himself drunk, he wanted to show his money off, not you. You were being responsible. You don't think that a race car driver faces those same challenges every time he gets behind the wheel? We do and we get paid for it. If you don't think a driver can accidentally grab the wrong gear, you're kidding yourself, and for David to dump this all on you...unbelievable." He was shaking his head, not understanding.

"It doesn't matter anymore whose fault it was, it will always be mine. David blames me every day for the loss of his leg. If I had just called Andrew, or his parents, or hell, paid the valet to take us home...he'd still be perfect. It took them over an hour to get him cut from the wreckage of the car, and once at the hospital, his leg from beneath his knee down to his foot, couldn't be saved."

"It isn't your fault."

"His mother and father think it is, along with my parents and the people I have to deal with for the company, our friends and business associates. They all give him attention for what he's been through and blame me. I see it on their faces every day."

"Were you injured in the wreck?" Releasing his hands from my face, an unwelcome pang of hurt washes over me.

"Yes...I had a seizure at the crash site and was transported by ambulance. Because I wasn't wearing a seatbelt, I sustained a head injury, and ever since then, I continue to have seizures that are brought on by a variety of factors. When I do, no one cares. They don't care if I'm alone and hurt myself. I've broken my arm, woken up with a large gash across my forehead, and one minute I was happily shopping in a mall, and the next, I'm lying in a hospital bed and I couldn't remember how I got there."

"Ems..." Van takes my head in his hands and hugs me to his chest. I breathe in his calming, familiar scent. I let the years of tears, the ugliness of it all unleash into his arms. The tears keep coming, but as they do relief comes too.

"Shh...shh..." he repeats over and over again until I quiet.

"I'm so sorry," I finally say into his t-shirt after I find my voice again, aware of his hard chest underneath me that's been the only source of comfort that I've ever known. I back away, swiping at my eyes.

"You need to stop apologizing for everything." His frustration is evident by him tugging at his hair. "Shit happens. We all have our own shit to deal with, it's how we handle it and who's there to help us get through it all that matters. For better or worse, sickness and health, right? David also took those vows, he has to honor them, if he's not...he isn't worthy of being your husband."

The tears start to creep in, but for another reason. "No one's ever said I'm worthy of anything. Not even my parents." The confession hurts to say.

"Leave him, leave them all." He lifts my chin so that our eyes are level, and I can't look away. "Listen to me." He pauses, stating slowly yet firmly, "They are *all* not worthy of *you*."

"You make it sound so easy."

"It is that easy."

"They'll ruin me. I've worked so hard ever since I can remember to make a name for myself, to not be seen as a Dawson, but as a smart, successful, competent woman. They threaten to ruin my career, my reputation, and my parents' name—anyone I care for. They'll do it, Van."

"Who gives a fuck, Ems? You're smart and amazing. Start your own damn company." I shake my head. He continues, "They've already ruined you, Ems, I see it every damn time you say his name or speak of home. They stole you. Don't let them keep you."

My bottom lip quivers at his words. So hurtful yet so beautifully true. They stole me, and Van has revived me.

"I'm scared," I confess.

"It's okay to be scared, but don't let it be this way because you made a marriage vow or because you feel guilty for something that was out of your control."

"I don't love him. I never have."

"Are you going back to him?" he asks. He leans in, coming dangerously close to my lips.

"I don't want to."

"I don't want you to, either."

"Van..." His lips press against mine, and I've never tasted anything sweeter. I can't control myself, and I push my mouth against his while he wraps his arms around me, pressing my body to his.

I rock against him, letting him know I want more, much more of him. He tugs me over so that I'm straddling him. His hands fall from my face, but land on my hips, digging in. Our kiss becomes more passionate with each stroke.

I wrap my arms around his neck, threading my fingers through his hair and tugging ever so slightly, causing a groan that makes my body respond, wanting more.

His hand grazes my sensitive skin as he sweeps my shirt over my head. In a split-second, cool air breezes across my breasts. Van's mouth leaves mine only to lean down and suck my nipple into his mouth.

I gasp at the sensation. I've never had this reaction before—instant, tingling, and primal. I want to see him, feel him, and make him mine.

As he laps his way around my chest, not missing an inch of my skin, his hands roam over my ass, caressing up my back and lightly trailing around to my front, brushing against my stomach.

His head rises from my chest. "You're beautiful, Emerson. Absolutely beautiful. I want to make love to you. I know you're not mine, but I want you to be. I'm sorry I've been all over the place with you. I've never felt like this, and I know you're off limits, but even if you don't want me the same way, I want you."

Placing my finger over his lips, I stop him. "I want you to make love to me. Everything that's happened has been perfect because it led us to this moment, to us, just us."

He guides us up till we're both standing. His eyes dance back and forth, glistening with the light of the lamp. He gives me his sweet smile, then it morphs into his sexy smirk as he tugs at the button of my jeans, releasing the zipper, tugging at them until they shimmy down.

Resting a hand on his shoulder, I steady myself as he kneels, helping me to step free of my pants. I stand in just my black cheeky panties as he presses his lips against the fabric. His hot breath is wreaking havoc on the one part of my body that's begging for him.

He runs his mouth and chin back and forth, teasing me, testing me.

I tug his hair. As I look down, his dark, hooded eyes stare back.

"You want me to take these off." He bites the tiny bow on the band of my panties and tugs it away from my body. I swear my eyes roll back in my head at the sexiest moment of my life.

I moan.

"Is that a yes, baby?" He licks his lips, and before I can answer him, they fall to my feet, and his warm, moist tongue licks a trail down until he tugs at my clit.

"Mmm..." is all I can say. Has anything ever felt like this? He sucks and licks and works magic until I can't take any more. My body shakes as I gloriously come with him lapping up what I've just given him

Before I can come down from the high, he tugs off his shirt, tossing it somewhere, and takes my hand. "Lie down."

I do as he asks while he slides his jeans down, taking his underwear with them, giving me the first view of naked Donovan Bradley...and he's absolutely beautiful in every sense of the word.

He hovers above me. "Are you sure?" he asks. "I hate to ruin this moment, I have to make sure. I don't want you to regret this." He swallows and continues, "Us."

I love how he's so concerned about how I feel, but right now all I want is him.

"I will never regret a single second I've spent with you."

As we join together, all I can think about is how this is where I'm meant to be.

26

After putting the beanbags side by side and covering our naked bodies with blankets, I've decided this is even better than my little chapel at home. Home? It isn't my home any longer. I don't want to go back, but I'm not sure where to go. I love where I'm at in this moment, but not sure what's next for me or us—if there's even an us.

"What are you thinking about?"

"Why you have blankets and pillows that don't smell musty, or like mildew, or like they've been here since you were ten? They should at least smell like dirt and not fresh flowers."

"Since a certain lady has entered my life, I've been coming out here to think or sleep." He winks at me. Van brushes his finger through my hair, repeating the motion, almost making me moan. We sit in silence under the low light of the lamp and gaze at each other. Never have I been so comfortable with someone. His hands are in constant motion touching me.

I start to close my eyes when he asks, "Do you want to go back to the apartment?"

"No, I'm happy right where I'm at, with you." I lean over and press my lips to his. He rolls me over so that I'm lying on his chest. It's so strong and muscular, but the comfiest pillow I could possibly imagine.

He lightly rubs his finger down my back, and I press a soft kiss on his pec to show my appreciation.

"You know, I would have never thought this would happen between us. I was so pissed when you showed up. Your asshole husband said he'd send someone who would make sure I knew how to do my job, and then this petite, businesswoman with a bun and a sour look comes walking into my shop...I was fucked. I knew it, you are literally the sexiest woman I've ever seen."

Lifting my I head, I rest my chin on his chest, looking up at him to get a better view.

"I tried not to pay attention to you, but when you had your seizure and the fucker told me to just leave you there." He shakes his head. "He doesn't deserve to be married to you." Van holds the side of my face, staring intimately into my eyes. "I'd never steal another man's wife or break up a home, but he isn't your partner or your protector or your home, he isn't a husband, he's a coward. I'm falling for you, Ems, I'm not exactly sure what all this means, but I do know I want to spend as many nights as I can lying next to you, exactly like this."

He couldn't have said those words any more perfectly. I kiss his lips and we lie on one beanbag for the rest of the night until birds chirp to wake us up.

***

Van slides on his jeans while I finish slipping on my shoes. "You know, I didn't expect this at all."

He walks toward me. "You mean spending the night in a tree house is unusual for you?" He raises an eyebrow.

"I do have my own hideaway at home. It's a desolate chapel in the middle of the woods. So, it does feel somewhat the norm for me."

Van bends down and lifts me off my new favorite piece of furniture. He lifts me up in the air and slides me down against his body, all while finding my lips with his.

Kissing him is so natural; it doesn't feel wrong or guilty. I know I should stop this now and head home, leave David, but I'm not sure how to pry myself away from Van.

"What do you want to do today?" I ask between kisses.

"Get that Bugatti out of my garage and never see it again."

"I have to go back and end things with him." Van looks down, his arms become rigid underneath my fingertips. "It's going to take some time." The Dawson's aren't going to let me go without a fight. I'm sure no one ever leaves a Dawson, nothing could be worse for their reputation.

"You ready?" All the fun from moments ago is replaced with a serious, cautious Van.

"Yeah," I return. Gathering up my jacket and taking a glance around. He puts away the blanket and turns off the lamp.

"Let's go."

As we start down the ladder, Callie comes running up. "There you are? Christ, we've been looking everywhere for you!" Ben stands beside Callie, out of breath, but with a knowing smirk on his face. "Why didn't you check your phone?"

Jumping down from the last step, I take it out of my pocket. I see eight missed calls from her and four missed calls from David. My stomach lurches.

She squints in my direction, "What's going on between you two?"

I look over at Van, but his expression remains stoic. "We spent the night in the tree house...talking."

"And?"

"And what, Callie?" Van snaps, taking all of us by surprise.

But she doesn't back down. "Are you two a thing?" She points between the two of us.

"I spent the night with her. I'm sure you can figure it out." With that he turns and walks in the direction of the lake, away from us and away from me.

"Sorry," Callie says quietly from beside me.

"I'm going too. We've got a lot of shit to get done to that Bugatti. We need to have it done if he's coming tomorrow," Ben adds, ignoring Van's comment.

"Who's coming tomorrow?" I ask.

"David," Callie answers with almost an apology.

My head drops into my hands. Could this get any worse? I never thought he would follow through on his threat. I'm never important enough for him to care this much.

On our way back, Callie rambles on how she woke up by the lake and no one knew where we went. She even went back to the garage and apartment. Thankfully, she hasn't quizzed me on what we were doing or if we're a thing like she tried to with Van. She must sense I'm in no mood to talk about it.

As we approach the garage, shouting erupts. Van's voice can be heard first, followed by another man's voice. We pick up our pace to find a stocky guy with a shaved head waving papers in the air while Van stands toe to toe with him, his arms crossed over his chest.

"Look what we have here, the bitch who's been snooping through our records. Maybe she can tell us all how Van's been bleeding this company dry, and everyone here will be out of a job soon." The stranger bellows with Violet smirking at his side.

All eyes go to me except Van's, his are locked on the stranger.

"Who's this?" I whisper.

Callie answers, "Teddy Donovan. The brother."

"I need to speak with Van," I say. With everything that went on between us, I should have mentioned my findings to him; I could kick myself for having to tell him like this and explain what Teddy's talking about.

"Go ahead, Van, talk to her, and tell that bitch how you use Bradley Restoration's money."

Before I can say a word, Teddy gets thrust forward by Van, his large body hitting a red toolbox.

Van grabs Teddy by the shirt, "Don't ever call her a bitch!"

Ben dives, tugging at Van's shoulder. "Come on, let him go."

"It wasn't Van. I can prove it!" I scream as Van lets go of him and shakes his head. "Let me see those," I say to Teddy to hand over whatever evidence he thinks he's found.

Teddy doesn't budge. "I'm not handing this over to you. This is my evidence, I don't want you doctoring it."

"Fine. Give me a few minutes." I hurry to the apartment to grab my bag with pages and pages of spreadsheets and receipts. When I return, Van's nowhere to be found, but Teddy's standing with a smug smile on his face.

"Where's Van?"

"In his office," Callie tells me.

"I'll be right back."

"Don't be long, we don't want you to have time to make up a fake plan," Teddy yells from behind me. I spin around.

Looking him in the eye, I tell him with more confidence than I've ever felt in my life, "I've never met you and I already don't like you." Trudging down the hall, I open Van's office door. He's standing, head bent down and hands on the desk, supporting him.

"Van?"

He looks up at me with sadness written all over his face. "I know he did it." How can I tell him this, it's his brother?

"Yes, he did." I lift up a stack of spreadsheets, bank statements, and invoices proving Van's worst fear, his brother embezzled from Bradley Restoration. "He took money from various accounts and transferred them to another account with a false name. He also racked up a hefty charge card bill under the company's name. All in all, a total of about five-hundred-thousand dollars."

Van pushes himself from the desk. "I should have done something sooner. But he's my brother. I knew no one would believe me. My dad and his wife are living it up in Florida. Mom's living with her boyfriend in Mexico. They left the company to my brother to manage the finances, and for me to do the work."

"You couldn't know your brother would do something like this."

"Yes, I could. He feels entitled to all of this..." Van puts his arms up, gesturing around the building. "He had a friend who worked on reality shows. His friend knew we did custom work and thought it would make a great reality special and it did. We got a ton of work from it. We started getting more prominent clients and attention. My parents didn't like all the attention and pulled the plug on the show. They were happy having some money in their pocket. Soon after their marriage fell apart and they went their separate ways. They always struggled, so they wanted to travel, but not together. They're better friends than a married couple. I didn't stop them. Needless to say, Teddy was pissed and blamed me for the show ending, their marriage failing, and anything else that went wrong. That's why he feels the money is his to do whatever he wants with."

"Does he do any of the labor around here? Or anything at all?"

"He does sales. He gets us some clients, but most of them are word of mouth. That's why we did anything your husband wanted. Even though he's an ass, he's a big name in the car industry."

"What do you want to do?"

"It's time to stop feeling sorry for him. Let's tell everyone what he's been up to."

Van and I head back into the garage. Not a single person has left. In fact, I think there might be more.

Van starts, "Why didn't you come to the race last night? Where have you been the last few weeks?"

His large frame hovers over Van. He's got at least fifty pounds on Van, and not in a flattering way.

"Getting clients. What the fuck else do you think I'm doing? Someone has to keep this place afloat. Mom and Dad are ignoring us, living the life while you're playing house with a client. Of course, you're taking money from this company and running it into the ground."

"He is not, and I can prove it," I speak up, defending him by holding a stack of papers in my hand. "I've got more if this doesn't convince you of his innocence and your guilt."

"Teddy didn't do anything wrong. You're a liar," Violet says from beside Teddy, arms crossed, poised to defend him.

"What did he promise you, Violet?" Van asks, narrowing his eyes on her, trudging closer to her, while Teddy backs away from her.

"Nothing."

"A new job title? Money?" He's close to her when he asks quietly but forcefully, "What did he promise you?"

She wilts under him, "He threatened me. He said he'd make it look like I took the money. If I kept quiet, nobody would ever know." She pauses, her eyes start to water. "I saw him take money from the drawer one day, and then it just kept happening. He told me it was his money to do what he wanted to with. He's an owner, so I believed him. I got suspicious one day and logged onto an online store and saw he'd purchased things for himself with the company's credit card. I confronted him and he said he'd tell you it was me." Tears cascade down her cheeks. "I'm so sorry, Van. I would have lost my job, and you...and I can't handle that." Her head falls into her hands.

"She's lying," Teddy spouts, pointing at Violet. "This is ridiculous. Van told her to say this."

But Van doesn't respond, only steps over to me, and takes the stack out of my hand. He thumbs through some paper until he finds what he's looking for. "I don't recall the shop needing a vintage guitar for eleven-thousand dollars, and the receipt is signed by Theodore Bradley." Van holds up the receipt for the crowd of Bradley Restoration supporters. "I've got plenty more transactions here if this isn't convincing enough." There's a gasp from almost everyone in the room.

"Teddy, is this true?" Ben trudges over to Van, parting the sea of people. He rips the receipt from Van's hand. Ben looks down and inspects it. "Motherfucker. You did it. You took all of our hard work and spent it on whatever the fuck you wanted."

Ben does the unexpected and pushes Teddy, pulling back his fist, ready to slug him, when Van intervenes.

"Stop it," Van screams, pushing Ben back. "It's fine. We'll deal with it as a family."

He looks over at Teddy, who's standing calmly with his fists at his side. I'm not sure how to read him. He's acting as if we're all in the wrong.

"Did you take money from the company that wasn't yours to take?" Van moves closer to him. "Tell me the truth."

"It was mine to take." He points to his chest. "I worked my ass off to get that money. I got that reality show started, and then you all wanted out—fuck you all! Call the cops and have them take me to court. I don't care. It's mine, all of it."

"No, it's not. Legally you're not an owner. Your grandfather is, he can press charges. You're listed as an employee, nothing else. Not an officer," I add, pointing out the evidence, line by line. The guilt on his face is evident.

"Are you telling Granddad?" Teddy asks Van, standing strong and confident but asking the question like a small, petulant child.

"I have to, but I won't go to the police unless Granddad wants me to." He sighs, "I think it's best if you resign from your position as employee," Van adds.

"What the hell will I do?"

"Work with your hands for a change." Then Van turns to Violet. "I'll deal with what he did to you later, but I think you should turn in your resignation too."

27

An hour later, Teddy and Van emerge from Van's office along with Violet. Mascara streaks down her face, and she turns and gives Van a hug. He whispers something in her ear and gives her a kiss on the cheek. She walks out the door with her head down and without a word to any of us.

Teddy apologizes to everyone. "I'll pay it back and make it up to you guys. I need to speak to my grandfather." We all watch in silence as Teddy walks out the door, and when he's gone, Ben speaks up, "We need to finish this car before her husband gets here." And just like that, they all turn their attention back to the car and get to work.

In this moment, I've seen the true side of Van. He's a forgiving, compassionate man who wants to make everyone around him happy. He could have raked his brother over the coals, but he didn't. Another piece of my heart just became designated for Van.

Neither David, nor my parents, would ever let anything like that slide, especially if it involved money.

Callie stands beside me. "Crazy, huh? Too bad Van's such a good guy, I was almost excited that'd we'd be rid of Violet, but she's part of the crew, just like Teddy."

"I know. How can they be trusted?" I ask, unsure of where they would go from here.

"They can't. We'll all keep an eye on them from now on. But they did lose what's important to everyone here—the shop and Van's trust." She places her arm around my shoulder. "Come on, let's pitch in and help."

"It's like nothing happened. Look at them all, working, doing their job, but most of all, helping you."

I smile at all of my friends.

"Let's join the fun. Maybe we can lend a hand."

Standing by Van, who's sanding the back rear fender, I nudge him and say, "Can I help?"

"Perfect timing. My arm is ready to fall off. Here, I'll show you how to do this." He takes my hand in his and places it over the sanding block. "Back and forth, like this." He makes even the littlest thing so...erotic. He places a soft kiss on my neck, and I tilt my head for more. He backs away quickly. I almost forgot where I was and who was looking.

I look up to see if anyone saw, and Ben smiles in my direction. Thankfully everyone else seems oblivious.

In a few hours' time, I've sanded, as well as learned how to change a tire and a spark plug. The basics for these guys, but for me, it's like a miracle.

"Ben needs to paint this last fender and we'll be able to assemble in the morning. What time is he coming?" Van asks me.

"I don't know. I haven't called him back."

He nods, but I can't read the expression on his face. He again remains stoic.

I grab my phone from my pocket and text David.

Me: I'm sorry I haven't returned your call. I lost my phone, but then finally found it. What time are you arriving tomorrow?

Within seconds he replies.

David: I'll be there the day after tomorrow. My car better be ready.

I hand my phone over to Van so he can see for himself.

He nods again.

I can't take the vagueness from him any longer.

"Can you say something?"

"What do you want me to say? Your husband is coming to pick up his car."

I roll my eyes, but I don't want to get into it while people can hear us.

"I'm going to bed."

"I've got a few more hours of work. I don't expect to be sleeping at the apartment tonight."

"Fine," I say and wish everyone else a good night. Callie tells me she'll call me in the morning.

Once inside I feel like crying. What a day and night? Van's a roller-coaster ride, to say the least. I need help figuring out my next step, and there's only one person I trust. Andrew.

"Hey, Emmy!"

"Andrew, it's so good to hear your voice. How are things with the Dawson's?"

"Weird. This has been the strangest trip. We've been everywhere in Europe. Cell phone service is non-existent. It's like they're purposely keeping me away from home. But after the last time I talked with you, I'm more worried about you than ever. What's going on?"

"I took your advice."

"What advice would that be?" I can almost hear his smile over the phone.

"I'm living. I'm ready to leave David."

He coughs. "What?"

"I am. I've learned so much about myself and realized that I don't want to feel guilty over something I couldn't control, and I don't want to live my life paying for it. I was shown how I should be treated. It's as if I've been living with a black cloth over my face, and it's been stripped away, revealing a bright blue sky."

"Van?"

"What?"

"Is that bright blue sky Van?"

"He's part of it, yes." My face flames at being caught. "But it isn't that, it's everyone. They make me feel alive and wanted and part of something important."

"David's coming the day after tomorrow. The Dawson's aren't going to make this easy, in fact, I doubt they'll let you go at all."

"They hate me. I don't care about my career or my reputation. I don't need it. I can't live like that anymore. My freedom is worth more than all the money in the world."

"Yes! I am so happy to finally hear you say it. I'm heading back tonight. I'll tell Mr. Dawson that I should help David with the retrieval of the car. I don't think he'll object since he's done with his meeting, and the only thing on his agenda for the next two days is getting piss drunk and fucking his mistress."

"Of course. I'll let you know what my plan is, but right now, I'm going to get some sleep. I've got a lot of planning to do tomorrow."

"You sure do. Just be prepared for anything, Emmy. I'm not sure what they're going to do when they find out about Van."

"They aren't going to." At least, I'm going to do anything to prevent that from happening.

28

—·—

I can't sleep. My mind won't quiet long enough for my nerves to calm and my eyes to shut. Plus, Van's still working on that damn car. Everyone else has gone for the night. I watched car after car leave from his window.

Slipping on my bra and shorts and taking a quick glance in the mirror, I take a chance that Van may want to talk to me. I can't take the silence any longer.

Approaching the parking lot, I double-check to make sure no one else is here. It doesn't take long to spot Van wiping down a tool with a cloth—or shop rag, seeing as I've been corrected at least a dozen times today. I learned how methodically he organizes his tools, and how he'll cut anyone who misplaces one of them. His words, not mine.

"Hey," I call out, but he doesn't respond, so I repeat it. He slams the drawer shut.

"Hi," he finally responds, almost sounding bored.

"Almost done?" I say cheerfully, hoping to lighten his mood.

"Yeah, just cleaning up." Van picks up more tools to busy himself. He seems to be avoiding me.

To hell with this...I can't stand here any longer and be ignored and not touch this man. The tension between us is making me sick. I don't want to feel this way around him. I'm not even sure what's causing him to act this way. He's been hot and cold all day. When everyone was here earlier and we were fixing the car, he acted as if nothing was wrong, but now...he can't even look at me.

His back is to me, so I do what feels like the most natural thing in the world to me, I wrap my arms around his waist, hug him, and rest my head against his back. *How can he smell so good when he's been working out here all day?*

He tenses, but I squeeze him, and he relaxes. I want him to know I want to be here with him. "You're going to get dirty if you keep leaning up against me."

"I don't care."

Van slams the drawer shut, spinning around but not breaking our connection. He brings his arms around me, holding me close to him.

"Are you okay?" I ask, not sure about the answer I'm going to get.

He sighs. "I don't want you to leave, and I don't know if you're coming back." His honesty takes me by surprise, but makes me hopeful that he does care for me. Now's my chance to let him know how I feel.

"I'm only going back to get a few things and to end some things I've been working on for my cosmetic line. It's my line, and I've been making sure that all of the things I've created can't be touched by the Dawson's. I know we haven't talked about us, but when I finish there, I'd like to come back here—with you."

Resting his head on mine, he hugs me tighter. "I'd love for you to stay with me. I can't give you everything you're used to, but I'll do my best to treat you right, make you feel special, you'll be my priority and I'll do my very best to be worthy of you. I've never had anyone do what you did for me today. If it wasn't for you, Teddy would have had everyone on his side. I couldn't prove it, but you could, and you didn't back down until they listened."

"Worthy of me? I've never met someone as caring as you are. Every time I've needed you, even if I didn't realize it, you were there for me. You're great to your friends, your granddad, and especially this whole situation with your brother. Kindness and forgiveness aren't something I'm used to."

I catch him blushing. "Come on, let's get you to bed."

"I was hoping we could, um, maybe..." I can't believe I'm even thinking of this, let alone going to ask him. "Never mind."

"What?" He leans back and gives me a stern look but doesn't let go. "Come on, something's brewing in that sexy mind of yours and I'm intrigued by it."

I wet my lips, trying to make the words come out easier. "The car's finished, right?"

"Almost...why?"

"I've never rode in it, and I think it's extremely sexy that you can race cars."

"You do, huh?"

"Yes," I answer, slowly nodding, biting my lip.

He leans down, releasing my lip with his teeth. My eyes close in response and a moan escapes. "Fucking sweet, baby." He pauses, staring into my eyes, the air heating between us, as he continues, "That's what you are, but I'm not taking you for a ride in that." He nods toward David's car. "I have my own ride, and that show-off car doesn't even compare. Besides, I don't want you in anything that prick owns anymore."

"I didn't mean to upset you. I didn't even think of it like that."

"Come here." He pulls me toward the door. We walk around the back, and there's a black car shining under the light. He lets go of my hand, eagerly opening up the passenger door to let me in. I scoot in.

Another Mustang, but this one is much newer and has different seats, I'm guessing a racing seat.

"Is this your race car?"

"I race it on the streets a few times a year, mostly to hustle money, but I'd rather keep the other guys racing. It's really just a hobby, but it's Ben's and Jake's life." He turns his head toward me. "Now let me show you how fun this can be."

He puts the car in gear as I buckle my seat belt, it's not a normal one, it's more of a harness. "This is different," I say, tugging at the belt.

"Five-point harness. I'm going to introduce you to a lot of new things, baby...get ready" Van guns the pedal and the car jets forward. I hold the top of my seat belt straps for leverage. The car jerks, and I lean far to the left and then back to right. A scream escapes me. "Donovan Bradley! Ahh...slow down."

We come to the end of the driveway, he slams the brakes and I whip forward. A huge smile rests on his lips, causing my matching smile. We drive in a comfortable silence. He turns off onto a deserted road.

His hand reaches my knee, causing a chill to race up my spine and heat at the spot where he's touching me. He squeezes my knee. "Are you ready?"

"Didn't you already show me how fast and crazy you can drive?"

"Awe...come on, darlin', that was just a little parking lot fun. Now we're going to drag race, but we have to pretend. You see, normally there's a guy with a flashlight, or a half-naked chick with a flag, who tells me when to stomp down, but I want you to count to ten and then hold on, pretty girl."

"Okay." I take a deep breath, giving my heart a second to calm down. Not because I'm in a car ready to do over one-hundred miles an hour, but because he's still touching me while rubbing his thumb across my knee, making the rest of my body jealous and lonely all at the same time.

His gorgeous face lights up. "Ready?"

I swallow. "If you are?"

"Good. Let's rock."

I can't help but get excited too.

He revs the engine. I brace myself, fingers digging into the side of the seat. "Okay...give me the countdown."

I count slowly one...two...three until I close my eyes, take a deep breath and say, "Ten."

I thought we were going fast before, but this...this is exhilarating, scary, and thrilling all at one time. My head jerks back against the headrest. I want to close my eyes, but I don't. Instead, I risk a peek over at Van. He's focused on the road, bottom lip trapped by his teeth and his hands white-knuckling the wheel. It takes mere seconds for the ride to end, but one second for my heart to know for sure I love this sexy, adventurous, caring, amazing man beside me.

The straps from the seat tighten as the brakes stop us. Donovan looks over with the biggest smile, and I can't help but mimic the childlike expression on his face.

He turns in my direction. "That was fucking amazing."

It takes a second for me to find my voice. "That was crazy."

"Crazy good?" he asks, hopeful.

"I loved it!"

Van releases his belt and leans in to kiss me. I'm trapped and he takes advantage of the situation. His kiss is forceful at first, but then as I meet his pace, he slows down, really showing me how he feels. His hand slides over my thighs, then across my waist to release the seat belt. As it does, I pounce. I immediately grab his hair and pull him closer, deepening our kiss.

"Baby...stop." I freeze as my stomach plunges. "No...no, don't worry. I just don't want this to happen in my cramped car.

I let out a breath. "Where then?"

"Aren't you turning into a bad girl? Do you want to do it in here?"

My face heats, something about him makes it impossible to keep my thoughts to myself. "I want you to fuck me on the hood of this car." I flash back to him with Kelly dancing on the hood of Ben's race car.

He swallows, almost choking. "Jesus Christ, you're unreal."

"Am I?"

"Get the fuck out of this car, now." He growls. I can't find the handle quick enough. As I fumble, the door opens. Van reaches his hand out. "Come on. I can't take any dirtier talk from you. Here I thought you were so proper and a prude, but you're the most seductive girl I've ever met."

Van yanks me out of the seat and lifts me up as my legs wrap around his waist. I rock against him, and he moves us over to the hood of the car. He sets me down and attacks me in the most delightful, erotic way.

He yanks down my shorts; all while his lips never leave mine. The passion between us is like nothing I've ever felt before, and I never want it to end. I lean back on the hood of his car and live a fantasy I never knew I wanted until I met Van.

****

I pull up my shorts while my wits return. Glancing around, I finally notice that we're in the middle of nowhere. Thankfully, no one is around. Van buttons up his jeans.

"What's that look for?" he asks, but I can't see the look on his face in the dark.

"I didn't even think of people seeing us."

"Do you really think I'd share you or that moment with anyone? Trust me, babe, I'll never let anyone see you coming for me."

I blush, looking down. Embarrassed for the first time at my loss of control.

"Hey." He lifts my chin with his finger. "Don't do that."

"What?"

"Worry. We're attracted to each other. You make me feel things I've never felt, and I'm not sharing you with anyone, in any way." He grabs my hand and leads me to the passenger side of the car. "Let's get out of here."

29

Waking up next to him is nothing short of heaven. I roll over to kiss him on the cheek. "Good morning."

"Am I dreaming?" he asks, his voice husky.

"Why would you say that?"

"Because you're in my bed and I don't have to pretend like we're friends, or that I was just being polite by letting you sleep on a comfy mattress instead of the couch."

"You aren't in heaven, but I'm in your bed." I kiss him on the cheek again and roll over, but he yanks me close to him.

"I'm hungry. I'm going to make you breakfast," Van says against my neck while placing gentle kisses on my skin.

"Maybe you'd enjoy something a little sweeter." I rock against his erection.

"I always want something sweet," Van says as his length rubs against me. The doorbell rings, stopping me mid-rock. I didn't even know he had a doorbell. Who would be ringing it at this hour? Looking at the clock, it is only six-fifteen in the morning. Van groans beside me, sweeping me up against his side. Something about spooning with him makes me think I'm the one who reached heaven.

"Are you going to just ignore that?""Mmhmm..." But he doesn't even open his eyes."What if it's about Granddad?" He opens one eye, lifting part of his mouth. "It's not. Whoever it is wouldn't ring the bell, they'd just barge in." Van squeezes me tighter. "It's probably someone selling Bibles or encyclopedias or something," he mutters, kissing my back.

I chuckle. "I don't even think they make encyclopedias anymore, let alone sell them door to door." Van starts to say something, but the ringing stops and turns to knocking as it gets louder, and more aggressive, and then turns into banging.

"Damn it!" he growls. "Stay here, I'll get it. I don't want anyone seeing you naked." He does this silly thing where he covers his open mouth, wearing a look of mock horror.

Van slips on his boxer briefs, while I admire his backside, wanting to pinch myself at the fact that I actually had sex with this man and woke up in his arms.Just in case it's one of his friends, I grab his t-shirt off of the floor to cover myself with it. I can't see who it is, but I hear Van saying something. I pick up a man's voice, then I recognize who it is...David.

"Some guy named Ace said this is your place and Emerson would be here." His voice is polite as ever, but I know better.

"She's not here. I couldn't tell you where she's at. And if you don't mind, it's too fucking early, man. I'll be at the shop around eight. We can discuss your car then."

"No...I want to see it now, and I want to know where my wife is!" he demands, his menacing voice sending ice down my spine. I tense under the covers. I wish he wouldn't have said I wasn't here. I could have dressed and acted as if I was sleeping. He doesn't know there's only one bedroom. I can still make that happen.

Sliding out of bed, I throw on my shorts, trying to find my courage to show my face. My knees feel weak and even a little shaky. Why do I let him make me feel that way?

"I'll see you at the shop around eight." Van slams the door in his face and turns the lock.

I start down the stairs as Van turns to walk up the steps. "I told you to stay in bed."

"David's not going away, I know that for a fact!" He shrugs, underestimating the seriousness of the situation. "You don't understand, he never gets told no."

"I just did. Now get your sweet ass in bed and let's finish what we started."

"No, Van. I can't. He's going to find some way to get in here."

"There isn't a way. Quit worrying about it." He sounds annoyed.

I stomp down the stairs past him. "I'm going to get a shower and then make my way to the shop. You should too."

He spins around, sighing at me. "Where are you going to say you were? A hotel? A friend's? Outer space? Come on, Ems. I won't let him near you. Look at you, you're scared shitless. Your whole attitude just changed, even your face is pale—all because of him."

Van walks in my direction, but I can't have him touch me right now. If I do, I'll let him change my mind, and I can't do that. I need to get out of here. I move to the bathroom and shut the door. No, more like slam the door in his face. Guilt overtakes me as the disappointment crosses his beautiful face.

Leaning my back against the closed door, I inhale some extra air into my lungs. David is here. He's going to find out about Van and me, and then he's going to ruin both of us. Am I ready to fight him and his family?

No, the answer is no. Now that the possibility is here staring me right in the face. I don't think I can. Van can't help me. He can't stop them. I can't stop them.

Van knocks. "Ems, stop this. He's not going to find out about us. Come back to bed."

"I can't, Van. Just let me be. I'll be out soon."

"Ems...don't do this. Don't let him scare you away from me." There's a pleading in his voice from the other side of the door that tears at every fiber of my being. The last thing I want is to go, but I have no other choice.

Turning on the water to the shower, I undress and let the hot water run down my cold body. Cold because of the way I treated Van. He cares for me. David's been here for only a few minutes, and I'm already pushing Van away.

Showering for at least fifteen minutes, the water runs cold, and I can't prolong getting out any longer. When the water stops, the voices begin.

"Why would you tell him that?" Van says, I can barely make it out.

I open the door slightly to listen in on who he's talking to. They answer him, but I can't tell who it is. Hurrying into my clothes, I try concentrating on their voices, but it sounds as if they've moved.

I pad down the hall as quietly as I can muster. The doors open. Van must be outside, so I follow the muffled voices until Ace and Van come into view. Again, they're standing toe to toe. "Why are you doing this to her?"

"She needs to know about your history, dude, before she leaves her husband for you."

"You mean before she picks me instead of you."

"You know as well as I do you're not the kind of guy who settles down, or who is a one-woman kind of guy. We both know you fuck everything in sight."

"You fucker!" he screams, grabbing Ace by his shirt. "You know nothing about me or her. I would never do that to her. And you sending her asshole husband over here to catch us makes you a piece of shit!" The words fly freely, but menacingly low.

That son of a bitch, I want to scream at Ace and ask him why he would do that and how he knows about us, but I also know that no matter how David treats me, I shouldn't be seeing Van behind his back. I need to tell David, and now I better tell Ace that I want to be with Van so he can stop this.

I trudge out the door. "Van, stop!"

Both of their heads spin in my direction. "Ems, you need to stop seeing him. Your husband is at Picture Rocks Inn. He asked me to find you and I told him I would. Unfortunately, I knew exactly where you would be. You need to go."

"No, I'm not going with you or David or anyone. Yes, I have feelings for Van, and I'm married and it's wrong, but I can't live a lie anymore. I don't love David, he's horrible to me and blames me for everything. From this point on, David, Van or I are none of your business. I appreciate your concern, but I don't need your help."

"You're being foolish. He doesn't care about you, he doesn't care about anyone but himself."

Van lets go of his grip, pushing him away. "You need to leave."

Ace nods. "I should have left a long time ago. Good luck, Ems," he says with disgust. "You're going to need it."

Van and I both watch as Ace gets in his car, then does a burnout to emphasize his point.

"He's wrong about me," Van says quietly beside me.

"I know," I say back, touching his arm in reassurance. "I need to find David. I have to tell him about us.

"Will you be back?" He looks up at me with the saddest eyes I've ever seen, like he expects my answer to be no.

"Yes, of course." Standing in front of him, I grab onto his shoulders. "I don't care what Ace, or David, or whoever says. I'm happy when I'm with you, and I want to see where this goes between us."

That puts a smile on his lips. The same lips I want to kiss, so I do. He crushes my body against his. As we turn to make our way back into the apartment, a cough interrupts. At first, I think it could be Ace, but the freshly colored bright purple hair tells me I'm wrong.

"Mr. Dawson has called the shop three times trying to find her." She rolls her eyes in my direction. "You two better come up with a plan because he'll be here soon."

"He just left. What did you tell him?" he asks her.

She crosses her arms over her chest "As much as I'd love to tell her husband that she's been screwing you, I don't want to hurt you, Van." Her voice becomes strangled. "I'm also sorry about the whole Teddy situation."

"I'm not screwing her, but thanks for keeping your opinion to yourself. She's headed over now to talk to him." I give Van a small smile and let go of his hand. As I walk away from him, Violet asks to speak with him in private.

Thankfully, I'm going to miss whatever crap she decides to spit at him, but I am going to have to speak with David.

30

Ben offers to drive me the five minutes it takes to get to the Picture Rocks Inn. I thought it would be best if Van didn't come. But no matter the outcome of today, I'd never trade the time I've shared with Van.

He doesn't say much, but as we reach the large white house with the picture-perfect wraparound porch and welcoming rocking chairs. Ben brings the car to a stop. "I don't know what your plan is, but Van's crazy about you. I've never seen him this way about anyone. I know you've heard some pretty shitty things about him, but he's a decent guy, and a fucking awesome friend. So, whatever you decide, I hope you don't fuck him over."

This is the most he's ever spoken to me, and it has taken me by complete surprise. "I won't."

"Let's hope not."

I exit the car and a quiet voice inside me whispers, "Me too."

I don't have to wait long to see David. He's sitting at a small table drinking a cup of coffee. He stands, unbuttoning a button on his jacket. His eyes widen as he sees me. "Emerson, darling, you look...different."

I should, I'm not wearing a suit or dress. Instead, I have on jeans and a tank top.

"How are you, David?"

He kisses my cheek. "I'm well, darling. I've missed you."

I bite my bottom lip to hold in a chuckle. He's so full of it right now. "Have you now?"

"Of course, I have." He gestures to the other chair at the table. "Please, sit."

Looking at the vacant chair, I yield to him and sit.

"Did you have a nice flight?" I ask, making small talk because that's what we usually do.

"I did." He leans in toward me in a hushed voice. "I don't like this new look you've got going, though. I take it you wanted to blend in."

Rolling my eyes at him, I feel a sense of courage that I haven't felt in a long time. "My look is just fine. The car is close to being finished."

He ignores me and asks his own question, "Where have you been?" His eyes narrow, waiting for my answer.

"I've been staying with Donovan."

"What do you mean, you've been staying with him? I was there this morning and you were not. Not to mention how this makes our marriage look."

"There were no openings here, at the Inn, when I arrived. Look, I don't want to get into this with you in the lobby. Can we talk in private, maybe in your room?"

"Let's go."

I follow him up the stairs. Thankfully, it's only two floors and we aren't stuck in an elevator together. My stomach starts to protest as we get closer to his room. I should have probably stayed in public with him. After all, I'm telling him that I'm leaving him.

David slides the key into the lock and opens the door, letting me in first.

The room is just as I would expect. Old south, flowery comforter, crisp white linen curtains, and white wicker furniture. David takes off his jacket and throws it over the arm of a chair.

His proper demeanor changes as he strides over to the bed and sits. "So, what do you need to tell me...in private?"

I'm finding it hard to talk now that he's here in front of me. I swallow trying to find my voice. "I... uh..."

David huffs, leaning back on the bed supported by his elbow. "Out with it, Emerson. We need to get back, and the sooner we do, the quicker I can be out of this dump."

Taking in a deep breath, I quickly speak the words I never thought I would. "I'm not coming back with you." The rest of my breath leaves with the words, and I almost need to bend over to regain my composure.

He leans forward, supporting himself with his elbows now on his knees. He puts his finger up to his mouth. "You're fucking him?"

"I'm not fucking anyone. I'm not happy, and neither are you. We don't love each other."

He lets out a cruel laugh. "You think I ever loved you." He huffs. "Love has nothing to do with our marriage. We're married because our parents gained money from our union. I gained money, and so did you. Then you had to go and ruin my life. I'm never letting you out of this marriage."

He stands, taking a few steps, and reaches me. He's so close, I can feel his breath on my face. Dread starts to creep over my skin. His eyes darken as he watches me. I know that look. Although he's not drunk, he's far worse, he's upset with me.

"I don't want your money or your family's money. I just want to be happy. I'm sorry for what happened to you, but it was an accident. I've tried to make it up to you, but there's nothing I can do to fix it."

"Fix it...you think I want you to fix me? No, I want you to be miserable. You don't get it, do you?" He snarls. "I don't want you to be happy. If you leave me, I'm going to do everything in my power to make your life hell. And that mechanic...I'll destroy him."

My knees go weak at his threat. "David...he hasn't done anything wrong. I've only stayed at his place. He's been nothing but a gentleman." I can't tell him I have feelings for Van, the truth will only add more fuel to the fire. I can't risk what he'll do to Van.

"You can't lie to me. Look at you." He grabs the strap of my tank top, snapping it. "You look like a whore. God knows you can't fuck like one, but you sure as hell look the part. The greasy mechanic only sees dollar signs."

I go to turn, but he grabs my arm to stop me. "You're not going anywhere. I'll send someone to get your things, and I'm sending you home. Now!"

"David...please, let's be rational. If I just leave without notice, they're going to think something is wrong. It's better to keep up appearances, don't you think?" My voice shakes.

"Do you really think these mongrels give two shits about you?"

"I think you give a shit about your reputation," I spit at him and add, "You can leave with your car and without me."

He stands, laughing. "You leave me and I'll make you hurt in every way that you've made me hurt. You don't deserve to be happy."

I suck in a breath, not sure what to say. I'm shocked, I knew he'd be upset, but this...this is my worst fear come true.

David must notice my reaction because he walks toward me, placing a cold hand on my face. "Now that you know how serious I am, let me just explain to you how this is going to go just in case you aren't understanding. First, I'll start here with this little town, especially since you seem to be so popular here. I wasn't here more than three seconds and people were talking about Ems and how beautiful she is and sweet and fun. Honestly, I couldn't believe they were talking about you."

I cringe as his fingers glide over my face. He's even worse than usual. He's completely sober and still acting as if the devil has possessed his soul. "Next, I'm going to destroy those trash friends of yours business. Of course, I'll make sure my car is on its way home before. And next...well, this is my favorite part of the whole plan...I'm going to ruin your reputation. Just imagine, the selfish whore who cheated on her poor disabled husband, then I'll ruin your career along with your family...and then take all your money."

"We signed a prenup, and you've been cheating for years. You can't touch me."

"I can and I will."

"You are the one who has been unfaithful and mean, and you've never loved me."

"I've never admitted to cheating, but there are some people in this town who can attest to the fact that you may have been sleeping with another man. I spoke with a gentleman named Ace. Strange name, but he was willing to tell me what I wanted to know." He threatens. "You'll get some, but you won't get what you're entitled to." He sweeps his finger away from my face and turns away from me. David opens the door to his room, exposing the hallway to my freedom. "We're finished here." He pauses, "Unless you're changing your mind?" His eyebrow raises.

I don't hesitate, taking less than a second to leave. Not looking back, I run as fast as I can. Getting away from him, that life. I don't care what he does, he can't make me stay with him anymore. I won't, no matter his threats. Nothing can make me stay.

Taking a left at the corner of Liberty and Vine, I keep the same pace. Ignoring the curious looks of the faces of the people I pass. Van's his next target, and if I'm not there to stop David, God only knows what will happen. I reach for my phone. Damn it! I left my purse at the hotel. I can't go back.

I run, the sandals giving my poor soles no cushion, but I continue on until I don't recognize where I am. I'm not sure where the shop is or how close I am to it. A gray-haired woman on her knees in front of her garden glances up from her flowers, tilting her head. She calls, "Dear! Dear! Are you all right?" She stands, concern etched on her face, coming in my direction as I'm hunched over, trying to catch my breath.

"Yes." I breathe. "No. I don't know."

"No?" The stranger lightly touches my elbow. "Come, dear, sit down."

I let my knees give, the grass jabbing at my skin. Placing my hands out in front of me for support, I finally say, "How close am I to Bradley Restoration?" using all the breath I have left.

"Bradley Restoration is three blocks over. I can drive you over if you'd like. I don't think you can continue to run in those shoes." Glancing down at my shoes, only one of the four straps is attached to the sole of the shoe.

"No...I'll be fine." Ripping the shoe off one foot, then the other, I take off again, thanking the woman, and try to remain in the grass as much as possible. The sidewalk is hot as hell, but I have to get to Van before David does.

Sweet relief washes over me as I see the Bradley Lane street sign. "Thank God," I huff out.

I slow down my pace, taking in my surroundings. There are so many damn cars in the parking lot and around the shop. I have no way of telling if David is here or not.

31

Van looks up from the Bugatti and smiles, but when he sees me his smile falters. "What happened?" Van asks.

I shake my head, unable to form words through my rapid heartbeat. "He's going to ruin you," I say quietly.

"Come on. Let's go talk in my office." He throws his rag down on the hood of the Bugatti and glances over at Ben who gives a nod of recognition.

His hands on my back, guiding me along. Reaching the office, he closes the door behind us. Immediately, I spin, bringing him close to me. Our lips crash and we kiss, feverishly. With each swipe of our tongues, he calms the hurricane brewing inside me.

Pulling away, his eyes rake over my features. Touching my cheek with the side of his hand, he asks, "What happened?"

"He doesn't want me to be happy. He knows I have feelings for you. Ace told him about us. He's going to do everything I told you. What are we going to do?"

Van swallows. "Are you staying?"

"Yes. I promise, I'm not going back to that."

His lip quirks up. "Then we'll get through this together. First, let's get this fucking car out of here. And deal with the rest later."

He wraps me up in his arms, I inhale his smell, calming and loving and home.

Leaving the office, we find the guys polishing the wheels of the Bugatti. It looks even better than when David first brought it home.

"Enough!" he yells over the tools buzzing. "We're done."

"We still have the other side to do," Jake protests, not even looking up at him.

"No, that's it. Push this motherfucker out of *my* garage now!"

"What's up?" Ben stands, confusion marring his face.

"I want this out of my garage."

Jake and Ben spring into action, and within minutes it's being pushed outside into the parking lot.

I stare at the car and it looks beautiful. I never saw it that way before, but now I know what it takes to make something that was so broken so alive again.

Van slips his hand around my waist, kissing my cheek, making me giddy. "I've never been so relieved to have a car out of my garage. But I'd never give up a second of it being here. It brought me you." I kiss him back, knowing I feel the same way.

"Wow," Jake says. "Is this the official coming out as a couple?"

Someone clears their throat, halting our kiss.

"Mr. Bradley…" a familiar voice booms. "Please, by all means, answer the man's question."

Van and I jump at the same time David speaks behind us.

Van lets go of my waist and stands. "Mr. Dawson." He takes my hand, pulling me up to his side, hand firmly placed again around my waist.

"It seems you have more than just my car in your hands."

"We'll load it on the trailer that was sent here earlier this week, then you can be on your way."

David laughs. "You think I'm just going to let you have her. Regardless of what you think, she's still my wife."

Ignoring his comment, Van tells him, "I'll get your keys."

"Do you honestly think I'm going to leave here peacefully?"

Ben stands, stepping closer. I can feel his presence behind me.

"No, I don't, but I'm trying to make this as easy as possible. I'm not asking for you to pay more than you've already paid. All I'm asking is for you to take your car and leave."

"And leave my wife with you?"

"The only thing I'm certain of is that she doesn't want to go home with you. After you leave, then it's her choice of where she goes." Van's voice is low but strong and fierce.

"She doesn't have a choice in anything. She seems to have forgotten that."

Ben pipes up. "Van, why don't you get some straps. I'll load up the car and we can get Mr. Dawson on his way."

Before I can react, the room shrinks as more of Van's friends surround us.

"Nah, I want to make sure this job is finished."

Ben practically growls at Van's response.

David scoffs, turning away from us and to his driver, Jones. "Jones, we're done here. Make sure Mr. Bradley is paid in complete for his work. Although, we are probably even on any additional repair charges since he's also been fucking the whore I've provided for him."

Before I can react, Van flies from beside me and directly at David, but Jones is there first, pushing Van back. "You motherfucker. I'm going to kill you. Don't you ever disrespect her again!"

David straightens his suit jacket, scoffing a laugh. "Jones, it's time."

He turns and walks toward his car. Jones shrugs Van loose, giving him a little push, but Van doesn't relent, he starts to charge at Jones again, but this time Ben puts his body between them. "Van, stop!"

Jones trots over to the car, opening the door. David turns to me and says, "You'll be sorry," before ducking inside, thankfully disappearing from my view.

I'm frozen in place. He's right I'll be sorry. Part of me wanted to yell, 'wait, stop, I'll go,' but I know that's only the fear talking. Van breaks free from Ben and turns to me. He grabs me in his arms, shushing me. I didn't even realize I was crying.

"We'll load it on their trailer. You go home. Both of you. We got this," Ben calls from behind us.

Van nods. "Let's get out of here."

He guides us outside, toward the house. Luckily, David's car is gone. The only thing left is the truck and trailer transporting the car back.

Once inside the apartment, Van pulls me close, wrapping his arms tightly around me. "I'm so sorry. I didn't want it to go down like that." He kisses the top of my head.

"It's over, that's all that matters. Can we just go lie down for a while?"

"Yeah, sure. Close your eyes and get some rest. We'll go visit Granddad when you wake up."

****

We step inside Granddad's house. The smell of tacos cooking saturates my nose. Teddy steps away from the stove. "He only eats my cooking now. You've been replaced."

Van moves to sit beside his grandfather. "You'd never replace me, would you?" he asks Granddad, almost pouting.

"Nah, I love you shitheads the same. Although, this one…" He wags his thumb at me. "This one I might love more."

I know my face is turning a bright shade of embarrassment. I love that I had such a horrible day, but I'm ending it with people who are my home.

Teddy hands Van a plate and then me. "Thanks," we reply in unison.

"It's the least I can do after everything that happened."

"I'm just glad Granddad has someone with him twenty-four-seven. I don't even have to look at my app…that much." Van winks at Teddy.

Thankfully Teddy agreed to his punishment, which isn't really much punishment at all, hanging out with his Granddad. He lucked out; instead of getting jail time, he's now a caregiver.

"How did the pick-up go?" Teddy asks while shoveling a taco into his mouth.

"He got his car back, paid me in full, but it didn't go as it should have." Van glosses over the important part where he almost beat the crap out of David. He would have been in jail right now.

Granddad rocks in his La-Z-Boy chair. "So are you divorcing your husband now that you're still here and the car isn't?"

"I am. He's not going to be easy on me, but I can't be married to him any longer."

He nods and continues to rock but doesn't say anything else. We all silently watch the TV, but I'm lost in my thoughts. I hate the look Granddad just gave me. It sort of said, "I know what you did?"

Did he really know? Does anyone know, no…only me. I didn't leave David for him. Van helped me see that I wasn't happy, and being away from the Dawson's, and even my parents, gave me the courage to leave.

After a while, soft snores fill the room. Every Bradley man is fast asleep. All with their heads back and mouths open. I can't help but giggle to myself. I take the opportunity to finish the dishes.

The sink is full. Teddy's food was delicious, but he's a messy cook. Pots, pans, and dishes are piled up high on the counter. It doesn't take all this to make tacos.

Scrubbing at the grime, I occasionally glance at the Bradley men. They're a great family, and even though Teddy and Van have not been getting along, they are now, and it makes me smile.

A loud crash pulls my attention from the pans, headlights flash by the kitchen window and tires screech along the pavement. Smoke billows from the store window that must have smashed. As I strain to see more, flames roar furiously in the showroom of Bradley Restoration.

Rushing away from the sink, I shake Van awake. I don't want to disturb Granddad, but I don't know what else to do. "Huh?" He jumps.

"There's a fire."

"What?" He scrubs his eyes. "Here?"

"The showroom!"

"Shit!" Springing out of his seat, he punches Teddy in the arm. "Get up, now! There's a fire!" Gritting his teeth, probably not wanting to alarm Granddad.

Van runs out of the house and toward the shop. Yanking the phone from his pocket, I overhear him telling the person on the other line the address. He frantically runs to the garage area. I don't think I've ever seen anyone run so fast in my life. I try and keep up with him, but I can't. Van disappears for a moment, my heart thuds in my chest. He can't possibly think he's going to put the fire out, can he? Seconds later he answers my question when he emerges with a fire extinguisher.

"Van! Don't go in there!" I scream, but he doesn't listen. "Wait for the fire truck!"

Starting to shake, I hold myself together. Van can't go in there. I yell for him as he passes by, but he doesn't stop, running to the glass door and kicking at the main entrance of the showroom. His boot hits the glass, again and again. Glass crashes around him, causing him to lose his footing and stumble back. He stands up again, this time he aims the extinguisher at the blaze. It doesn't do any good. The fire keeps roaring.

Teddy moves from beside me and runs toward Van. "Stop! You're going to get yourself killed. It's just a fucking store. Stop!"

Teddy tackles Van, and the foam shoots straight in the air forming a cloud around them. I can't see, so I run closer. It's so hot that my hands come up instinctively, shielding my face. I can't get as close as they are. "Van!" Panic overcomes me. I can't see where they're at because of the smoke. I can only hear coughing in the distance. I scream for him again.

There is a break in the foggy air, and Teddy emerges with his arm around Van's waist while the other is holding Van's arm that's slung around his neck.

"Oh my God, is he okay?"

Van coughs. "I'm fine. I'm fine," he promises, sitting up as he wipes the soot from his face.

Teddy lays him on the gravel parking lot, dropping beside him and rolling on his back. Van's face is covered in black ash from the fire. He coughs while trying to prop himself up. "Don't. Lie back and try to catch your breath."

He doesn't listen and fights to get up. The showroom is now completely engulfed in flames. My heart breaks as I glance at the expression of loss on Van's face. "Where the fuck is the fire truck?"

As he says the words, the sirens blare off in the distance. Turning around to see how close they are, I spy Granddad sitting in a chair from the porch. My heart breaks again as he's wearing the same look as Van.

32

— • —

The firemen reel in the last of the hoses. The lights are still flashing on the vehicles; red and blue swirl around us. I'm starting to get extremely dizzy, overwhelmed, and coming down from my adrenaline high. I look away hoping that a seizure doesn't happen.

Van remains standing next to me as person after person approaches him with questions. His jaw is tense, his face is still covered in soot, and he hasn't focused on anything other than his dreams crumbling in front of him.

"Thank God you guys had sprinklers in the garage and offices. No telling what might have blown up." The gray-haired police officer tells him. "We found this purse and phone by the door. Do you know who it belongs to?"

Recognizing the black crossbody purse, I nod. "It's mine."

"Did you leave it outside, it wasn't touched by the fire."

"There it is, you must have," Van chimes in, like he's happy to see it.

I take the purse from the officer's hand and peek inside. My phone is there along with the rest of my belongings. I know that I left it in David's room. Did he leave it here when he left?

"The showroom's pretty new. I'm not sure why the sprinkler system didn't go off," the officer blabbers on and gives a small laugh. "Just my luck. Good thing we have insurance."

The officer removes his hat and then places it back on his head. "Do you have any cameras that would have picked up the guy she thinks she saw?"

Van glares at the officer. "She has a name. It's Emerson Dawson, and she saw a man get out of a car and throw a Molotov cocktail into my fucking business. And yes, I fucking have it on camera. My guy's going through our surveillance footage right now and he'll give it to you as soon as he can." Frustrated, Van grabs my elbow and leads us away from the officer toward his group of friends.

"Van...are you okay?" Violet asks, her sincere concern for him is apparent and makes me jealous. I shouldn't be, but I am. She's looking at a person on the brink of losing his business, and so am I. She wraps her arm around his neck, ignoring the fact that he's still touching me.

Shrugging her away, he answers, "I'm fine. We have insurance. No one got hurt. Let these guys do their jobs and we'll deal with it in the morning. I'm headed to bed, and all of you should too. There's nothing left for us to do." Violet backs away, scowling at me.

"I think we should stay. I'm sure we can do something," Jake adds.

"No, there isn't. It was arson. It's the police's job now. Besides, we can't get back in there until we're given the okay. Just go home and go to bed." He nods, not letting anyone give him a response, moving his hand from my elbow and interlacing it with my fingeres, tugging me along.

"Van! Wait!"

"What?" He turns and yells back at Violet.

"Are you fucking her or something?"

Van lets go of my hand and closes the gap between him and Violet. I stay where I'm at, but he's in her face. "Yes. For anyone who thinks my life is any of their business, yes. I care for Emerson, and I have feelings for her. She left her husband today and she's staying here until she decides what's next. If you have a fucking problem with that, I don't give a fuck!"

Even in the dark, I can see her eyes bulge and her mouth open. He spins back around, taking my hand again, giving it a quick squeeze.

He stood up for me, for us, and I couldn't be more content. Whatever this is between us is going to be complicated, but I think as long as he's by my side, we can get through anything.

Inside the apartment, Van grabs a glass from the cupboard, filling it with water from the faucet. He takes a huge gulp, and it's gone within seconds. Watching his throat bob, thoughts of licking it and taking his mind off of this horrible night flash before my eyes.

"When did you see your purse last?"

"At the hotel."

Van takes another gulp and gently places the empty glass in the sink.

"He must have brought it with him when he picked up his car." Giving an explanation that I can only hope is true, because I can't admit what I really think happened, I shake my head because I know he brought it when he started the fire.

"I'm getting a shower first." He kisses my forehead and stalks off toward the shower. Changing my clothes, the smell of smoke permeates my nose. "Ugh?" I whip the shirt over my head and throw it in the corner. I need a shower, too, but I'm wiped out. I can't help but think David had everything to do with this. Van hasn't said a word about suspecting David, but maybe he's afraid to admit it too.

Slipping on my nightgown, I file into the bed and cover up with the blanket. Moments later, Van walks up the stairs, water still glistening down his chest. My mouth waters at the sight. His hair freshly toweled. Roaming over his body, I want to feel him on me, in me, everywhere. I need him to wash away this day.

"You see something you like?"

Nodding slowly, I deliberately bite my lip and crook my finger in an invitation.

His face changes from playful to serious. With hooded eyes, he swipes his tongue over his bottom lip, wetting it along the way.

He stalks over to the bed, ripping his towel off and tossing it somewhere across the room. He slides over my body, and I'm unable to deny that this man is made for me. I don't care what we have to deal with, he's mine, and I'm his.

Van's lips devour mine and his hands go straight to my underwear. Tugging at them, I help him pull them down. "I need this right now. I need you to make it all go away," he whispers against my lips.

"I'll take it all away. I promise." He slides down and his soft, warm mouth places kisses along my belly. I'm about to come undone when my phone blasts a ringtone.

"Ignore it."

I do, I ignore it while his tongue dances along my skin. Lost in the sensation, the phone rings again. I try my best to ignore it, and finally the only sound is a soft moan escaping his mouth.

Ahh. This man can wreck me, destroy me, and completely obliterate me in every way. I've never felt this or had this with anyone. I've reached my heaven.

My phone vibrates beside me. Van grumbles as he moves from me to reach for my phone. "Here," he says, staring down at David's name on the screen.

I nod.

"Did you like the show?"

"What?" I ask, hearing the ice in his voice.

"I told you how this was going to go. Bit by bit," he says. "Don't worry just yet. Your boyfriend didn't get hurt this time, but this was just a warning."

He hangs up.

My throat dries waiting for Van to read what's written all over my face, to confirm what I already know.

"He did it. David was behind it. Wasn't he?"

The way Van confirms my worst nightmare hits like a wrecking ball. This is how he's going to ruin the Bradley Restoration, and he won't stop here. He's never going to stop. I left him and now he's going to make everyone pay.

The passion has melted away, followed by fear. Fear for Van, his business, his family, and for me. He won't stop at just me, everyone I know is in the path of destruction.

"Hey." Van leans over, eyes focused on me, wiping the hair from my face. I close my eyes at his touch, savoring him. He calms and soothes me in a way no one ever has. I can't explain it, nor do I want him to stop. "It's going to be fine. I'll fix everything. We'll be all right, Ems. I'm not going to fight it as long as I have you by my side."

Giving him a half-hearted smile, I agree only to appease him. He doesn't return his fingers to where they were or his mouth. The atmosphere has changed. With one little phone call, the entire night has been altered.

He lies next to me, pulls me so that our bodies are facing each other. His hand rests in my hair, moving his coarse but gentle hands, tracing my hairline around my ear. I close my eyes, savoring his touch.

A tear streams from my eye. Van's thumb wipes it away. "Shh...no worries. He got his revenge on me for taking his girl. He's done. I've got insurance, no one was hurt, and you're free of him."

"How can you be so calm about this? A fireball was thrown into your business. He could have killed you or Callie or Ben or Teddy, anyone. He destroyed your business, all those restored beautiful, one-of-a-kind cars. This isn't something to sweep under the rug or to shrug off. I've seen you worked up over much, much less. I just..."

He places his finger over my mouth. "Hush. I'm not going crazy because I deserve it."

"Van?"

"No... listen. He sent his wife here for a fucking stupid reason, but he did, and I'm so fucking glad he did. I knew you were forbidden, and I tried to resist you, but I couldn't, can't. I tried, but every time you're near me, I'm happier than I've ever been. I feel things I don't even know how to explain. Safe, content, hopeful." He sighs, "Happy."

Unable to contain the smile that comes to my lips. Another tear falls, but this time it's because of his sweet words.

"I took you from him. I wanted to show you what a life with me could be like. What a life without rules, obligations, or worries could be like. It was wrong and it's not something I'm proud of, but I know if he would try to take you away from me...after I've had you. I'd move heaven and earth and destroy everything in my path to make you mine. I love you, Ems. You don't have to say it back or even feel it. It's the only word I have to tell you how I feel."

I move to cover his mouth with mine. Feelings of peace, contentment, happiness, and love overwhelm my senses. I love this man and his confession. He thinks he should be punished for wanting to be with me. I know all about living with punishment for your actions, accepting punishment because you feel you deserve it for something you want, searching for something to make you happy, when all you really want is to be loved.

"I love you too. I do."

He kisses me softly, love pours from his kiss. It's nothing that I've ever felt before. He loves me, he does. And I love him, and because I love him more than I've ever loved anyone, that's why I need to leave. David isn't going to stop at just a fire; he's going to keep going until he destroys my life and everyone around me.

Van's head rests on my chest. His breathing slows, his body weight becomes heavier as he relaxes, falling asleep. I'm so thankful he was able to fall asleep so fast. I'm so thankful he wasn't hurt, or anyone else. He has insurance and can rebuild, but I've known David and the Dawson's most of my life, and they aren't going to stop here.

Unable to keep my mind from racing, I go over the events in my head.   I can't let him hurt Van more than he has, or let Van blame himself or think he deserves to have all his hard work ripped from him. Maybe if I put some distance between me and Van, David will back off. I can get my affairs in order and maybe come back to Van someday. If he'll still have me.

In his sleep he adjusts, squeezing me tighter. My throat dries. I have to leave him before he wakes or he'll never let me go, and I won't be able to make myself leave. I decide to savor at least another hour or so with him.

When my time is up, I'm going to have to break his heart and destroy mine in the process.

****

At three-seventeen, it's time for me to leave. Van doesn't move as I slip from under him. He moans but doesn't wake up. I decide to only take one bag with me. Leaving all of my clothes and shoes. With my duffle bag in hand, I pad quietly down the steps. Taking the only thing that I want, I open the cupboard and take one of the matching *'fuck off until I have a cup of joe'* mugs. It's silly, but at least I'll have something of his.

The night breeze chills my skin as I close the door behind me, careful not to make a noise. I've contemplated a million different ways to leave, what I would say, and then take it all back, but I can't. I'm not going to have Van hate me. If I don't leave, David won't stop. It'll ruin him, and then he'll blame me and regret ever knowing me. I can't live through that, especially not with Van. If there's a chance he could hate me while being with me, I'll avoid that hell at all costs.

The headlights come into view. Padding down the steps, I wait for the car to stop. When I open the door, a solemn Ace stares back at me. "Hey." he says, quietly greeting me.

"Hi," I respond, having a difficult time hiding my sniffle. I slide in the passenger seat with my bag on my lap. "Thanks for coming to get me. You said if I ever needed a ride." I shrug. "I definitely need one."

"I wasn't expecting your text, especially one to take you to the airport and to tell me that David is responsible for the fire."

Shrugging my shoulders in response, I say, "It's time to go home."

"I'm sorry I told Dawson about you guys. I was so pissed, but I never thought he'd do something like trying to burn down the shop."

"David isn't one to be underestimated. It doesn't matter now. You should salvage your friendship with Van after I'm gone. He'll forgive you. It's who he is."

"I'm sorry, Ems. I didn't mean for it to go this far."

"Yeah, well, neither did I. It doesn't matter anymore. I'm going back to him."

"What about Van?"

"He doesn't know I left."

Ace steps on the brakes, grinding the car to a halt. "Are you kidding me? You can't just leave without saying goodbye. What the fuck? His place went up in flames tonight and you're just leaving him."

"Ace...I...can't say goodbye to him. If I had to say it, I'd never leave. I'm so thankful for the time I got to spend with him and getting to know him, but David burnt down his business. He won't stop. It's for the best. Besides, I think I made a rash decision. I'm not even divorced or separated. I need to go home and fix my affairs."

He huffs out a sigh. "I think you're making a huge mistake."

Ace puts the car back in gear and we're driving again. "Please, it's better this way, for everyone."

"I disagree. I can't say I'm happy that you and Van had something. I'll admit I was...am...a bit jealous. I was hoping maybe something, I don't know. It doesn't matter, I've never seen Van act the way he has about you with anyone else. He's a fuck 'em and leave 'em type of guy, but with you he's completely different."

Just like that, my heart cracks a little more...

33

"**M**rs. Dawson, the last of the account information has been entered. Is there anything else I can get for you this evening? It's after seven." Marissa, my assistant, tells me while standing by the door. She taps her watch for emphasis.

"I know. I'll be leaving soon. You can go, if you like."

She moves away from the doorway to make her way over to my desk. Her young face crinkles. "I wouldn't normally pry, but is everything all right? Ever since you returned from your trip, you've barely left your office, working till well after midnight every night."

Tilting my head, I say, "How do you know that?"

"Fred. He leaves in the morning as I'm coming into work."

Of course, the security guard.

"Everything's fine." Looking away from her, I concentrate on the paperwork in front of me.

She stands and I try my best to ignore her so she'll go away. We've never been friends, and I don't want to start now.

"Don't forget about the fundraiser tonight. It starts at eight."

I sigh, the event completely slipped my mind. "Shit!"

Standing, I pack up my things. I have to go to this event. The Dawson's will have my head if I don't.

Marissa walks over to the closet, pulls out a dark pink ball gown, and a pair of matching sandaled heels. "I knew you wouldn't have time, so I called Margo from Mary's Boutique."

I exhale a sigh of relief. "Thank you. I'm sorry I've been so busy, but you've saved my life tonight."

She nods and smiles, exiting my office.

How did I manage to forget about tonight? It's the Dawson's annual fundraiser. This event makes them almost look like they care about others.

Van's beautiful face enters my mind. The way he cared for me, loved me. I could be with him, but instead...I can't even think about it, so I do the only thing that helps ease the pain.

Placing my phone up to my ear, I listen to his voice.

"You promised you would stay. I love you, Ems. You don't have to go back to him. Please tell me you're somewhere else, anywhere but with him. I don't trust him. He's going to drown out your spirit, Ems. Please, if you ever felt anything for me, please leave him and go someplace safe. Please. I love you." His pleading stops, but a sniffle comes through.

I wipe tears from my damp face, for the hundredth time since I first listened to it.

****

As we pull up to the Dawson mansion, David's Bugatti sits front and center in the driveway. I've been back for weeks, and it's as if nothing has changed. I've been able to keep to myself. I've only seen David one time, and I said absolutely nothing to him.

If it wasn't for the event tonight, I'd be locked up in my bedroom. I've immersed myself in work, trying to forget about Van, but it hasn't worked. He's on my mind every second of every day. He's tried calling, but I blocked his number. I couldn't trust myself that I wouldn't answer. The only solace that I have is that he did call me. He did care for one moment why I'd left. Callie and Ace both called to check on me, and I told them it would be better if they forgot about me.

Both protested, and I blocked their numbers as well. In a few weeks I went from finding a group of friends to having absolutely no one. Andrew has been with Mr. Dawson, and I haven't been able to reach him. They're coming home from Europe today...of course, only for this event. Dawson Jewels is making a sizable donation to fund the local art history museum.

While it's a worthy cause, my heart's not in it, nor will it ever be.

Jones opens my door, nodding in a friendly manner. "Mrs. Dawson."

I glare. I haven't had the guts to bring up the fire yet with him or David. I don't want to make it worse for Van. However, the first thing I did was pay a visit to our attorney, draw up a contract, and had five-hundred-thousand dollars sent to Teddy's account. I sent a contract stating he would use the money for Bradley Restoration, and I would give him another hundred thousand if he agreed. Needless to say, appealing to his greed worked. I received a signed copy within minutes by email.

I knew if I sent the money to Van, he'd refuse. Though, I can't make Jones or David pay for what they did, I can at least make up for it in some way.

Gathering the bottom of my fuchsia ball gown in my hand, I make the journey out of the car. Releasing the silky material to the ground, Jones extends his elbow, but I ignore him once more and straighten my shoulders, walking into the mansion alone.

"Rosa, I'm glad you're here tonight, but you should be home. You worked at our house all day." I give her a brief hug.

Her cheeks flush. "No. It's good. I need the extra money, and besides, all staff are required to work this event."

"Oh...you should have said something. I would have managed just fine on my own today."

"Emerson, dear, come in. You're late." Mrs. Dawson nods toward the kitchen and scowls at me. "We need some more champagne." She's clearly unhappy with Rosa speaking with me.

"Good evening," I say, blandly. Her gray hair is twirled up into a perfect updo. She's wearing a gold gown that shimmers in the sunlight.

As I pass, she leans close to me. "I'm glad you changed your mind. We've all been tempted by other men, but I'm glad you made the right decision. David's happy to have you back." She chuckles, then continues. "Who would have thought you of all people would have had an affair."

Glowering back, I don't respond. "It was nice seeing you." My manners firmly in place, I head toward the main room where the usual guests gather. David stands talking to two beauties whom I don't recognize. Before I would have been jealous or concerned, now I just wish he'd tell me he loves one of them, or both, and want to leave me.

The dark-haired beauty in the red dress, with more cleavage visible than polite society necessitates, gestures in my direction with her glass of champagne. David turns to acknowledge my presence. We haven't spoken since I returned. We've only been in the house once at the same time. He spends most of his time at the country club, or so he says.

"Darling. You look lovely." His sickening eyes land on me. He smirks, then leans in to kiss me on the cheek, I stiffen as his lips touch my skin.

"Thank you," I reply, only because it's what's expected of me. Part of me is dying more and more with each second that drones on.

The music filters between us. David holds out his hand. "Shall we?"

I lift my hand, placing it in his while cringing at his touch.

Wrapping his arm around my waist and pulling me close to him makes every inch of my body recoil. I can't remember the last time we danced.

We sway to the music. He drags us away in the middle of the dance floor; soon we're in the midst of the crowd. His breath brushes against my cheek. My eyes close bracing for whatever he might say or do.

"You've been hiding," he says with that disgusting, appalling smirk on his face. It makes me sick even looking at him. I swallow hard trying to think of the words to say to him.

I suck my bottom lip. "I haven't been hiding, just been busy. I guess I could say the same for you since I haven't seen you either."

"After paying a visit to that quaint little town, I decided to take a break, ride in my newly fixed car, and think of ways to make you pay for having an affair."

David's arms grip dangerously painful around my waist, fingers digging into my skin. Trying to push away seems like the only answer, but he won't let me. "No worries, darling. I'll think of something," he whispers close to my ear. His grip loosens, mercifully releasing me, but his words still ring in my head. I'm going to pay in every way possible, only he doesn't realize I already have by letting go of Van.

Making my way over to my table, my mother-in-law sits among her squad of stupid rich housewives with nothing to do but compare diamond sizes. Josephine Blair sits on her right, positioned to kiss Mrs. Dawson's ass. I can't stomach their conversation, but it's better than having David's hands on me.

"Emerson, we were just talking about you. I was telling them how we sent you on that marvelous trip down south where you were studying Civil War artifacts. It was truly amazing, wasn't it?"

Where does she come up with this stuff? Rolling my eyes, I agree with her. I don't even try to hide it. They'll only see what they want to anyway.

"Yes. Very unique experience. I'd recommend it to anyone."

"You look awfully pale, dear, you should probably turn in for the evening. I think that would be best, don't you?"

"I think you may be right. I've had enough adventures for tonight." Getting out of my chair ever so eloquently, I nod and leave the ladies, or monsters depending on the situation. Walking away from them isn't as hard as it used to be. I don't really care what they think of me or my dress or my hair or anything else about me. I'm almost dead inside, going through the motions, biding my time, waiting for the right moment to leave again. How long will I be trapped in this life? Dead on the inside while the only thing I have to hold on to are the memories from my time with Van, Callie, and even Violet. I was alive and cared about. Now I'm just a puppet for them to control.

Walking past the hall mirror, I catch a glimpse of myself. Noticing my shoulders collapsed, I try to straighten myself as if that's going to help my mood. Nothing's going to help me.

Reaching for the door of the exit, my name is bounced off the walls. When I look up, familiar eyes meet mine.

Chapter Thirty-Four

"Andrew!" I scream, wrapping my arms around his neck.

"Emmy. Doll?" He pulls back, and takes me in. "You look so pale." He frowns, his gaze roaming over my features.

"I'm fine." Trying to reassure him, while brushing the strand of hair from my face, I adjust my stance to be more casual and relaxed.

He takes my hand and we walk out into the cool night breeze. People are milling around the front porch while Andrew leads me over to the large white gazebo on the main lawn.

We stop and sit on the swing. "It's so good to see you, Andrew. I missed you. I've barely talked with you. How was Europe?"

"Horrible. Mr. D kept me busy. I was worried about you. I talked to Van a few times. I thought you were fine." I shrug, not committing to anything.

"Cut the shit, Emmy. You look awful. I got off the phone with Van an hour ago. He's a fucking mess, and if I wouldn't have seen you with my own eyes, I'd say you're just as bad."

It's dark outside, but I can still see the dismay in his features. He's got me, he knows me all too well, but that isn't what's got my heart beating out of my chest...Van, he's talked to him.

"He's a mess?" I barely squeak out.

"Yeah. He said that David showed up, set his place on fire and you ran. What the hell happened?"

I can't lie or stop the tears from falling in front of Andrew. "I did what you told me to do...I had fun and fell in love."

He lets out a sigh. "Christ. The one time you listen to me." He almost lets out a laugh. "You really did a number on him. I had to reassure him over and over again that you were okay. But I don't think I'm right, am I? Did you leave him because you wanted to, or because of David?"

I glance up and know I don't have to answer him. He already knows. Rubbing his scalp with his hands, he lets out a breath.

"He's really a mess?" I can't help but asking again. I need to know he's still thinking of me in some way.

"Of course, he is. You have that effect on people, you just don't realize how special you are. He told me he thinks he's in love with you." The roof of my mouth dries, preventing me from speaking. He continues to torture me. "He's worried that David's going to hurt you. I had to stop him from coming here. You need to tell me how you plan to leave David."

Finding my voice, I admit, "I don't know. I thought I'd wait for him to get over this whole Van situation. He'll get bored and move on to something else. Once he feels like he won, it's over. If I leave too soon, Van's won, and it only gets worse for him."

"What about you?" He shoots back.

"I'll be fine. I've lived with him for this long. I'm used to living like this." As I say the words, the reality is far worse than the meaning behind what I just said.

"David hasn't hurt you, has he?"

I scoff. "Of course, he has, but not in the way you're thinking. He ruined Van's business. He wouldn't stop unless I came back. So here I am. I just have to be patient."

Andrew practically lets out a growl. "Patient? You've been patient forever. He's always going to find an excuse." His voice deepens to mock David. "You made me lose my leg. I'm nothing because of you. You deserve to pay for what you did to me."

Widening my eyes, I can't believe he knows David's exact words to me.

He nods as if reading my mind. "Yeah, I know what he says to you. I hear it all the time, and so does everyone else. You need to leave him soon. He's always going to find something to hold over your head to make you stay."

"That's enough, Andrew! I think your employment has officially ended as of tonight." David emerges from the shadows behind us, along with his father.

Andrew stands, positioning himself in front of me while I sit in shock. How did we not see them?

"No. No..." I speak up. "He hasn't done anything wrong."

"Emerson, dear, telling you to leave your marriage is grounds for termination. Andrew has taken an oath to serve this family. His behavior does not exhibit that oath," Mr. Dawson speaks for his son.

"I'm sorry you feel this way, but I've only stayed this long with you to protect Emerson."

"She doesn't need your protection. You've crossed a line, and it's time for you to leave."

I get up from the bench swing and move in between David and Andrew. "Please, don't do this. He cares for all of us. He's been a wonderful employee and friend. It's my fault. Let's just forget this happened and go back inside."

"No. I'm done. I can't in good conscience let them treat you this way." Andrew turns to face me, gripping my shoulders, almost shaking some sense into me. "Come home with me, leave them. You don't need to stay." Looking past him, and at the two Dawson men with hate in their eyes and knowing what they're capable of...I know what I need to do.

"I have to stay. I'm sorry, but your employment here has officially ended." I look down at the ground, there's no way I can bring myself to see the look of disappointment on his face, but it rings loud and clear in his voice.

"Emmy, you don't have to stay. Come with me. Please."

With my head unable to move, I concentrate on my pink heels, until they're next to David's. I've chosen whose side I'm on, and on the inside, I'm furious and ashamed of Emerson Dawson, but above all I need to protect Andrew and Van.

When David's arms wrap around my waist and he whispers "Good girl" I glance up to Andrew retreating away from us and getting into a black SUV and pulling away. Tears well in my eyes, but I refuse to let them fall or let the Dawson men see me cry. They may have hurt me, tortured me, and ruined my life, but I refuse to let them do the same to the people I care for.

"I'm going home. I'll have Jones take me."

David kisses the top of my head. I can't remember the last time he's done that, but this doesn't feel like a loving gesture. No, this is a possessive gesture as if to say, well done.

"I'll be home when the party is over," he tells me and I walk away as fast as my feet can carry me.

On the way home, Jones doesn't speak to me. I don't think I could handle any type of fake conversation with him. I've already had to act enough tonight. I have nothing left to give.

He opens the door for me, and without a glance, I head inside. My bedroom door is closed, and I reach in my purse for the key. Keeping it locked is the only control I have left.

The key turns and momentary relief appears. Slamming the door shut and locking it behind me, I fall onto the bed and finally let the tears fall.

Hours, seconds, minutes later, I remove myself from the bed. The clock blazes four-fifty-seven. I can't sleep, only replaying the hurt I've caused the two most important people in my life. I let Andrew down. He's only wanted to protect me. I hope he knows that he did. That he was more of a protector than anyone has ever been, but most importantly, a friend. The only real friend I've ever known until recently.

Pulling myself from the bed, I slip out of the dress, releasing the chains of the night with it. There's only one thing left to do. Changing into yoga pants and my Superman t-shirt, I slip on my shoes and grab my mug, leaving my room behind, but not before locking it.

****

I haven't been here for weeks, and for the first time, it doesn't hold the same peace it once had. The chapel is exactly the same, but I'm not. In the past few weeks everything about me has changed. I wish I had the power to stop David and his family from hurting Van, his family, and Andrew. The only way I can stop David, I know, is to stay with him.

I decide to take a nap in a spot that I feel safe. Lying down with my head on the pillow and covering myself with an afghan, I cuddle up with the only thing of Van I have left. As silly as it is, a mug is the most comforting thing I own in this moment.

Waking up to a bang, I sit straight up. Wiping my eyes, the crashing comes again. Focusing on the door, David stands before me. I know that look. It's the same look I've seen several times. He's drunk and he's mad and ready to take it out on me.

34

—·—

"**Y**ou." He points in my direction, slurring the word.

"David, what are you doing here?" I ask, sliding the mug down on the pew and slipping the afghan off my body.

"I wanted to sleep next to my wife...but...you weren't there. Bed. No Emerson." He pouts as if he's a small child.

"I couldn't sleep." Holding up a book, I explain. "It helps me fall asleep."

His childlike expression falls into a scowl. His voice changes and is no longer slurring. "Did that mechanic put you to bed, or did he keep you up by fucking you?"

"I think you should get some rest. You've been up all night."

He sits down beside me, too close, setting alarms off all over my skin.

"I set his store on fire. I mean, I didn't throw the ball of fire into the window, but I did enjoy watching the replay of him trying to put it out. Although, it was a shame no one got hurt." His voice clears and it dawns on me that a completely different David is here.

"What's wrong with you?" Slips unbidden from my mouth. I cover it as soon as I realize what I've said.

"Bolder. Huh? I kind of like it." Sliding closer, his breath touches my ear. "I like fucking a girl with a dirty mouth. I think the mechanic taught you new tricks."

"You need to leave."

"Leave? Oh no, baby. I'm just getting started. See, I've had some time to think this over and you've embarrassed me. You've made me look like a fool twice. I'm not dealing with it well. Thankfully no one in our circle knows about your mechanic. He's a piece of shit. A low-life, low-class, low-income...piece of shit."

Trying to stand, he grabs my arm and yanks me toward him. I'm sitting on his lap with his arms wrapped around mine so that I can't move. Moving my shoulders isn't working. He squeezes tighter. "I'm not letting you go."

"Yes, you are. I came back. No one knows what happened while I was gone. Your image is still intact. But don't worry, people know you're an alcoholic who lives off of Mommy and Daddy and..."

The whole side of my body meets the floor in such quick fashion that I don't even realize that he's thrown me off of him. My arm aches, and the side of my face throbs. "David?" I whisper.

He crouches down beside me. "See what you make me do to you? Why can't you just listen to me? Everyone listens to me but you. You try to be better than me, the company, with clients, with friends and family...but I hate you. I hate you for driving that night. For not seeing the other car coming, and above all, for giving them permission to amputate my leg. You let them take it!" Drool cascades down his chin while hate spews from his lips.

"I had to...your leg was so mangled...it would have been so painful." My voice is strained, my mouth so dry I can barely get the words out.

His hand comes around my throat, cutting off my breath. "You wanted me to live like this...and knowing you went ahead and fucked around with that fucking mechanic. I should just let you be with him, let you go and have little trash babies..." He lets out a growl and lowers close to my face while still squeezing the air from me. "I don't ever lose, so..." By the grace of God, he lets go.

A cough escapes, letting in air. I can breathe. I inhale every molecule of air I can. Coughing is good, it means I'm going to be okay. I mentally repeat over and over, but when my eyes meet his...they're cold, dark, and dead, and I know he isn't finished with me.

David backs away, unbuckles his belt, and rips it from around his waist. In a faster motion than I can process and fight off, he's straddling my hips, wrapping the belt around my wrists, the leather biting into my skin, but the metal buckle is sealing my fate. "There, now you can't fight me off. You haven't lived up to your obligation in pleasing your husband. Tell me, did you please the grease monkey?" I freeze, unable to understand what's happening. Who is this man with such contempt for me?

As if I've detached from my body, I feel like I'm in a dream world. I don't want to stay here. Unable to stop him, there's no fight left in me. Instead, Van's face comes to mind, the concern on his face when I woke up from my seizure. I vaguely notice my body jostle, ignoring it, I focus on Van. A voice is there, but I don't want to listen. Van's voice is the only thing I hear. "I love you, Ems. I love you, Ems." Over and over, I recall his words.

A pain rips across my cheek, pulling me from my fantasy. David's trying to get inside me, gripping my hair, spit dripping from his mouth as he grits through his teeth, "You're mine, I own you. Did he fuck you this good?" His hand tries separating my thighs, but I squeeze them as tight as I can manage. David grunts, frustrated at my attempt to stop him. Something inside me awakens. *Why am I giving in?*

Looking up, my eyes meet his scrunched face, his hardness pressing against me, trying to gain access. "Stop," I scream, but it's nearly a whisper. "Stop!" I say but this time it's audible. Again, I say it. Over and over, each time louder and louder, but he keeps pushing, ignoring me. He isn't listening. "Please, stop!"

His hand holds both my tied hands above my head. Struggling against his grip, I try to move them, but it's as if he's got superhuman strength. A pain rips from my knee up to my thigh, causing my leg to weaken. David takes advantage, and his hard length presses against my entrance. I summon every bit of strength I have left. I scream. "Noooo! Noooo!" Thrashing from side to side, taking advantage of every inch of space between us. "Nooo! Stop! Please!" As if by some miracle, my name's called as a heavy weight crashes onto my side for a split second. Then the weight is gone, replaced by a fierce growl, the sound of crunching, and a bone-chilling scream.

Pulling every ounce of strength, I roll over to see Van above David. Pounding his fists into David's face. Blood splattering with each hit. He's here. Thank God. "Van!" I call again. "Van." But he doesn't stop. His fists pound into a motionless David. Another person enters, then another, then another. It's as if everything starts working again in my body. Andrew, Mr. Dawson, and Mrs. Dawson come into view. Andrew pulls Van off of David, breaking his grip from where it was wrapped around David's neck.

"Van. Enough!"

Mr. Dawson is at his son's side. "What have you done?" His eyes roam over to me. He gasps. "Emerson?" His face softens as he takes me in. It's at that moment that I feel cold and aware of how naked and broken I am. It crashes like a wave over my body. Rolling back onto my other side, facing away from them, hoping to disappear.

"What has he done?" is said across the room. Vaguely, I recognize Mrs. Dawson's voice.

A blanket covers me along with a scent I'll never forget. Van. "Ems, talk to me. Can you hear me? Say something."

I can't. I'm so tired.

"Emerson!"

The weight's too heavy. Focusing on the floor in front of me, it starts to move as if it's asphalt on a scorching hot summer's day. Heat races up my body. The all-too-familiar tingling sensation takes over my body. My vision blurs as I fade into darkness.

35

Opening my eyes, the light is too bright. Bringing my hand up to cover my face, I say, "Turn off the light," to whatever monster decided to turn on a bright light.

"Morning." The light dims.

I freeze. Focusing through the haze, beautiful dark eyes peer into mine.

"Donavan?"

"Hey. Sorry about the light, but I had to get you up. We're worried about you."

"Who?"

Andrew steps beside him. "All of us."

My room is suddenly filled with people I would have never imagined being in the same room together—let alone my bedroom—peering over his shoulder, staring at me as if I were an alien. Mr. and Mrs. Dawson stand out the most, next is Jake and Callie. None of this makes sense.

"What's going on?" I mutter, barely able to recognize my own voice.

"You had a seizure...well, actually three in a row, but we finally got them to stop. How are you feeling?"

"Confused."

"I know. We'll explain everything, but you're safe, and all right," Van reassures.

Trying to sit up, I want my explanation now. "What's..." A head rush stops any other thoughts.

"Shh...close your eyes. Rest. Everything will be okay. Is okay."

I believe him. I'm not sure what's going on, but for right now, everything's fine. I fall back into darkness.

****

The bed dips beside me, jostling me awake.

Opening my eyes, I see Van is staring back at me. He's shirtless, with messy hair and stubble covering his perfect face. I've never seen a more beautiful sight. "Hey."

"Hi," I answer in a hazy state as he takes my hand in his.

"How are you feeling?" About to answer as if he's not lying in my bed at the house I share with David, I sit up in a panic. "It's okay. Everybody knows I'm here."

"What? They do?"

"Yeah. Sit back and I'll explain everything in a minute."

"But..."

"Sit back." I do as he asks only because I'm so damn confused. I don't know what to think. He rolls on his side to face me, and I mimic his position.

"Do you want me here?" he asks, concern and a bit of hesitation in his voice.

"I'm so sorry." He's here. I can't believe it. He's here for me. "I didn't want to leave. I didn't know how to stop him. He wouldn't stop until he ruined you and your family and friends..." His finger presses against my lips to stop me.

"Don't apologize. I get it, I do. I shouldn't have let you go. I love you, Ems. If you don't love me anymore, it's okay...I just knew that he'd hurt you because of me."

"I love you, Van. I do." Tears cascade down my face. "I'm so sorry I left you." His lips are on mine before I can explain another word.

He pulls away sooner than I'd like. Caressing my cheek with his thumb, he asks, "Do you have any idea how relieved I am to hear you say that?" He smiles. "I was sure you'd tell me to leave when you woke up."

"I'm so sorry...for everything." My voice is strained, coming out hushed. Leaning down, he kisses my cheek softly. Automatically my eyes shut, my whole body savoring his touch.

A knock at the door interrupts. As it creaks open, Mr. Dawson appears, followed by Mrs. Dawson.

Van moves back but doesn't let go of my hand.

"I'm so glad to see you awake and hopefully feeling better," Mr. Dawson says politely, which is a tone unlike anything I've ever heard from him.

I nod but stiffen because I'm not sure what the hell's going on, or why they would all be in the same room together, without David. David?

"Where's David?"

Mr. Dawson takes a few steps closer, causing Van to tighten his grip.

"Do you remember what happened?" Van asks.

Searching my memory, I can't recall anything but being in the chapel.

"No."

Relief consumes Mr. Dawson's features. "Good. That's good."

Taking a moment to glance at Van, his jaw is clenched, and he doesn't seem at all happy that I don't remember. What am I forgetting?

"You had a seizure," Mrs. Dawson tries to explain but Van cuts her off.

"No. You had three. If you're going to lie to her, then I'll have to ask you to leave."

She places her perfectly manicured hand on her chest, a bit appalled, I'd guess, but she recovers with an apology. "I'm sorry, three. David was drinking and on some medication. He's in a rehabilitation facility."

Shaking my head, I'm unsure what she's talking about. I'm so confused. He always drinks and takes unprescribed medication. Why is this different? Why?

His face flashes quickly in my mind, breaking through the fogginess like a wrecking ball. My hand flies up to my mouth as my lungs squeeze. He hit me, tried to rape me, and Van...he stopped him. I reach for Van. Seeing the bruises on his face and the cut on his bottom lip confirms what I already know happened.

A sob escapes, and Van has me wrapped up in his arms before I even realize it. Hushing me and kissing the top of my head. In the distance, the door shuts. "It's okay...baby. He can't hurt you anymore." He rocks me back and forth in his arms. When my tears slow, he begins to talk.

"David's in jail right now but will be transferred in the morning to a rehabilitation facility for alcoholism and depression, among other things. He hurt you pretty bad. I almost didn't get to you in time." His voice cracks.

"Thank God you did. I should have never left you," I whisper as more tears break free.

"He's getting help. Mr. and Mrs. Dawson finally get it. They were worried about you, or maybe their reputation...either way, they're being decent human beings..."

"I don't understand." They never cared about me.

"When you finished seizing and were calm, Mr. Dawson and Andrew were having a hell of a time containing David, even with a fucked-up face and broken bones. He was high on something. He wasn't listening to anyone, and Mr. Dawson saw how much he'd hurt you. He called the police on his own son."

"What?"

"Yeah, I couldn't believe it myself. Of course, I think it might be more to save their image, and they'll spin it whatever way they want, but the end result is he's not a threat to you anymore."

I wince as he kisses my cheek. "How do I look?"

"Beautiful but hurt." His forehead crinkles, and I think he almost cringes. "But a doctor is here at your beck and call and is taking good care of you."

The pain radiates through my body. My face must be twice as big as normal, my side and back are killing me, but the worst is the sting between my thighs.

"How did you find me?" I ask, moving my thoughts away from the pain of what happened to me.

"Andrew called. He said they fired him, and you were going along with everything. He said you were cold and lifeless. I knew, I had to come and get you. I didn't trust David, and I'm glad I came for you, even if you may not have wanted me to come."

He swallows and continues. "Anyway, Andrew told me how to get around the property, and I was able to remain undetected until the chapel came into view. Mr. Dawson ran for me, and his guy, Jones, knocked me down, but then I heard the screams. I managed to get up and I ran." He shakes his head, as if he's shaking away a memory. "The screams from you were..." He swallows, "They just kept getting worse the closer I got. Then when I finally got in, he was on top of you, and I knew..."

I squeeze him tight. This time I stop him. "No more. Please."

"I'm so sorry I didn't come for you sooner."

"I should have been stronger. I should have stayed with you. I'm sorry."

"No. No more apologies. He was wrong. There was no reason for any of this. I'm just thankful you're all right." He kisses my forehead. "Whatever happens next is up to you. If you want me to go, I will."

"No. I don't want that. I need you. I love you. I'm coming home with you."

"But don't you think you should stay here, get your business settled..."

"No. I can start my own business. I don't want anything to do with David or the Dawson family. They made me a robot, someone who would hide instead of facing their fears. What kind of life have I been living? I met you...but it wasn't just you, it was your family, your friends. They all treated me with kindness and respect. I haven't been treated that way for a long time. I finally felt like myself. I'm sad that I let myself live that way for so long, but I'm so thankful now that I realize I'm free."

"You are free. You can do anything you want. No one owns you. And I'm so damn proud of you."

"I don't feel proud. I was going to let it be. Just keep living my life like a robot or martyr. I thought it was my fault for David acting the way he did. I knew starting a relationship with you was wrong, but I did it anyway. The guilt is what I let rule my life. I thought if David was happy, it would make me happy. But he was never going to be happy.

Then when I met you. I became alive. I felt wrong for feeling that way since I was married to him. But in reality, our marriage ended a long time ago, and if he ever loved me, he wouldn't have been able to hurt me the way he did."

"No, love doesn't hurt like that."

I lean back, settling beside him. Wrapped in his arms. "When are we going back to Bradley Restoration?"

"As soon as you're ready, princess."

36

"I can't believe it's been weeks since you've been back, and you still haven't worn a suit. I'm not used to it," Callie teases me.

"Ha, ha, very funny. I don't need to wear a suit. I'm working from the apartment."

"I still can't believe the Dawson's gave you the whole cosmetic company."

"They didn't. Don't go all crazy on me. They did give me the rights to the products that I developed, which are now being called Emerson Rose Cosmetics."

Callie jumps up excitedly, even with a little clap. "I love the name. I'm so happy for you, Ems."

Van crawls from under the hot rod he's been restoring since we got back. "I'm proud of her too." He kisses the top of my head. Turning to face him, I wrap my arms around his waist.

"Ew...can't you two keep your hands off of each other for just a few minutes?"

"No," we say in unison.

Ben chimes in, "Let them go. It's nice that two people who actually like each other can show affection in front of others." I don't miss his sarcasm, or the fact that it's directed at Callie. She rolls her eyes in response. The whole room suddenly becomes awkwardly silent.

Thankfully, my phone chimes in my pocket. Taking it out, I answer the call from my lawyer. "Ms. Dawson. How are you today?"

"Good, Paul," I say and walk out of the shop into the cool night air. Pinks, oranges, and yellows blaze off in the distance, letting me know night is near. "What can I help you with? I wasn't expecting to hear from you."

"David's court date has been set. We need you to testify against him. It's most likely he will have to do some sort of community service, or house arrest since he's still in a rehabilitation center. The final results of his toxicology test haven't come back. He was on a mixture of drugs. We won't know for sure which ones or the amounts he ingested, but honestly, he shouldn't even be alive. The doctor is guessing heroin and Ecstasy. I'm sorry this has all happened to you, but I'm thankful you're alive."

"Thank you, Paul. I'm much better now. I'll testify if you need me to, but I just want him to get the help he needs."

"I believe he is. There was one other thing. The divorce papers have been filed, and pending David's signature, will be approved in two months. Also, his parents have agreed to give you everything you asked for in the divorce decree."

It feels like a thousand pounds release from my shoulders. "They did. No problems?"

"None. They said with everything he, and even they, have put you through, you deserve to have the money and all the chapel belongings." My mouth dries, I don't have to fight any longer. They've been so kind and accommodating. Nothing that I ever expected from them, but I guess they're doing what they've always done—enabling and fixing his mistakes.

Van startles me as he wraps his arms around my waist.

"Thank you, Paul. Let me know if there is anything else you need."

"I will. And you will receive the first installment on Monday. One-million dollars and thirteen cents."

I can't help but chuckle at the cents. Only I would calculate everything down to the last penny.

"Good to know."

He wishes me well and hangs up.

"Good news?" Van asks with a bit of hesitation.

"Great news. It's almost finished. What do you say we go check out the tree house?"

"Why?"

"I've suddenly fallen into some extra furniture, and I need somewhere to put it."

"You got everything?" he asks excitedly, pulling me tighter against him.

"Yes. Everything, but the most important thing is standing in front of me. Thank you, Van. Thank you for not just letting me be okay with my life. You showed me that my happiness matters."

"I love you, Ems."

"I love you too. Now we have some work to do. That tree house isn't going to get painted white by itself."

"Oh no, it stays as is. I'll build you a tiny house for that stuff. You're not touching my tree house."

"Okay. I knew I'd get one out of you eventually. You do owe me since you did sell the one, I was sleeping in and then made me sleep in a dilapidated trailer."

He laughs and slides his hands in his pocket. "Yeah, I did. I'll never forget your face either. All over a little mouse."

I slug him in the arm. "Jerk."

"Ahh...you love me."

"Yes. Yes, I do."

***

Are you ready to read Callie and Ben's Story? Click here for Beautifully Built.

Scan the QR Code for Beautifully Built and all my social media and website links!

— · —

Acknowlededments

I want to thank my girls, Madison and Hayley. They are always so proud to tell someone that their mom is an author. Although they are not old enough to read my books, I write so that they know whatever they want to do in life, no matter how challenging, they can accomplish it.

To my mom, no words will ever be enough to express the strength she has shown throughout her life, but I've learned so much from her. Love you, Mom, and I'm so proud of you.

To Nana, thank you for being the first person to read my books and helping me become the person I am.

Kathy Blinkiewicz, my second mom, who is the best Trisha Madley book promoter and one of my biggest fans! Thanks for all you do for me.

To Jason, the love of my life, my partner and best friend. Thank you for supporting my passion.

Most of all, to you, my readers:

Thank you to all of you who have read and purchased *Safer With You* and *Fearless With You*. I can't tell you how much it means to hear people ask me, "When is your next book available?" Thankfully, I can finally answer, "Today!"

Thanks to Allusion Graphics for *Beautifully Restored*'s amazing book cover. https://allusionpublishing.com/

The editor of *Beautifully Restored*, Allusion Graphics. https://allusionpublishing.com/

Amy Dobbs is a wonderful author, and the proofreader of *Fearless With You* and *Beautifully Restored*. Thank you for the countless things you did to help make these books possible. I can't wait to see your books in print.

My beta readers: Nina Faieta, Mary Balmer, Kathy Blinkiewicz, Amy Dobbs, Maria Longo, and Amanda Zickafoose

Thank You, Everyone!!!

Enjoy!!!

Visit trishamadley.com for more information.

SAFER WITH YOU - Book One

Nora Skye must start her life over again. She notices that her boyfriend Luke has become distant and secretive, leaving her with no other choice than to spy on him.

When Luke learns of what she has done, he discards her. Forcing her back home. Upon her arrival, she attends her sister's wedding where she meets the sexy, charismatic, and outrageously out of her league Jase Madsyn.

She knows his reputation, the mystery that surrounds him, but that doesn't stop her from experiencing the best night of her life. But she soon discovers that he may be the person responsible for her pain.

FEARLESS WITH YOU - Book Two

Nora Skye has survived the unimaginable. Now that the chaos has settled, she is free to enjoy her new life, with the man who saved her in more ways than one—Jase Madsyn.

Jase killed the man who hurt Nora, but now new obstacles arise. His career starts to wear on their relationship, but the problems don't end there when Samantha, his ex-fiancée, shows up with a surprise of her own, and his mother disappears without a trace.

Nora tries to be supportive, but too many secrets cause their fragile relationship to crumble. Can their love survive his secrets...but most of all, his past?

I'd love to hear from you!

To sign up for updates and my newsletter, go to www.trishamadley.com.

Website: www.trishamadley.com

TikToc: https://www.tiktok.com/@trishamadleybooks

Facebook: https://www.facebook.com/trishamadley

Facebook Group - Madley's Mob

https://www.facebook.com/groups/437792053399452/

Instagram: https://www.instagram.com/trishamadley

ABOUT THE AUTHOR

I live in a small town in Pennsylvania with my husband, two amazing daughters, and two dogs, an unlikely pair: Pomsky and a Maltese. I spend my time writing, editing, reading, and graphic designing. Visit me at www.trishamadley.com.